DESIRES OF THE DEAD

Kimberly Derting is a full-time writer who lives in Western Washington state with her husband and three children. DESIRES OF THE DEAD is her second novel. You can visit her online at www.kimberlyderting.com.

Kimberly Derting

DESIRES OF THE DEAD

headline

First published in 2011 by
HarperCollins USA

First published in Great Britain in 2011 by
HEADLINE PUBLISHING GROUP

1

Cataloguing in Publication Data is available from the British Library

ISBN 978 0 7553 7896 8

Printed in Great Britain by
Clays Ltd, St Ives plc

Headline's policy is to use papers that are natural, renewable
and recyclable products and made from wood grown in sustainable forests.
The logging and manufacturing processes are expected to conform to
the environmental regulations of the country of origin.

HEADLINE PUBLISHING GROUP
An Hachette UK Company
338 Euston Road
London NW1 3BH

www.headline.co.uk
www.hachette.co.uk

To Amanda, Connor, and Abby.
Always.

PROLOGUE

VIOLET LEANED FORWARD ON HER HANDS AND knees over the frozen landscape. Inside her boots, her toes felt as if icy shards were burrowing beneath her skin and slithering into her veins. Her fingers were very likely frost-bitten within her gloves.

The flashlight's beam slashed through the veil of blackness that had settled over the wintry forest, creating a spotlight where Violet had been trying to uncover the ground beneath the soft layer of snow.

In her drugged state, she couldn't be certain that she wasn't hallucinating as she stared at the man who towered over her. His weathered skin seemed to glow with an unnatural life of its own. It was both strange and beautiful.

But her thoughts were thick, and she struggled for each one, dredging them up from the swampy depths of her confused mind.

He spoke to her, unaware that her brain filtered his words, jumbling them and making them something less than coherent. She tried to concentrate as the tranquilizing sensation bled through her, deadening her senses.

But she was cognizant enough to be afraid—*terrified*, even—of this man. She could understand enough of what he was saying to recognize that he was disturbed. And dangerous.

He'd followed her. In the middle of the night. And even through the haze that distorted her awareness, she realized that he must have known why she was there. That he somehow knew she had found the body.

She glanced down at his hand, at what he held there, and her tangled thoughts immediately cleared.

She watched while he gripped the handle of the shotgun tightly in his fingers, and then he looked at her. "I'm really sorry that you found her," he explained sadly. "I didn't want anyone else to die."

CHAPTER 1

January, Five Weeks Earlier

CHELSEA LEANED DOWN TO VIOLET LIKE SHE HAD a secret to tell, something she didn't want anyone else to hear. "Check out the new eye candy!" Chelsea shouted, making Violet jump.

Violet was pretty sure that everyone in the cafeteria had just heard her friend. As usual, Chelsea's internal filter seemed to be turned off.

Come to think of it, Violet couldn't remember Chelsea ever screening her words.

The *boy* Chelsea was referring to happened to be walking

right past them and, like everyone else, he'd heard her too—he would have had to be deaf *not* to hear—and he looked up in time to catch Violet glancing his way. Chelsea turned back to Jules and Claire, and pretended to laugh at something funny they'd said, giving the impression that it had been Violet who'd made the outrageous comment.

He smiled sheepishly at Violet and kept on walking. Violet felt her cheeks burning, and she was grateful that he at least had the good sense to look embarrassed by all the attention he was drawing. As humiliated as Violet was, she also felt a little sorry for him. It must suck to be the new kid in school. Even a really good-looking new kid.

As she watched, a girl joined him. Violet might have guessed from the resemblance—the similarity in coloring between the two of them—that they were related, except she didn't have to guess; Violet already knew that the girl was his younger sister.

They had a new student every now and then at White River High School, but in a town as small as Buckley, Washington, the fact that there were *two* new students on the very same day was cause for major gossip. Even if they were brother and sister.

Violet watched the pair until they found a table at the far end of the cafeteria, away from the activity and the busier tables at the center of the large, noisy space, and then she turned to Chelsea.

"Thanks a lot, Chels. I'm sure that wasn't *at all* awkward for him." Violet glanced down and examined the contents of her plastic tray. The pizza looked greasy and runny, and the applesauce had a faintly grayish hue to it. The food made her lose her appetite altogether.

Chelsea grinned back at her. "No problem, Vi. You know me: I'm a giver. I just wanted to make him feel welcome." She shoved a spoonful of the grim-looking applesauce into her mouth, smiling around the flimsy plastic utensil. She gazed over Violet's shoulder to where the two new students sat by themselves. "If he didn't want people talking about him, he probably shouldn't look so tasty." She was still gawking at them when her face wrinkled up and she pulled the spoon from her mouth. "What's your boyfriend doing over there?"

Violet twisted in her seat so she could see what Chelsea was talking about just as Jay joined the two new kids at their table. He sat beside the girl, but he was already talking to her brother like they were old friends. And then he turned and pointed in Violet's direction—*right at her, in fact*—and smiled when he saw that she was watching him. He waved at the same time the new guy looked up to see her studying them.

It was the second time she'd been caught staring at the new kid.

Violet tried to smile, but it didn't actually reach her mouth. She thought about pretending she hadn't seen them but realized it was too late, so before turning around she gave a halfhearted wave. She hoped the new boy wasn't telling Jay that she'd just called him "eye candy" . . . especially since *she* hadn't. Jay had been her best friend long before he was ever her boyfriend, so she hoped he would know she wasn't the one who'd said it.

"Oh, look," Claire announced, typically unaware of anyone else's discomfort. "I think Jay's inviting them over here."

Of course he was. Why wouldn't he be?

"Great," Violet muttered under her breath. She didn't bother turning around this time; instead she just glared at Chelsea.

Chelsea feigned innocence. "What? You don't want New Boy to come sit with us? Claire and Jules don't mind, do you?"

Jules was too busy eating to get involved in their conversation. The lanky tomboy looked like a prison inmate as she leaned over her tray, one arm wrapped protectively around it, shoveling the less-than-edible-looking food into her mouth.

Claire shook her head. "Of course not."

Chelsea continued, "You are one lucky girl, Violet. That boyfriend of yours has a heart of gold. He's just trying to make the new guy feel at home." And then she added, "Yet, when I do it, you get all bent and give me dirty looks. You should try being a little more like Jay and me. Try opening up your heart . . . just a little."

"Oh wait. Never mind," Claire announced, ignoring Chelsea. "The new kids are staying where they are. But here comes Jay."

Violet shot a warning look at Chelsea as Jay sat down beside her. He slipped his hand beneath the back of her shirt, tracing his thumb across the small of her back. It was so familiar, his touch, yet disarming at the same time. Violet leaned into him and he kissed her forehead. His lips were soft but left her skin tingling. She could hardly believe that her stomach still did somersaults whenever he was near.

"What are you guys talking about?" Jay asked, and Violet wondered if she only imagined the implication she heard in his words.

Chelsea smiled sweetly. "We were just curious about your new friends over there. Well . . . more about him than her."

Chelsea Morrison was a pretty girl. She had smooth skin; a slim, athletic body; and shiny, chestnut-colored hair. It wasn't until she opened her mouth that the near-perfect illusion of femininity was shattered. Fortunately for Chelsea, she couldn't care less what people thought of her . . . one way or the other. Chelsea refused to conform to what anyone else expected her to be.

Jay chuckled at Chelsea. "You mean *Mike*?" he asked, giving the new kid a name. "I was just asking if he wanted to come sit with us, but for some reason"—he glanced at Violet with raised eyebrows—"he didn't want to. Is there anything you want to tell me? Like why Mike might prefer *not* to sit at the same table with you?"

"It wasn't *me* . . . it was *her*!" Violet, nearly choking on the bite of soggy pizza she was trying to swallow, pointed at Chelsea.

Chelsea laughed, and even Jules stopped stuffing her face long enough to smile appreciatively. Claire was the only one who remained straight-faced, mostly because she didn't seem to be listening anymore. Her fingers worked viciously over the keys of her cell phone; she was absorbed in a long series of text messages . . . probably to someone sitting only a few tables away.

"I know," Jay admitted. "Chelsea's the only girl at this school who would actually have the balls to say something like that right in front of someone."

Chelsea did her best to look indignant, her eyes widening in mock outrage. "*Whatever!* Why couldn't it have been Jules? Or Claire?"

"*What? I* didn't say anything," Claire piped in, suddenly paying attention.

Chelsea rolled her eyes at Claire's serious tone. "Paranoid much? No one was actually accusing you of anything. Besides, what do I care if he knows it was me? There's nothing wrong with noticing that he's . . . *mmm*, delicious. If he plays his cards right, he could end up as Mr. Chelsea."

"As if that's even possible, Chels," Claire declared. "The guy doesn't change *his* name; you'd have to change yours."

Chelsea rolled her eyes again, this time so that Claire couldn't see her, as she visibly bit back her irritation. "Thanks for the lesson in social convention, Claire-bear."

Claire shrugged and smiled ingenuously. "No problem."

Violet glanced at Jay, grinning over Claire's innate ability to annoy Chelsea without repercussions.

Violet envied Claire for that. But she knew that the only reason Chelsea didn't turn her wrath on Claire was because, more than anything else in the world, Chelsea hated apologizing. So somehow, with a strength of will that she was unable to find when dealing with anyone else, Chelsea managed to curb her temper when it came to Claire's sensitive feelings.

Violet found it highly entertaining.

But Jay was grinning back at Violet for an entirely different reason. He bent toward her, and sparks of anticipation crackled through her body. His lips quietly brushed over hers, right there in the middle of the crowded cafeteria, just the whisper of a kiss. Yet Violet was powerless to stop him.

Even if she'd wanted to, her body never seemed to follow the simplest of instructions when it came to Jay. He was like her Kryptonite.

Chelsea stared at them disgustedly. "Will you guys stop it already? I think I just threw up in my mouth a little bit." She shuddered exaggeratedly. "If you can't wait until you're alone, I'm gonna have to ask you to find another place to sit." And then her short attention span got the best of her, and she nodded her head in the direction of Mike and his sister. "So what's their story?"

Jay shrugged. "I have no idea; I just met him today. He's in my first-period class. His family just moved here. That's about all I know."

"Why *here*?" Jules asked, and Violet had to admit that she was wondering the exact same thing.

It wasn't as if Buckley was a first-choice kind of town. And it didn't have particularly easy access to anywhere important. It was more of a pass-through city on a small stretch of highway that headed nowhere in particular.

Jay shrugged again.

"That's weird. You should find out," Chelsea commanded. "What about her? Does she have a name? Not that I care really, but it would be rude to call her 'new girl' once Mike and I are dating."

"I have an idea," Jay suggested, leaning toward Chelsea from across the table. "Why don't you put together a list of questions, in order of importance, and I'll have him fill out the answers? Kind of like *new-kid homework*." He smiled innocently. "You don't have to do it now, of course; just try to get it to me before the end of the day."

"Ha-ha." Chelsea made a face. "You're freakin' hilarious, Jay." And then she turned to Violet. "That must be why you like him so much. 'Cause other than that, I just don't get it."

Claire's brow creased, as though Chelsea's statement didn't make sense. She decided to help Violet out. "No, he's cute too." And when Jules started laughing, she added, *"Well, he is!"*

Chelsea was unmoved by Claire's explanation and, as usual, had to have the last word. "No offense, Violet, but no one's *that* cute. That's all I have to say about it." And then, in usual Chelsea fashion, she changed the subject before Jay had the chance to remind them all that he was sitting right there. "Hey, don't forget, we've got a date on Saturday."

"I didn't forget," Violet assured her. "I'll take any excuse I can to go into the city."

Besides, Chelsea might be obnoxious, but Violet knew they'd have fun. Plus it was a chance to get out of Buckley for the day. . . . She wasn't about to turn down an opportunity like that.

At the sound of her uncle's voice coming from the back door, Jay threw Violet off his lap.

Violet giggled as she hit the cushions on the back of the couch.

"What are you doing?" she complained. "It's just Uncle Stephen."

Jay sat up. "I know, but ever since the Homecoming Dance, I feel like he's always watching us. I just don't want him to think we're doing anything we shouldn't be."

The Homecoming Dance. It had been almost three months since that night, but the memories still made Violet shudder.

Not a day went by that she wasn't grateful Jay was still alive. Grateful the bullet from the killer's gun had only grazed his shoulder, despite the fact that the man—one of her uncle's own officers—had been aiming directly for Jay's heart.

If her uncle hadn't shown up at the dance when he did, firing the fatal shot that took the killer down, neither she nor Jay would have made it out of there alive.

Jay had always liked her uncle before then, but now it was something closer to worship. And even though Jay would never admit it out loud, Violet suspected that Jay felt indebted to her uncle for saving his life . . . a debt he knew he would never be able to repay.

A debt he wouldn't even owe if it weren't for Violet. It was Violet's fault that he'd been in that situation in the first place. Violet and her . . . *ability*.

All because she was different. In more ways than most people could, or would ever, understand.

The dead called to Violet.

They used echoes that only Violet could sense, pulling her onward, steering her to their locations. These echoes came in many forms. Smells, sounds, sometimes an inexplicable color. *Anything*.

Yet not all the dead had echoes, only those who had died prematurely, their lives cut short by the actions of others. And it wasn't just the dead who stood out to Violet but also those who had killed. They bore a mark as well: an imprint identical to the echo of their victim.

The imprint might fade, yes, but only over time. And only slightly. It would remain with them forever, in some form, an unambiguous reminder of the life they'd stolen. A reminder they would unwittingly carry with them.

And Violet was the only one who knew it was there. She was the only one who would ever see, or feel, or taste, what they had done.

They couldn't hide it from her.

"What are you two doing?" Her uncle's teasing voice came into the room before he did. But his voice was the second warning that they were no longer alone, since Violet had tasted his presence long before he'd actually stepped into her house. Ever since saving her and Jay at Homecoming, her uncle carried an imprint of his own. The bitter taste of dandelions still smoldered on Violet's tongue whenever he was near. A taste that Violet had grown to accept. And even, to some degree, to appreciate. "Nothing your parents wouldn't approve of, I hope," he added.

Violet flashed Jay a wicked grin. "We were just making out, so if you could make this quick, we'd *really* appreciate it."

Jay jumped up from beside her. "She's kidding," he blurted out. "We weren't doing anything."

Her uncle Stephen stopped where he was and eyed them both carefully. Violet could've sworn she felt Jay squirming, even though every single muscle in his body was frozen in place. Violet smiled at her uncle, trying her best to look guilty-as-charged.

Finally he raised his eyebrows, every bit the suspicious police officer. "Your parents asked me to stop by and check on you on my way home. They won't be back until late. Can I trust the two of you here . . . alone?"

"Of course you can—" Jay started to say.

"Probably not—" Violet answered at the same time. And then she caught a glimpse of the horror-stricken expression on Jay's face, and she laughed. "Relax, Uncle Stephen, we're fine. We were just doing homework."

Her uncle looked at the pile of discarded books on the

table in front of the couch. Not one of them was open. He glanced skeptically at Violet but didn't say a word.

"We may have gotten a little distracted," she responded, and again she saw Jay shifting nervously.

After several warnings, and a promise from Violet that she would lock the doors behind him, Uncle Stephen finally left the two of them alone again.

Jay was glaring at Violet when she peeked at him as innocently as she could manage. "Why would you do that to me?"

"Why do you care what he thinks we're doing?" Violet had been trying to get Jay to admit his new hero worship of her uncle for months, but he was too stubborn—or maybe he honestly didn't realize it himself—to confess it to her.

"Because, Violet," he said dangerously, taking a threatening step toward her. But his scolding was ruined by the playful glint in his eyes. "He's your uncle, and he's the police chief. Why poke the bear?"

Violet took a step back, away from him, and he matched it, moving toward her. He was stalking her around the coffee table now, and Violet couldn't help giggling as she retreated.

But it was too late for her to escape. Jay was faster than she was, and his arms captured her before she'd ever had a chance. Not that she'd really tried.

He hauled her back down onto the couch, the two of them falling heavily into the cushions, and this time he pinned her beneath him.

"Stop it!" she shrieked, not meaning a single word. He

was the last person in the world she wanted to get away from.

"I don't know . . ." he answered hesitantly. "I think you deserve to be punished." His breath was balmy against her cheek, and she found herself leaning toward him rather than away. "Maybe we should do some more *homework*."

Homework had been their code word for making out before they'd realized that they hadn't been fooling anyone.

But Jay was true to his word, especially his code word, and his lips settled over hers. Violet suddenly forgot that she was pretending to break free from his grip. Her frail resolve crumbled. She reached out, wrapping her arms around his neck, and pulled *him* closer to *her*.

Jay growled from deep in his throat. "Okay, *homework* it is."

He pulled her against him, until they were lying face-to-face, stretched across the length of the couch. It wasn't long before she was restless, her hands moving impatiently, exploring him. She shuddered when she felt his fingers slip beneath her shirt and brush over her bare skin. He stroked her belly and higher, the skin of his hands rough against her soft flesh. His thumb brushed the base of her rib cage, making her breath catch.

And then, like so many times before, he stopped, abruptly drawing back. He shifted only inches, but those inches felt like miles, and Violet felt the familiar surge of frustration.

He didn't say a word; he didn't have to. Violet understood perfectly. They'd gone too far. *Again*. But Violet was frustrated, and it was getting harder and harder to ignore her disappointment. She knew they couldn't play this unsatisfying game forever.

"So you're going to Seattle tomorrow?" He used the question to fill the rift between them, but his voice shook and Violet was glad he wasn't totally unaffected.

She wasn't as quick to pretend that everything was okay, especially when what she really wanted to do was to rip his shirt off and unbutton his jeans.

But they'd talked about this. And, time and time again, they'd decided that they needed to be sure. *One hundred percent.* Because once they crossed that line . . .

She and Jay had been best friends since the first grade, and up until last fall that's all they'd ever been. Now that she was in love with him, she couldn't imagine losing him because they made the wrong decision.

Or made it too soon.

She decided to let Jay have his small talk. For now.

"Yeah, Chelsea wants to go down to the waterfront and maybe do some shopping. It's easier to be around her when it's just the two of us. You know, when she's not always . . . *on.*"

"You mean when she's not picking on someone?"

"Exactly."

Jay's brow furrowed, and for a moment Violet wondered what he was thinking. Then he smiled at her as he tucked his hand behind his head, getting comfortable again. His eyes glittered mischievously, reminding Violet that he was still her best friend. "You know she made me a list, don't you?"

"What do you mean?"

"A list. Chelsea made me a list of questions to ask Mike."

Violet laughed, pulling herself up. It was too ridiculous to believe. But it was Chelsea, so of course it was true.

"What did you do with it? You didn't give it to him, did you?" Violet asked, her eyes wide with shock.

Jay sat up too and grinned, and Violet was sure that he had. And then he shook his head. "Nah. I told her if she really wanted the answers, she'd have to give it to him herself."

Violet relaxed back into the couch. "Did she?"

Jay shrugged. "I dunno. You never know with Chelsea." He leaned forward, watching Violet closely as he ran his thumb down the side of her cheek. "Anyway," he said, switching the subject, "I get off work at six tomorrow; maybe we can hook up after that." He moved closer, grinning. "And you can tell me how much you missed me."

He kissed her, at first quickly. Then the kiss deepened, and she heard him groan. This time, when he pulled back, there was indecision in his eyes.

Violet wanted to say something sarcastic and sharp-witted to lighten the mood, but with Jay staring at her like that, any hope of finding a clever response was lost. She could feel herself disappearing into the depths of that uncertain look.

She ignored the common sense that warned her *not* to lean in for another kiss. She much preferred giving in to that other part of her. The part that wanted more, the part that told her: *Don't stop.*

And when Jay didn't back away either, she realized that she wasn't the only one who was disregarding logic tonight.

Her heart skipped beats, fluttering madly, as their lips finally touched.

CHAPTER 2

VIOLET WAS SITTING AT THE KITCHEN TABLE WHEN her dad came down, already dressed for work. According to the clock, it was only five fifteen. On a Saturday.

"I made coffee." Violet kept her voice low, even though there wasn't a chance in hell they'd wake her mom at this hour.

Her dad ignored her comment and instead sat beside her. "What's the matter, Vi? Couldn't sleep?" He frowned, looking even more serious than usual. "Was it the dream again?"

Violet gritted her teeth. Of course it was the dream. It was always the dream—a faceless man chasing her—waking her night after night, a scream wedged painfully, noiselessly, against the hollow of her throat.

She hated the dream.

"Third night this week," she sighed. "At least I almost made it till morning this time."

Her father pressed his hand over hers. It was a gentle, reassuring gesture. "You're safe, baby. No one can hurt you now." He squeezed tighter, trying to convince her. "You and Jay, you're both safe."

"I know it's just a dream." She shrugged, drawing her hand away. She took another bite of her cereal, smiling weakly and pretending that she believed her own words.

If only it didn't feel so real. . . .

But she knew he was right; it was just a nightmare, nothing more. It didn't *mean* anything.

Besides, it wasn't like she was psychic. Psychics had abilities that were actually useful; they could predict the future, see things *before* they happened.

Violet's skill was something else altogether: She could only locate the dead. And only *after* they'd been murdered.

It was a painful ability to have—one that she'd been able to use once, when a pair of serial killers had hunted girls in the area. But, of course, she hadn't been able to save their victims. She had only helped locate the killers, to stop them from killing again.

Yes, maybe she was special, but if she'd had her way, she would have chosen to be psychic. Or, better yet, completely normal.

Unfortunately, Violet was never given a choice in the matter.

* * *

Chelsea was only a half hour late. Not bad by Chelsea standards.

She honked from out in the driveway, a long, inconsiderate blare. Even Chelsea's car was obnoxious.

Violet made an apologetic face to her mom before heading out the door.

Chelsea honked a second time as Violet jumped down the front porch steps.

"Nice, Chels. What if my parents were still sleeping?" Violet accused as she slid inside the car's warm interior.

"Yeah, right. Your dad's like a farmer. He's the early-to-bed-early-to-rise kind of guy. And I really doubt your mom sleeps past ten, even on a Saturday." She gave Violet a sideways glance and raised her eyebrows. "Am I wrong?"

"Not this morning," Violet admitted. "But you could have been."

But it was pointless to argue; Chelsea was already turning up her stereo.

Late January was not the usual tourist season downtown, especially not on Seattle's waterfront. In the summertime, it was bustling with activity: shoppers, tourists, impromptu street concerts, artists, and restaurants all squeezed in tightly along the piers. This time of year there was still activity, but the crowds were anemic, people nestled inside their warm winter coats and clutching umbrellas beneath the low-lying gray clouds.

Chelsea didn't seem to notice the weather or the lack of fanfare on the streets. "We should totally take a ferry out to one of the islands," she begged breathlessly.

Violet grinned. "All right. Which one should we take?"

Violet could remember riding the ferries with her parents when she was little. They would buy her hot cocoa from the concession stand and then huddle up at the railings and watch the choppy black waves of the Puget Sound.

Chelsea jumped up and down, the enthusiasm on her face making her look younger, less jaded. "Let's just take the first one we can get!"

Violet laughed. This was why she liked hanging out with Chelsea by herself; she was a different person when no one else was watching.

According to the schedule, there was an island run due to leave in a little over an hour. They bought their tickets and wandered around the piers before it was time to board.

They stopped at Ye Olde Curiosity Shop, a tourist favorite crammed with freakshow oddities, where Chelsea bought a necklace with a creepy shrunken head dangling from the chain. And before they left, they asked the guy behind the counter to take a picture of the two of them standing in front of a petrified pig that was on display.

Once they were outside, it was just starting to drizzle, and Violet tugged the hood of her coat over her head.

The *feeling*, the quivering vibrations, struck her long before the sound.

That unmistakable shiver beneath her skin was followed immediately by the inexorable sensation of being summoned, as if something reached into the very core of her and tugged. She could no more ignore the pull than she could deny what it was.

Something dead was calling to her.

The noise that chased the vibrations, reaching her at last, was distinctly out of place along the edge of the Puget Sound's rough winter waters.

In the summertime it might have found an anonymous place among the street performers who set up along the piers to attract tourists. But now, in the dead of winter, the instrumental sound of a harp, like the one Violet imagined angels might play, was at odds with her surroundings. It would have been soothing—the acoustic whispers—had it not been for the fact that it signaled the presence of a body . . . human or otherwise.

Violet was rooting for *otherwise*.

"Where are we going?" Chelsea asked, piercing Violet's concentration as she struggled to hold on to the precarious sounds reaching out to her.

Violet hadn't even realized that she'd been walking away from the waterfront shops. She paused, lifting her hand. "I think I heard something," she explained absently.

She thought about resisting the urge to follow the sound, just ignoring it, especially here . . . with Chelsea, who knew nothing about her friend's "gift." Besides, what did she think she would do once she found the body that beckoned her? There was no place to bury it, and she certainly couldn't take it with her.

Sometimes when she was near a body, she felt drawn

toward it, compelled to find it.

Usually when Violet found an animal, the casualty of a feral predator, she could take care of it herself. She had her own graveyard. Grim, yes, but a necessity for any girl with the ability to locate the dead.

If it turned out to be a person, however, that was another story altogether.

Once an echo called to her, and before the body was suitably buried, no matter how long or short that span might be, Violet remained unsettled. It wasn't until the body was given a final resting place of its own that the echo would fade, falling into the backdrop of her consciousness, never disappearing altogether but weakening, becoming something less . . . *haunting.*

On that day, Violet could breathe again.

Instead of trying to resist the pull she felt now, she heard herself saying, "Stay here, Chels. I'll be right back." She didn't wait for her friend to answer as she wandered away.

It took a moment for Violet to locate the direction again, as the sound drew her away from the piers.

It was farther than she'd expected, and she was only moderately aware that the scenery around her was changing dramatically. Beneath her skin, the stringed harp continued to strum.

On the other side of the road, across the street from the waters of the Puget Sound, she walked past the charming antique shops and faded brick facades of old Seattle. She moved toward the shipping docks ahead of her. Tall chain-link fencing topped with barbed wire appeared, in stark contrast to the cobblestone sidewalks and worn timbers of the wharves she left behind. Large cracks split the uneven concrete she trod upon.

Signs hanging from the fencing read: *Trespassers Will Be Prosecuted.*

Behind the chain-link, huge steel shipping containers were stacked on top of one another, end to end, creating impenetrable fortifications, shielding from view piles of industrial-grade pallets and an army of forklifts. Massive red steel cranes stood high above the containers. Several cargo ships floated in the waters beyond.

Seagulls, some vivid white and some the color of dirty dishwater, landed intermittently on the grounds, scouring for scraps of food.

It was Saturday, and the shipyards were practically deserted, with only a few cars parked in the outer lots. But the large central gate stood open.

Violet slipped inside without notice. She was too preoccupied to care if anyone spotted her. The gentle sound of the harps grew stronger until the vibrations were nearly painful and Violet found herself gritting her teeth. It was compelling, this echo . . . this death. And Violet was so close.

She moved around a towering row of cargo containers that were painted in dull shades of red, blue, and steel gray.

The briny smell of salt water was crisp in the air, and she wondered at how it had gone unnoticed by her before now.

Now it seemed so significant. The salt water and the harp. *And the body.*

She stopped, suddenly aware that she was no longer alone.

The skin at the back of her neck tightened, prickling. Someone was behind her; someone was watching her.

She held her breath, afraid to turn around. And even more afraid not to. She'd felt this before, this sensation of being stalked. Every muscle in her body was strained and tense.

But she had no choice; she had to find out who was there.

One . . . two . . .

Before she reached three, she felt someone grab her arm, gripping her tightly.

Violet jerked, her heart crashing inside her chest.

And Chelsea shrieked, worry clouding her face as Violet turned to stare at her, her eyes wide. Chelsea's hand shot up to cover her own mouth.

"Chels, what the hell? I thought I told you to wait!" Violet hissed, dragging Chelsea closer to the containers, where no one would be able to see them.

Chelsea reached for Violet's hand. *"What did you think you heard, Vi?"*

Violet lifted a cautionary finger to her lips, warning Chelsea to be silent as she moved in front of her, concentrating once more on the sound of the harp. She could hear Chelsea breathing heavily directly behind her, and she wondered if the other girl was afraid. . . . It *felt* like she was afraid. But Violet didn't pause to find out.

Violet was confused. She was in the right place; the sound was practically within her now in the same way the reverberating echo was, beating soft strings from inside her chest and spreading out to her head . . . her fingers . . . her toes.

But there was nothing here.

Only shipping containers stranded on a vast expanse of blacktop. All solid. And sealed.

She looked up at the red cargo container in front of her; its corrugated steel walls were impassable.

She moved around it, reaching out to brush her fingertips along the rough surface, examining the faultless seams and *feeling* the sound beneath her scalp. Her skin prickled. She finally found the door of the shipping vessel, but it was apparent that it was not an opening Violet could access. It was sealed tight, a large, rusty padlock hanging securely from a thick metal loop.

It's in there, Violet thought silently. Whatever was calling to her was inside the massive container.

"What are we doing here?" Chelsea questioned her again, and Violet could hear the alarm tracing her friend's voice.

Violet glanced up, momentarily forgetting the body trapped inside the steel tomb.

What could Violet say to her? She wasn't about to tell Chelsea what she could do. Jay was the only person outside her family who was aware of her strange ability for discovering the dead . . . the *murdered*. And Violet planned to keep it that way.

Besides, even if Violet could find plausible words to explain her ability, Chelsea would never understand.

How could she? She would think Violet was some sort of freak.

She looked at the container one last time, feeling defeated by its massive, impenetrable surface. She glanced around her and tried to push away the buzzing inside her head, tried to ignore the sounds, the ones that only *she* could hear, coming from within the steel box.

"I thought I heard something," Violet repeated.

"We're gonna miss our boat," Chelsea said.

Violet finally gave up. What choice did she have? It wasn't the same as finding a body in the soft earth of the forest around her house. This body was sealed, unreachable. And she didn't even know *what* it was.

It was probably some animal—a seagull or a rat—accidentally trapped inside the cargo vessel, starved to death.

Could that be an imprintable offense, a death caused by mistake?

It must be, Violet thought as she followed Chelsea back out of the shipyards.

The salt hung heavily in the air, clinging to the sound waves . . . and the haunting resonance of the harp that drifted after them.

★ ★ ★

The ferry ride was more fun than Violet had expected, especially in light of her discovery in the shipyards.

They only stayed on the island for about an hour, walking from the dock to an ice-cream shop, the kind that made real old-fashioned ice cream and served it in warm, handmade waffle cones. They ordered the most ginormous, two-scoop cones and somehow managed to eat every last bite.

Chelsea talked about Mike, the new kid—*again*—and Violet mostly listened. It wasn't like Chelsea to obsess over a boy, and Violet found it sort of hilarious to hear her going on and on about him. Not that there was much to go on and on about. They still knew barely anything about him except that his sister's name was Megan, and their last name was Russo. In the three short days he'd been at their school, he and his sister had managed to stay pretty much to themselves.

Aside from Jay, Violet had hardly seen Mike talk to anyone. So Chelsea was forced to repeat the few things they did know about him and to wonder aloud about the rest.

During their trip back, Violet fought against the persisting discomfort from the echo in the shipyard. And even though she could no longer *feel* it physically pulling her, or even hear the sounds of the harp out there in the open waters, that didn't mean it had left her alone.

Already the familiar sensation settled over her, the uneasiness she'd grown so accustomed to when a body was desperate to be laid to rest.

The dead didn't always want to be forgotten. And that need to be discovered could be so powerful that it became

Violet's only thought, her only purpose, until she could locate the remains, and if possible bury them properly, giving both the victim and herself a sense of completion.

Closure, her mom called it.

Closure was a good word for the relief she felt when a body was safely buried. *Quiet* was another. Better still, Violet thought, was *peace*.

She did her best to ignore the draw that tugged at her as soon as they docked again in the city, so near the body once more. And the drive home was no better. Just like on the ferry, there was that ever present feeling of discontent that refused to release her.

Chelsea dropped Violet off at home, honking one last time for good measure as Violet got out of the car.

Violet laughed, maybe a little too hard, as she tried to chase away the tension that settled over her more heavily with each passing minute.

By the time Jay called, Violet was in a foul mood. She thought about telling him about it, about what had happened in Seattle, but all she really wanted to do was to curl up in a ball and ignore that it had ever happened at all. If she could have willed it all away, she would have.

Even though Jay tried to change her mind, he knew better than to push too hard. Violet needed some space.

She was sure she would tell him about it eventually. Just not now.

For now, she wanted to rest. And to forget.

CHAPTER 3

THE BLACKNESS WAS STIFLING, OVERWHELMING. She was afraid it was going to suffocate her. But it was the cold that was unbearable.

She searched around her once more, exactly as she'd done every few moments for the hours—or days—that she'd been trapped inside. Time had stopped holding any tangible meaning as seconds stretched into minutes, stretched into hours. Stretched into days.

It was useless, her efforts futile. There was no escape, and she already knew it, but her waning survival instincts refused to allow her to surrender . . . to accept her fate.

There was no light. Not a trace. Not even a flicker.

And no light meant no openings.

But she searched anyway, because she couldn't give up, feeling with her fingertips along every surface she could find . . . the floor . . . the walls . . . the corners. They were all too familiar to her now, and her skin was raw from probing the unyielding and punishing metal.

Panic took hold, again, and she screamed, beating her bruised fists against the walls that confined her. The voice that came out of her mouth was foreign, even to her own ears. It was weak and small. It sounded like someone who had already conceded to death.

The darkness closed in on her, filling her lungs until it was hard to breathe and impossible to scream any longer. The sounds of her stranger's voice rasped and echoed around her until she found herself gasping to catch real air . . . clean air . . . *undark air.*

She collapsed into the corner, wrapping her arms around her knees and rocking herself.

It was so dark.

And she was all alone. And so very, *very* afraid.

She cried into the void between her legs and her chest, sobbing at first and then fading to a diminutive, almost inaudible, whimper as she curled into herself.

She wanted to go home.

Violet didn't wake quickly. Instead she woke on a slow sob, crying into the damp surface of her pillow, clutching it tightly as she tried to smother the lingering terror.

She felt confused, stunned. At first she couldn't recall the dream, so unlike the ones that had haunted her in the past, or the reason this one had brought her to tears. But as she lay there, struggling for composure, it came back in fragments.

The smothering blackness.

The fear. Sheer panic.

The devastating feeling of defeat.

The glimmer—although pale and fleeting—of hope.

It was as if she'd been buried alive. Entombed in total darkness with no escape. Violet was shaken by the nightmare, even as she assured herself that it was just that, a bad dream.

But this time she didn't believe it; she wasn't buying it at all. This was more than just a dream.

And she knew why. It was the voice. It hadn't been *her* voice. It was small. Frail. And it belonged to someone else.

She closed her eyes, struggling to give the haunting images meaning. Why had she dreamed she was another person, trapped and alone in the dark?

And why had it felt so real?

But she knew the answer. Of course she knew. She'd known it even in her dream, in the deepest voids of sleep. And now, as she danced between knowing and not wanting to admit the truth, it fractured her tentative grip on her own well-being.

It felt real because it was real.

Someone was in there. Isolated and afraid.

She blinked, trying to make the idea go away, but it refused to budge.

There was a person inside that steel container.

She shook her head, even though there was no one to see her. Still, the voice inside her head refused to be silenced. "No," she whispered, "there isn't."

But saying the words aloud didn't make them true; even she knew that.

The tears came again, but this time they were hers and hers alone. Because even though she knew what her dream was telling her, that there was a person in there—a dead person—she also knew she had to go back to make sure.

The sky was the shade of polished ebony when Violet crept out of her house, leaving only a brief, and vague, note so her parents wouldn't be alarmed when they got up and discovered she was gone.

She held her breath, listening to the crunch of gravel beneath her tires as she eased her car out of the driveway with the lights still off. When she reached the road, she double-checked her pocket to make sure her cell phone was in there, and she flicked the headlights on, casting an unnatural glow through the mist that had settled over the deserted back roads around her house.

The air was brisk, and since Violet hadn't taken the time to let her car idle before leaving, too worried her parents would hear the noisy engine, the interior was frosty. She could see her own breath in front of her face as she drove toward the main highway out of town.

It was early—or late—depending on how you looked at

it, and the roads were empty at this hour. Violet felt like the only survivor in some sort of postapocalyptic movie, alone in the abandoned shell of a town. The illusion was shattered when she saw a car coming toward her on the opposite side of the narrow highway. She wondered briefly if they were coming home or heading out like she was.

Because she hadn't slept much, she was tired. Fatigued was more like it. And the darkness had a lulling effect on her senses as her car moved across the pavement, rocking her gently. She stopped at a small drive-through espresso stand that was open all night to pick up a double-shot vanilla latte, hoping to shake some of the weariness out of her system for the long drive to Seattle.

As she got closer to the city, and night edged toward dawn, the sky gradually shifted from ebony to a deep, smoky charcoal. More cars crept onto the roadways, and suddenly Violet was no longer alone.

But that didn't mean she was any less afraid. She was terrified about going back to the shipyard, about standing in front of that cargo container for a second time, knowing what might be inside. And she had no idea what she could do about it once she got there.

Unfortunately there was no way she could just ignore it either. This echo would never leave her alone.

She came to a stop, parking her car right outside the tall chain-link fencing that guarded the perimeter of the shipyards. Even from where she sat, it was obvious: The gate was definitely *not* open this morning.

Violet got out of her car and approached the closed entrance. Crystalline puffs of steam were visible from her mouth as she zipped up her coat and stuffed her hands deep inside her pockets. It was still so dark, *too dark*, and Violet scanned the area for any sign of life.

Yesterday there had been only a few people milling about, but this morning there was no one. The silence was nearly complete, except for one thing: the tremulous vibrations of the harp.

It only added to the mysterious calm that drifted like fog through the vacant grounds.

Her heart pounded recklessly as she reached the gated opening. Part of her hoped it was locked, had probably been hoping for that the entire drive. And now, that desire nearly overshadowed the nightmare that had drawn her here in the first place.

The coward in her thought about leaving, about just turning around and heading back. But she knew she couldn't. This wasn't something that would just go away on its own. She knew that much for certain.

Getting through the gate turned out to be simple. There wasn't a lock, at least not like the padlock she'd seen on the shipping container. She reached out to touch the seemingly simple, garden-variety U-shaped fence latch. Her fingers clasped it and she lifted. It opened easily.

She glanced around to see if anyone was watching, but there was no one in sight.

Every fiber in her body was on alert as she held her

breath and shoved the gate.

It inched open. It was tall, and heavier than it looked, and Violet had to lean into it a second time, using her shoulder to push it far enough so she could squeeze through.

The resonance of the harp eclipsed the noises around her, the waking city at her back, and the ocean in front of her. It was vaporously surreal. Ominous. It was like the sound track from a horror film.

But this was no movie, Violet reminded herself; she was here to find a body.

She crept as quietly as she could around the containers, despite the fact that she seemed to be all alone, following the ghostly echo of the harp that drew her. When she saw the container in front of her, looking exactly as it had the day before, she was assaulted by that same sense of alarm, the sudden grip of panic, that she'd felt during her dream. The terror, she recognized, of being trapped within the solid steel walls.

She was shaking all over, her body mimicking the vibrations that quivered through her like electrical currents. She wanted to get closer, but her feet felt heavy and she struggled with the weight of them.

When she reached the container, the musical echo that just yesterday seemed eerily harmonic now felt menacing. It tore through her senses like an out-of-control chain saw, ravaging her.

She tentatively reached out to touch the steel walls, afraid that they might scald her. But just like yesterday, her fingertips brushed the icy-cold metal unscathed. From her nightmare, she knew exactly what it would feel like from the inside, and that memory stayed with her as she stroked the exterior.

The vibrations were jarring; the harp's echo was invasive and painful.

He, or she, was in there. And even though it was too late to save the person, the body still wanted to be found.

Violet shivered against the cold as she tried to withdraw into the warmth of her thick coat. But nothing could warm her now; the chill was bone deep.

She wondered why she'd dreamed about this individual. Her ability had never led to that before. What was it about *this body* that made it infiltrate her dreams?

Violet wasn't sure what to do now. Who should she call? Who could she tell?

Not her uncle Stephen. Even setting aside the fact that Seattle was way outside his jurisdiction as a cop, he was still her uncle, and that meant, without a doubt, he would feel obligated to tell her parents that she'd come out here—alone and practically in the middle of the night—in search of a dead body. They would never let her out of the house again.

And, for almost the same reasons, she couldn't tell Jay either.

But she had to do something. She would never sleep again if she didn't help whoever was in there.

She fingered the cell phone inside her pocket.

She could call the local authorities . . . anonymously. She

could make up some excuse for them to come out here and look for the body and then leave without giving them her name.

But even she knew she couldn't use her cell phone; it would be too easy to trace the call, to track it right back to her. And then they'd want to know how she knew where to find the body. A question she did not want to answer.

What she needed was to get out of here. To find a pay phone.

She moved quickly now, backtracking through the shipyard. She stole through the opening at the entrance and raced toward the sidewalk, scanning up and down the road for a pay phone.

It didn't take long to find one; there were two, in fact, that she could see from where she stood. One was just at the edge of the shipyard's parking lot.

She jogged across the short space and picked up the receiver. The handset was cold and dirty, but Violet barely noticed. She surveyed the silver face of the phone for dialing instructions. She didn't have any change, so she hoped this would work.

She dialed quickly, her fingers trembling.

There was a soft click, and then . . .

A woman's cool voice spoke from the other end. "911, what's your emergency?"

Violet paused. *This is a mistake,* she thought; *I should hang up.* Her thumb hovered over the large lever on the phone.

"911 operator, please state the nature of your emergency."

She hesitated, but she had to do something.

"Hello?" she said flatly, her mind spinning in a thousand different directions, grappling for a coherent explanation.

"Please state the nature of your emergency."

"I . . . I think I heard something . . . some*one* . . ." Violet started, still unsure. Her hands were shaking, and so was her voice. "It was coming from inside one of the shipping containers on the waterfront."

"Do you have an address?"

Violet shook her head, even though the dispatcher couldn't see her. "It's near the ferry terminals. The ones at Pier Fifty-two. There's a sign that says *Puget Sound Shipyards*."

She was jumpy about placing the call. Maybe she'd made a mistake. She glanced around uncertainly, suddenly wondering about what kind of person could put someone inside one of those containers. What if that person was still here? What if he was watching her? What if he'd followed her?

She took a step away, and the hand holding the handset fell to her side as she strained to listen to the sounds around her, searching for any sign that she wasn't alone. The metal cord that connected the receiver to the pay phone reached its limit and she froze. She could hear the operator speaking on the other end, but she couldn't make out the words.

She needed to get out of there, but that need was outweighed by the desire to make someone come . . . to find whoever was trapped inside the steel box.

She lifted the receiver back to her ear, ready to bolt at a moment's notice. "That's all I can tell you. There's someone in there, a person . . . locked in one of the containers. A *red* cargo container. Please . . . *send help*. . . ." She was whispering now, afraid that someone besides the operator might be listening to her.

"What is your name—"

Violet hung up, ending the call with an eerie sense of foreboding.

She ran as quickly as she could to her car. Once she was inside with the doors locked, she leaned her head back and fought to catch her breath. She started the engine and listened to its rough purr as she waited for the heat to catch up—and for her heart to slow down.

Outside the car, the echoes of the harp were muffled now, but the quivering aftershocks stirred all the way to her soul. She could hear the distant sound of sirens. She wondered if this was their destination . . . if they were coming because of her call.

She didn't wait to find out; she put the car in gear and drove out of the parking lot, a little surprised that her tires didn't squeal as she stomped on the accelerator.

And as the watery dawn broke across the sky, she was haunted by the nagging sensation that she'd just made a terrible mistake.

CHAPTER 4

IT WAS STILL EARLY AS VIOLET PASSED THE TURN to her house, but she kept on driving. She wasn't quite ready to go home, not ready yet to face the questions from her parents about where she'd gone to so early on a Sunday morning.

Her note had simply said she was going out and would be back soon. Violet knew it was a lie, even if only one of omission. To her parents, however, a lie was a lie; the distinction wouldn't matter. She only hoped they wouldn't ask too many questions.

She drove, instead, to Jay's house and parked next to his shiny black Acura.

He'd bought the car in the fall, right before the Homecoming Dance. Violet couldn't recall ever seeing it when it wasn't polished to a high-gloss shine, which was no small feat in a climate where it rained more often than not. Jay spent so much time at the do-it-yourself car wash that Violet was afraid he might buff away the top layer of paint. But so far it managed to sparkle even on the gloomiest of winter days, and Violet's car just looked sad and dull sitting beside it.

Even though it was a Sunday morning, Jay's mom answered the door ready for work. She was a nurse at the hospital in the next town over, so her schedule was irregular at best, but the flexible hours were perfect for the single mother. After Jay's dad had left, Ann Heaton had moved to Buckley, the town where she'd grown up, to raise Jay on her own.

"Hey, Violet, you're up early," Ann said, letting Violet inside. "Jay's up in his room, still asleep."

"Thanks. I'm glad I didn't wake you."

"Oh, honey, even if I didn't have the early shift this month, I'm not one to laze around in bed all day. Even on a weekend."

"I'm not sure it counts as *lazing* when it's only seven thirty in the morning," Violet teased. Her eyes watered as she followed Jay's mom inside, and she blinked against the familiar sting that Ann Heaton always caused her. Jay's mom carried an imprint of her own.

Violet had only confided in her own mom about Ann's imprint; she'd never told anyone else. Her mother had explained to her the difficulty that nurses sometimes faced when watching their terminally ill patients suffer agonizingly slow deaths.

Violet had decided *not* to tell Jay that his mom had killed, even out of mercy.

Now, years later, the smoldering scent of burning wood that Ann carried had dulled, and the sting that hit Violet's eyes, like smoke from a campfire, had lessened. Although not by much.

"You know what I mean, young lady." Ann smacked Violet on the behind, the same way she did to Jay whenever he was giving her a hard time. And then she winked. "You can go on up, dear. I'm sure he won't mind if you wake him." Ann grabbed her purse and car keys from the table beside the door. "Will you please tell him I'll be home after dinnertime, so he should feed himself?" Without waiting for an answer, Ann gave Violet a quick peck on the cheek, and the smoky scent wafted around both of them . . . only Ann couldn't smell it. "I gotta run or I'll be late. See ya later, sweetie."

Violet watched her leave. She liked Ann, loved her even. She was quirky and funny, and she never made Violet feel unwelcome. Their home was a place that was as comfortable to Violet as her own.

She dropped her coat on the back of a chair and crept quietly up to Jay's room. She did her best not to wake him as she pulled the door closed behind her. She watched him sleep, stretched out on his back, feeling herself coming back to life in his presence.

"What are you doing?" he mumbled without opening his eyes.

Violet startled, feeling like she'd been caught doing something she shouldn't have been. Like when they were little and they were busted for looking at a dirty magazine one of the other kids brought to school.

Jay rolled onto his side and squinted one eye open at Violet, grinning. "Come over here," he growled, lifting the corner of his sheet up, inviting her in. He looked rumpled and messy and alluring.

Violet slipped off her shoes and climbed in beside him. He wrapped his arm around her back, pulling her close. His breath was warm, his body warmer, and she felt herself thawing for the first time since she'd stepped out into the shipyard that morning. Even the heat blasting inside her car on the way home hadn't helped.

She tucked her feet between his legs.

"What are you doing here so early?" His voice was rough from sleep but it sounded like soft velvet. He stroked her back lazily. "Are you feeling better today?"

Neither question really needed an answer; they were just Jay's way of letting her know he'd been worried about her.

"I didn't mean to wake you," she whispered as she let herself get comfortable against him. She'd been cold and tired, and now that she was warm again she thought she might actually be able to fall asleep, right there in his arms.

He rested his chin against the top of her head. "You didn't," he assured her. "I was already awake."

Violet sighed. It felt so good to be here. It was the first time she'd felt comfortable since she'd gone to Seattle yesterday with Chelsea. Jay made her feel safe—*among other things*—and she needed that right now.

She closed her eyes; they were gritty and raw from lack of sleep. She breathed deeply, inhaling him, and relaxing as she sank further into him . . . and into the pillow beneath her head.

She fell asleep like that, wrapped in warmth.

Wrapped in Jay.

When Violet awoke, she was alone.

She was in Jay's bed, and even though he was gone now, she could still smell him in the blankets around her. She stretched long and hard, waiting for the blood to start flowing so she could find the strength to get up.

She rolled onto her back and stared up at the familiar cracks in the faded plaster above her. Bright daylight strained to get through the closed curtains. Violet stretched again, and then reluctantly threw back the covers.

Jay was in his kitchen when she came downstairs.

"Hey, Sleeping Beauty," he said, looking up from the beat-up laptop he was working on at the kitchen table.

Jay's mom was a lot of great things that Violet admired; technologically savvy was definitely not one of them. She was one of those people who were loath to move into the twenty-first century and embrace all things modern. She was the only adult woman that Violet knew of who didn't own a cell phone, and she refused to buckle beneath the pressure to pay good money for high-speed internet, so Jay was forced to plug his secondhand laptop into the phone line and use dial-up. Not because they couldn't afford such luxuries, but because Ann Heaton wasn't going down without a fight.

Violet smiled lazily at him. "Thanks for letting me sleep."

"I figured you were pretty exhausted."

"Yeah, sorry about waking you so early. I probably should've gone home." She wrinkled her nose, hoping it looked adorable, so he would forgive her.

Jay grinned, and suddenly *he* was the one who was adorable. "You didn't wake me. Your mom called before you got here to see if I knew where you were."

Violet cringed as she glanced at the clock. She was surprised to see that it was already after lunchtime. "*Oh, crap!* I better call and let her know I'm alive. She's probably freaking out!"

"Don't worry. I called her after you fell asleep. She's fine." And then his face became serious. "So? Where were you?"

Violet bit the inside of her cheek. She hadn't planned on telling him, but she couldn't lie either. He would know. He always knew.

She lifted one shoulder, trying to play it off as nothing. "Seattle."

From the look on his face, it was the last thing he'd expected her to say. "So you went all the way to the city and back before, what, like eight o'clock? What time was it when you got here anyway?"

"A little after seven thirty," she confessed, gnawing on her cheek again.

"Really, Vi?" He ran his hand through his messy hair, a sure sign that he'd moved from confused to irritated. "Why? Did you forget something yesterday that you had to go back for?"

Violet nodded halfheartedly, noncommittally. "Something like that." She turned around so she didn't have to face him. She grabbed the kettle from the stove and filled it with water.

"Mm-hmm." Jay's voice was filled with skepticism. "So, *what* exactly?"

She set the kettle back on the burner and turned around, leaning against the stove. She was going to have to tell him. There was no way around it.

"I sensed something, Jay. Down by the ferry terminal, when Chelsea and I were there yesterday. That's why I didn't want to go out last night." She sighed. "I think I might have freaked Chelsea out. She had no idea what was going on."

He scowled at her. "So why the hell did you go *back*?"

She rubbed her temples with the thumb and forefinger of one hand, covering her eyes so she wouldn't have to see the worry on his face. Even with a good dose of sleep, she still felt uneasy . . . unsettled. And she knew she wouldn't feel any better until they found whoever was inside that steel crate, and he—or *she*—was laid to rest. "I had a dream, and I needed to go back and find out for sure if something—someone—was there."

When she glanced up, Violet saw the muscles in his jaw flex. "So?" he asked through clenched teeth. "Did you? Find something, I mean?"

Violet's cheek was getting sore from where her teeth were ripping it apart. "N-no," she stammered. "I mean, kind of."

"Well, shit, Violet, what's *that* supposed to mean?"

"It means there's someone locked inside one of those gigantic shipping containers down on the docks. But I couldn't get inside, so I still don't know for sure. I mean, not in any way I can prove."

Jay jumped up from his chair. It was more than he could take. "Are you telling me you went down to the shipyards before it was even light out? In the middle of the night? *All by yourself?*"

Violet smiled then. She didn't mean to, but she couldn't help herself; she felt the corners of her mouth twitching upward before she could stop them. She was never going to get used to this, his worrying about her.

"Yeah," she challenged, taking a step toward him. "Something like that." She walked to where he was standing, barely containing his frustration. She didn't try to hide her grin. She put her palms against his chest and could feel his heart beating wildly. "You think you're gonna be okay? Do you need to sit down? Do you want me to get you a cup of tea or something?"

"Hell, Violet, it's not funny. I swear to God, you're asking for trouble when you do things like that."

She dropped her hands, her eyes narrowing. "*Things like that,* Jay? Things like what? I *never* do *things like that.* And it's not like I *wanted* to go; I *had* to go." She wasn't smiling anymore.

Jay exhaled loudly. "You should have called me. I

would've come with you. *You know I would have.*"

The teapot started to hiss behind her. "I know," she admitted. "But you also would've told my parents. Or my uncle. And I didn't want them to know. Please don't tell them, Jay." Steam whistled through the kettle's spout, and Violet turned around to slide it from the burner.

She kept herself busy for a moment, pouring hot water into a mug and giving Jay a chance to absorb what she'd just asked of him, letting him consider her request.

Before the dance and before they were a couple, there would have been nothing to think about; he would never have told on her. They'd kept each other's secrets. No matter what.

But now everything—*everything*—had changed, and Violet was sometimes surprised by how far he would go to keep her out of harm's way. She knew that, for him anyway, it meant that he would even betray her secrets if it meant she'd be safer in the end.

She carried her steaming mug, with the tea bag steeping inside, and set it on the table as she sat down.

Jay reluctantly sat too. He leaned forward and rested his elbows on his knees, watching her warily. Finally he sighed, "I won't tell . . . *if* you make me one promise."

She met his eyes, hesitating at the look she saw on his face. The unusual mixture of tenderness and fear were at odds, but it made Violet feel warm and soft inside. He reached out his hand to her, and she took it, letting him pull her toward him. She settled onto his lap as he wrapped his arms around her. He nuzzled her neck, inhaling deeply as if the scent of her was somehow reassuring.

"Next time . . ." he insisted in a voice quieter than before, "you call me."

She nodded, satisfied that he would keep her safe . . . secrets and all.

It was completely astonishing to her—even after all these months—being in love with her best friend.

Violet survived the surprisingly brief interrogation by her parents. She and Jay had come up with a lame story about going to Chelsea's to get the cell phone she'd left in her friend's car the day before. But as it turned out, she really hadn't needed the lie. Her parents didn't seem all that concerned about where she'd been. They were more worried about how she was feeling today, knowing that she'd locked herself in her bedroom the night before.

Later that evening, once again alone in her room, Violet turned on the TV and scoured the local news for reports that a body had been discovered on the waterfront. When she found nothing on the news, she checked the internet. She was afraid that it would be there, that her darkest fears would finally be confirmed, that someone *had* been murdered and left behind for her to find.

And she was equally afraid that there would be no news, that she would remain in this tormented state indefinitely. Either way would be devastating.

But in the end, she knew nothing more than she had that morning.

So it was another rough night for Violet, and it took her

hours to drift into a sleep that was too light to be restful. But it was a dreamless night and, for that at least, Violet was grateful.

When morning finally came, Violet wanted to stay in bed and skip school. But somehow the idea of her mother hovering around her all day, asking if everything was okay, was even less appealing than trying to make it through another sleep-deprived day.

She managed to drag herself out of bed, feeling fatigued and unenthusiastic. The shower helped—a little. But breakfast only made her queasy. She felt off, out of sorts. And it completely sucked, because she knew she would be sleepwalking through this day, and probably the next, and the one after that. Until whoever was inside that container could be found and properly buried.

Her phone buzzed just before she walked out the door; she had a new text message:

Check the news. It was from Jay.

As she stood, Violet grabbed the remote and flipped through the local TV channels. It didn't take long to find what Jay wanted her to see; it was on all the stations.

A four-year-old boy had been found on the Seattle waterfront late last night. Inside a cargo container. They flashed a picture of the blond-haired, cherubic-faced little boy.

Violet recognized the photo; she'd seen his face before, on the news, a story that she'd too easily ignored. An Amber Alert had been issued when he'd first disappeared—several weeks earlier—after he'd gone missing from his home in Utah.

And even then, she remembered thinking . . . vaguely . . . in the back of her mind, that the boy on the screen reminded her of her little cousin Joshua.

Violet felt sick. She had to sit on the edge of the coffee table to calm her suddenly shifting equilibrium. She felt like all of the air had been sucked from her lungs.

But at last she understood her dream on Saturday night.

She had dreamed of a dead boy. A *real* dead boy.

She dropped her backpack on the floor, deciding to give in to her exhaustion and stay home from school.

If only she'd been wrong, if only the container had held nothing more than a dead animal, then everything would be different now. But as it was, knowing that she hadn't been mistaken, that she'd somehow known what—or rather *who*—had been in there, she felt crushed by the burden.

She turned off the television and headed back to her room. She knew there would be no peace for her until this boy's family was able to reclaim and bury him.

She sat on her bed. At least in the privacy of her bedroom she didn't have to go through the motions of normal, everyday life.

Here, she could hide away without pretending to be anything other than what she really was:

A girl who found dead bodies.

CHAPTER 5

VIOLET STOOD OUTSIDE THE CAFETERIA, WISHING Jay would hurry up. She needed him to anchor her, to make her feel safe.

She felt raw, exposed. Her skin ached and her teeth were on edge, making them hurt all the way down to her jaw.

She knew, of course, why this was, but knowing didn't make it more bearable.

Violet heard her name again, and she glanced up. She recognized Lissie Adams and her friend, even though she couldn't immediately dredge up the friend's name—her brain was too fuzzy, her thoughts too muddled. But that didn't stop her from trying to interpret the look on Lissie's face. Disdain, maybe. Disgust. A mixture of both, most likely.

Apparently, Chelsea and Jules, who'd been waiting with Violet, saw it too.

"Go away, Lissie," Chelsea said, standing in front of Violet. "Shouldn't you be feeding with your own kind?"

"Stay out of it, Morrison. This has nothing to do with you. I was just tryin' to talk to Violet."

Chelsea took a step forward until she was practically nose to nose with Lissie. "Yeah, well, Violet's not interested in listening to any of your crap. Besides, we all know you're just pissed because Jay doesn't like *skanks* like you."

Lissie's lips tightened, but her face paled. It was a low blow, Violet knew that much, even from behind the curtain that buffered her from the real world.

She couldn't watch, but only because it was too difficult to concentrate. She turned away; her friends would handle it; they would take care of her until Jay arrived. Beside her, an unfamiliar girl stood quietly, waiting without saying a word. Violet had the distinct feeling that the girl was part of their group, that she should recognize her, but, again, the confusion that plagued her made her uncertain.

The girl smiled, a nice smile, but Violet just turned away, staring at the floor, trying to tune out everything around her. It was easier that way, not thinking, not noticing.

And then her heart fluttered—the first sign that it was still beating—as she heard Jay's voice. She didn't look up; she didn't even acknowledge that he'd joined them except to herself. Except to feel fleetingly grateful that he was there. At last.

She listened to the chatter going on around her as Jay's arm slipped over her shoulder and he steered her toward the lunchroom. She heard Chelsea and Jules. She heard Claire giggle. She heard the voice of the new boy—Mike, she remembered—deep like Jay's. And she heard Jay.

She didn't hear the girl, but she knew she was still there.

They were all just noise to Violet.

Background.

She felt Jay squeezing her hand with his. It was warm. It made her feel safe and attached to the world.

He reminded her that *she* was still alive.

LUST

SHE STOOD AT HER LOCKER, ONLY PRETENDING to sift through its contents, when in reality she kept her focus on the students hustling through the busy hallway behind her, not wanting to miss him amid the after-school activity. She knew she couldn't wait for too long, or she'd miss her ride. Not that she really cared. She'd walk home if it meant she could spend a few extra moments—even in passing—with him.

Just thinking about him made her heart flutter within the walls of her chest.

Casually she bent down to adjust the laces on her shoe so she could get a better view. And that was when she saw who she was looking for.

Jay Heaton.

Her heart beat a joyful rhythm as hope blossomed anew. She had to stop herself from grinning; she was all by herself and she didn't want to appear crazed.

What she wanted was for Jay to finally notice her. She willed him to glance her way, to come to her, but he just kept walking, his eyes searching the crowds for someone else. What she wouldn't give to be that person, just this once.

And then the look on his face changed, and a smile so sweet that it made her forget to breathe reached all the way into his eyes. He'd spotted the person he was waiting for, and her bloom of hope wilted.

Of course. The girl he was always waiting for . . . Violet Ambrose.

Envy rooted, spreading like a disease. Everyone had always told her how pretty she was, but what had being pretty ever gotten her? No matter how hard she tried, she couldn't get Jay to look at her like that.

Her jaw tightened as she ground her teeth together, trying to imagine what it was that Jay could possibly see in that shell of a girl, why he had ever decided to call Violet his "girlfriend" in the first place. She looked like a zombie, like one of the walking dead. Her skin was gray and slack, her expression . . . well, it was nothing. Violet was empty.

But he didn't seem to notice. He lifted the backpack from Violet's shoulders and curled his arm around her, guiding her protectively through the hallway as he led her outside.

She followed at a reasonable distance, trailing the two of them to the parking lot, trying to appear relaxed, like she was just another student. There were so many others around her that it was easy to blend, easy to go unnoticed.

She counted her steps, concentrated on keeping her breathing steady and her head low.

One.

Two.

Three . . .

When they reached Jay's car, she slowed, keeping her distance so she could watch as he opened the door and helped Violet inside. Her stomach convulsed when he leaned down and pressed a gentle kiss on Violet's forehead. She reached up and touched her own cold forehead in that same exact spot as she, once again, tried to imagine what it would be like to be in Violet's place. . . .

For just a minute.

For a week.

Or maybe even forever.

CHAPTER 6

EXACTLY SIX DAYS FROM WHEN VIOLET HAD placed her anonymous phone call, the boy was taken home and buried by his family.

Six days.

She could almost pinpoint the moment it happened, the moment that he felt released, and that her burden was lifted. She was like a comatose princess in some fairy tale when the spell was broken by the kiss of her prince. Except that in *her* grim fairy tale, the kiss was the funeral of a four-year-old boy.

And there it was . . . that *closure* she'd been waiting for.

Only three days later, she was back among the living

again, sitting in the cafeteria with her friends like the normal girl she wished she could always be. Yet she couldn't help but notice the absence of her boyfriend.

Apparently, Jay and Mike had been practically inseparable since they'd started hanging out, right after Violet had discovered the boy's body in the shipyard. *Inseparable* was probably too strong a word, but to Violet it felt damn close.

She hated being jealous. And of a guy, no less.

She wasn't exactly sure *why* it bothered her so much. Jay was allowed to have other friends, wasn't he? And it wasn't as if Violet didn't like Mike; he seemed like a nice enough guy. She just didn't really know him.

Besides, Chelsea sure liked him. That said something for him . . . even if it was just that he was absurdly hot. From what Violet could tell, *everyone* seemed to love Mike.

And maybe that was it; maybe she was feeling left out. While everyone else had been getting to know Mike, *falling in love with him* for the past week or so, Violet had been sort of . . . *checked out*.

But it wasn't her other friends she was worried about. It was Jay. She missed him. She missed being *alone* with him. It seemed like everywhere Jay was, Mike was.

And wherever Mike was, Chelsea wanted to be.

So they'd created an odd foursome, and Violet was feeling crowded. Like the misfit of the group, the only one who *wasn't* wild about Mike.

And worse, she was beginning to feel like she was competing for Jay's attention. It was something she'd never done before . . . and she had no intention of starting now.

She found herself secretly hoping that Mike and Chelsea would hook up already, just to give her and Jay some breathing room.

"What are you thinking about?" Jay asked as he plopped down next to her.

She blinked, wondering if she was wearing her frustration on her face. "Nothing," she lied, pushing her salad around her plate.

She wasn't sure why she didn't just tell him.

"Doesn't look like nothing," Jules interrupted from across the table.

Violet cast a quick glare at her friend for inconveniently pointing out the obvious.

"What?" Jay asked, nudging Violet with his shoulder. "Tell me."

Violet hesitated, suddenly embarrassed over her new insecurity. Yet, inside her head, she bitterly referred to Mike as "Jay's boyfriend."

Ironically, though, it was Mike who saved Violet from having to confess those very thoughts, when he slid into an open space on the other side of the table. "What'd I miss?" His lazy smile reached all the way into his tawny-colored eyes, and even the dimple on his cheek made a fleeting appearance.

Violet could see the draw for Chelsea; he *was* sort of stunning to look at.

So then what was Jay's excuse? She jokingly hoped it

wasn't the adorable dimple too.

Sitting next to Jules, Chelsea, who'd been unusually quiet, immediately perked up. "Nothing. We were just wondering what was taking you so long." She beamed at Mike.

Mike paused, not sure what to make of her comment, and then shot a half smile in Jay's direction. "Well, I guess it's a good thing I showed up when I did then."

Chelsea giggled, a strange, high-pitched sound that nearly caused Violet to choke on her food. *What the hell is going on with her?* Violet thought, eyeing Chelsea warily. *Someone needs to check her meds!*

"Anyway," Chelsea announced, as though she'd been interrupted by Mike's arrival, rather than moping over his absence, "what do you guys think about all of us getting together tonight? Maybe going to the movies or something?"

Violet's heart sank; a night out with "everyone" was definitely *not* what she'd been hoping for. Her shoulders fell as she sighed.

But it was Jay who cut Chelsea off before she could firm up her playdate. "Actually, Violet and I already have plans. We're gonna do something by ourselves tonight." He nudged Violet with his knee beneath the table. And to soften the blow with Chelsea, he added, "Maybe we can all go this weekend instead." Then, keeping his voice low, he said to Violet, "Besides, we've got some *homework* to do."

Violet sighed again, this time an entirely different kind of sound. He hadn't forgotten about her after all. And she wasn't losing him to a new guy with great dimples.

His barely subtle use of the word *homework* didn't escape her notice either.

She smiled to herself.

"Sure. No problem, man," Mike agreed as he took an enormous bite from his sandwich, making nearly half of it disappear at once. He was completely unfazed by Jay's announcement, and Violet suddenly liked him a little more.

Chelsea, on the other hand, looked crestfallen, like she was shriveling, and Violet actually felt sorry for her friend, something that took her entirely by surprise.

But as bad as she felt for Chelsea, Violet wasn't about to turn down the opportunity to be alone with Jay.

Violet was sitting in the passenger seat of Jay's car after school when the first call came in. It was a Seattle area code, but she didn't recognize the number, and she wasn't in the mood to find out who it was, so she hit Ignore on her phone.

The caller didn't leave a message.

Jay dropped her off at home, kissing her sweetly with a promise that he'd be back as soon as he finished up the to-do list his mom left him every afternoon.

Generally the list consisted of picking up around the house and taking out the garbage, but Jay was like the man of the house, and occasionally his mom threw in an odd handyman job or two. He'd become rather skilled with a screwdriver and a roll of duct tape.

As his car pulled away, Violet's cell phone rang again.

She checked it . . . it was the same number.

She hit Ignore for a second time, and, still, there was no message.

As she stood outside her front door, Violet glanced toward the street and watched Jay's car disappear. She tried to disregard the nagging sensation that had been plaguing her over the past week or so. She'd been aware of it even while she'd been lost in that in-between haze, awaiting the boy's burial. It was the disturbing feeling that she wasn't alone, that someone was following her . . . watching her.

It's just your imagination, she told herself for the umpteenth time, *nothing more.*

She scanned her driveway once more before ducking inside her house and dumping her backpack by the door. Her mom was still out in her art studio—a converted shed in their backyard—working. But there was a note on the kitchen counter waiting for Violet.

It was a message. A name and phone number. The same number that had called her cell phone twice already.

Apparently someone *really* wanted to talk to her, but Violet didn't recognize the name her mom had written down.

She pocketed the note, grabbed a can of soda, and wandered up to her room to find out who was so desperate to reach her.

She sat cross-legged on the bed as she scrolled down to her missed calls and hit Enter.

It rang twice before a woman's voice answered on the other end. "FBI, Seattle Field Office. How may I direct your call?"

Violet jerked the phone away from her ear as if it had just caught on fire. She hung up and threw it against her pillow.

What the hell was that? Why was someone from the FBI calling her?

Blood rushed noisily through her ears as she pulled the message out of her pocket and reread the name.

Sara Priest.

Who the hell was Sara Priest? And why was she calling Violet?

Violet felt momentarily staggered. She thought about all of the law enforcement people she'd had contact with over the past year.

After the shooting at the dance, she'd given statements to the police, repeating her words over and over again to more officers and detectives than she could count. She'd even spoken to the prosecutors who were handling the case against the other serial killer, the partner who'd been captured alive.

But *never* to the FBI. *Never* to anyone named Sara.

She wondered if somehow the FBI had become involved in the case. But why now? They already had one of the men responsible in custody, probably imprisoned for the rest of his life. And the other was dead.

So what had happened to change all that? Had they uncovered more victims? More missing girls, buried and forgotten? But surely, if that were the case, it would have been on the news.

Which left something else, something more recent.

She quickly ran through the reasons why that should be impossible.

She'd used a pay phone.

Anonymously.

With no witnesses around to see her.

It had to be the serial-killer case.

Her cell phone rang again, jolting her back to awareness. She leaned forward and pulled the phone toward her with one finger, as though it were something repulsive . . . something to fear. She glimpsed down at the screen.

It was the same number.

Violet was assaulted by the lingering, stomach-clenching sensation that she was missing something.

She briefly thought about answering it, to find out once and for all. But she couldn't bring herself to do it, and, instead, she shoved the phone away.

She decided that, for now, ignorance really was bliss.

CHAPTER 7

BY THE TIME JAY FINALLY SHOWED UP, VIOLET couldn't wait to get out of her house. She was a nervous wreck from waiting around all afternoon, afraid that the FBI was going to call again. And even though she'd silenced her cell phone, there was nothing she could do about her home phone.

It only rang twice, but each time she practically jumped out of her skin, worrying about who might be on the other end.

Fortunately neither was her mysterious FBI caller. Once it was her dad calling to say he'd be home late from work. Typical. And the other was Jay, since he couldn't reach her on her cell, telling Violet that he'd pick her up at six.

Violet was surprised that they were going out, mostly because she'd assumed they'd be staying in, "doing homework," among other things. But apparently Jay had other plans.

She was waiting outside when he pulled up.

He hopped out of his car and held open the passenger-side door for her. Violet eyed him suspiciously; he was acting really weird.

"All set?" he asked when he got in again.

"I don't know," she answered. "You tell me. Where are we going?"

He grinned, trying to pull off laid-back but a little too anxious to sell it. "It's a surprise."

"Really? What is it?" Already she could feel the tension lifting. Jay was a great distraction.

"Do you understand the concept of 'surprise,' Violet? Telling you would kind of defeat the purpose."

"Can I guess?" she asked, suddenly giddy.

Violet hated surprises. Christmases and birthdays had been like torture when she was a little girl. She would drop hint after hint about what she wanted, making long, elaborate lists for her parents, usually in numerical order. And after handing them over, she would resort to pleading, cajoling, and searching for whatever they'd gotten for her. She'd spent hours of her childhood combing through closets and scouring beneath beds in search of their secret hiding places, only to be disappointed that her parents had outsmarted her yet again.

A part of her—albeit a really, *really* small part—had even learned to dread the arrival of the holidays. She was certain it was some sort of sick Pavlovian response to the Christmas season, knowing that she would, once again, be afflicted by her crippling inability to wait patiently, while she counted down the days until the big fat man in the red suit made his annual appearance.

But tonight was different. Tonight she was with Jay, and almost everything, even a surprise, was tolerable when they were together.

He considered her request before answering, and she could tell he was enjoying this. Jay loved this particular weakness of hers. "You can guess, but I'm still not telling."

"What if I guess right?"

"Then you'd be pretty freakin' amazing."

She pretended to be offended. "So, what if I don't figure it out . . . ?"

His uneven grin made an appearance. "You're still pretty freakin' amazing, Violet." He lifted her hand, pressing it lightly to his lips.

Violet felt herself blushing. She knew how to handle his teasing, but she still hadn't gotten used to this gentler, sweeter side of him.

"You're such a girl," she chided, but somehow the words came out too soft . . . too tender, and ended up sounding like a compliment.

Jay just laughed. "So what does that make you, the guy?"

He squeezed her hand even tighter, keeping it buried in his.

"Or some sort of lesbian," she teased, raising an eyebrow. "Maybe we should try out a little girl-on-girl action."

"*Nice*, Violet. Do you kiss your mom with that mouth?" His eyes glinted as he watched her.

She leaned closer to him in the darkness of the car's interior. "No, but I'll kiss you with it."

He set her hand back in her lap. "Watch it, Vi, or I might pull over right now and we'll never make it there."

She raised her eyebrows. "Make it where?"

"Nice try, but you can't distract me that easily. . . . It's still a surprise."

He drove the rest of the way in silence, pretending to ignore her, even though she knew she'd gotten to him. And then he flipped on his blinker and turned again, coming to a stop in the deserted parking lot of a lakefront park. It was an odd location for this time of year, made stranger by the darkness that was shrouding the crisp night.

Violet looked at him curiously. "What are we doing *here*?"

"This is your surprise." He pulled a thick winter coat out from the backseat. "You might want to put this on," he recommended as he jumped out and popped the trunk.

Violet got up, shrugging into the warm, down-filled jacket. The sleeves hung well past her hands, hiding her fingers inside the soft, pillowy fabric. She felt like a little girl playing dress-up in her dad's clothes. But she was glad to have it when Jay met her on the passenger side, carrying a small cooler in one hand, a fleece blanket tucked beneath his arm. He was grinning mischievously.

"A picnic?" Violet asked, looking at him like he'd lost his mind. "Isn't it a little cold? And dark?"

She took the blanket and he slid his arm around her shoulders, pulling her against him. "I promise I'll keep you warm. And well-lit."

He led her toward the park, and when she stole a look across the grass, in the direction of the lake, she froze in her tracks, unable to move.

Her heart stopped, and she reached for his coat, drawing him back. "Jay . . ." she whispered. She was sure she was witnessing an echo—a strangely beautiful echo.

"It's okay, Vi." He leaned down, his nose tickling her ear. "I see it too. I did this. It's for you."

She relaxed her grip, finding her breath again.

Jay pulled her forward and, as he did, she was able to see the splendor of what he'd done. Just for her.

This time, when her breath caught in her throat, it was for an entirely different reason.

At her feet, a luminous path lit the way through the grassy field. It was made entirely from glow sticks; each of the radiant lights had been painstakingly set into the ground at perfect intervals, tracing a curved trail that shone through the darkness.

Apparently, Jay had been busy.

Near the water's edge, at the end of the iridescent pathway and beneath a stand of trees, Jay had set up more than just a picnic. He had created a retreat, an oasis for the two of them.

Violet shook her head, unable to find the words to speak.

He led her closer, and Violet followed, amazed.

Jay had hung more of the luminescent glow sticks from the low-hanging branches, so they dangled overhead. They drifted and swayed in the breeze that blew up from the lake.

Beneath the natural canopy of limbs, he had set up two folding lounge chairs and covered them with pillows and blankets.

"I'd planned to use candles, but the wind would've blown 'em out, so I had to improvise."

"Seriously, Jay? This is amazing." Violet felt awed. She couldn't imagine how long it must have taken him.

"I'm glad you like it."

He led her to one of the chairs and drew her down until she was sitting before he started unpacking the cooler.

She half-expected him to pull out a jar of Beluga caviar, some fancy French cheeses, and Dom Pérignon champagne. Maybe even a cluster of grapes to feed to her . . . one at a time. So when he started laying out their picnic, Violet laughed.

Instead of expensive fish eggs and stinky cheeses, Jay had packed Doritos and chicken soft tacos—Violet's favorites. And instead of grapes, he brought Oreos.

He knew her *way* too well.

Violet grinned as he pulled out two clear plastic cups and a bottle of sparkling cider. She giggled. "What? No champagne?"

He shrugged, pouring a little of the bubbling apple juice into each of the flimsy cups. "I sorta thought that a DUI might ruin the mood." He lifted his cup and clinked—or rather, *tapped*—it against hers. "Cheers." He watched her closely as she took a sip.

For several moments, they were silent. The lights swayed above them, creating shadows that danced over them. The park was peaceful, asleep, as the lake's waters lapped the shore. Across from them, lights from the houses along the water's edge cast rippling reflections on the shuddering surface. All of these things transformed the ordinary park into a romantic winter rendezvous.

Violet reached for one of the tacos, amazed that it was still warm.

Jay watched as she took a bite. "Is everything okay, Vi?"

She swallowed, setting the rest down. "It's perfect. . . ." She wrapped her blanket around her and went to Jay's chair. She leaned over him, her curls falling around her shoulders like a dark curtain. "*You're* perfect." She smiled as she collapsed on top of him, kissing him.

He groaned and pulled her closer, making room for her as the kiss deepened.

She'd wanted to be in control but had too quickly lost the upper hand. Her breathing became uneven, and she pressed herself against him, squirming to get closer. The warmth between them spread through her like a fever, making her restless and impatient.

He stopped her then, before there was no going back,

drawing his face away to create the most microscopic fissure between them. "You taste like tacos."

Violet gasped as she tried to catch her breath. "What?" She blinked, trying to gather her thoughts. "Really, Jay? Is that a complaint or something?"

He shook his head. "Of course not."

"Good. Because this is: *I hate it when you stop like that.*" She pushed herself away from him and sat upright, crossing her arms in front of her.

"Come on, Violet, that's not what I meant." The dazed look in his eyes only made Violet feel slightly better. She was glad he was at least a little bit bothered. "It's just that I wanted to talk to you . . . you know, before we get *distracted*."

"God, I really *am* the guy," she glowered, but her shoulders slumped.

He hauled her toward him, dragging her into his arms. "Stop it. You are *not* the guy." He kissed her on the mouth, ignoring the fact that she wasn't kissing back. But as annoyed as she was, it was hard to stay mad. Especially here . . . now. It truly was magical.

So when he pulled out the Oreos and dangled them in front of her—a peace offering—she shook her head and sighed. "You're impossible." But there was no real fight in her words, and she couldn't stop her lips from twitching when he grinned down at her.

He took her reluctant smile as surrender and settled back, bringing her with him until they were curled up against each other.

Violet took a cookie and twisted it apart, eating first one half and then the other, the way she'd always eaten them since she was a little girl.

Jay waited a moment before breaking the silence. "I know you really don't like to talk about this stuff, but I want to make sure you're okay. Ever since that day in Seattle with Chelsea, you've been going through something. I haven't asked you about it, because I knew you needed some time to work things out, but now . . . I just thought . . . you know, that maybe you'd want to talk about it. Maybe tell me about the boy."

Violet froze. The silence that followed could have swallowed her; it seemed to deepen with each second that passed. She wanted to say something, just to make the hush between them vanish, to replace it with something. *Anything.* But she couldn't. Her voice was gone; words escaped her; her thoughts had gone astray.

She didn't want to think about the boy. Not now. Not ever again.

She'd spent so much time trying to erase him from her memory, so much time trying to banish him, that she was unwilling to reopen that door, even at Jay's request.

She didn't know why he would want her to. Why he would ask her to do that.

Violet tipped her head back, struggling for the right thing to say but coming up empty. Finally she just shook her head. "I can't."

She thought he'd argue, try to convince her. But he didn't. Of course he didn't. He was Jay, and Jay wouldn't push her like that. She should have known better.

He smiled sweetly, crookedly, and her pulse hammered out of control. "Okay," he answered, pressing a whisper-soft kiss to her brow. His hand spread over her hip, his fingertips gentle, reassuring.

They lay there like that, in a different kind of silence now, watching the lake and the stars, listening to the night, each basking in the warmth of the other. Violet listened to the muffled sounds of his heart until her breathing slowed, becoming steady and even. She let him wrap his arms around her. He kissed her, but with more restraint this time, more caution than before.

And even though she hated to be the one to end their evening, she knew that someone had to.

"We should probably go," she finally said, pulling her cell phone out to check the time. "It'll be after ten by the time we get home."

"Do we have to?" Jay grumbled, trying to hold on to her.

"Unless you have a better idea . . ." she hinted suggestively, only half-joking.

But she knew that Jay wouldn't take the bait, much as she wanted him to. Instead he gathered the leftovers while Violet folded the blankets and helped carry everything to his car.

"Do you mind if we stop at Mike's house on the way back? He helped me run my errands this afternoon, and he left his wallet in my car. I just need to drop it off." He slid the cooler in the trunk.

Violet sighed, wishing they could have this one evening without anyone else. It didn't seem like too much to ask. "Can you take me home first?"

He looked at her like she was crazy. "It's right on our way," he explained. "Besides, it'll only take a sec."

"Whatever," Violet muttered under her breath. She didn't slam the door, but she'd wanted to.

She hated feeling this way, and hated it even more because she definitely was *not* supposed to act like this . . . pouting over a quick stop on their way home from the perfect date. What the heck had gotten into her anyway?

She knew she was being irrational, but she couldn't help herself. She crossed her arms over her chest when they stopped at what she could only assume was Mike's house, and when Jay promised he'd be right back, she refused to look at him.

Clueless to the wrath she was mentally raining down upon him, Jay left her there, bounding up the short porch steps in two long strides and pounding on the front door. When it opened, he disappeared inside.

Only once she was alone did Violet pay any attention to her surroundings, to the dilapidated little house where Jay's *new boyfriend* lived. It was set back in the woods, down a long, single-lane dirt driveway that afforded them complete privacy. And it was dark, with only the porch light to break up the blackness that settled bleakly over the property. Tall trees encroached all around the tired-looking house. The paint was faded and peeling, and there were rusty window screens propped alongside the rickety front steps. There was something about the isolated location, the spooky house, and the absolute darkness that gave Violet the creeps.

But just as he'd promised, Jay was back out within minutes, and Violet was relieved to see him, despite the fact that she was determined to keep her oath of silence where he was concerned.

It was then, however, that Violet felt the unexpected whisper of *real* jealousy shoot through her. Mike's sister, Megan—not Mike—poked her head out the front door, waving to Jay. She said something that Violet couldn't hear, but the tone of her voice, which Violet *could* hear even through the closed windows, was something that Violet would have recognized anywhere.

It was the same voice she'd heard too many times before, from girls who were flirting with Jay. Her good-bye was a little too eager, a little too choreographed, as if she'd planned her moves before Jay had arrived.

Violet noticed too that Mike's sister was cute, almost at the same time she realized that the other girl had no idea that Violet was sitting there, in the dark, watching them while she waited for Jay.

The girl cocked one foot up behind her. It wasn't an obvious gesture, but Violet recognized it for what it was meant to be: coy and endearing. And then she saw the girl twirl a strand of hair from her ponytail with her finger as she spoke again, trying to capture Jay's interest.

Jay was just opening the car door as he turned around

to respond to her. That was when the interior light blinked on, and Violet was suddenly aware that she was no longer cloaked by darkness.

Mike's sister saw too.

Violet bit her lip as she raised her hand and waved innocently at Megan, who was standing motionless, like a statue, her foot kicked up behind her. She almost felt guilty as Megan visibly slumped, her foot dropping back to the unstable-looking floor beneath her. Almost.

Jay smiled at Violet, oblivious to Megan's flirtations, as he climbed in and closed the door. "See, I told you I wouldn't be long."

Violet felt better, realizing that Jay didn't seem to notice the other girl. Although Jay wasn't off the hook that easily, she was still mad at him.

Now, not only did he have a new boyfriend, apparently he had a new admirer too.

Just as they reached the mouth of the driveway, Violet felt the sudden stab of a headache coming on. She massaged her fingertips over her temples, and then at the base of her neck, trying to rub away the tension.

A pair of headlights met them at the junction of the road, and just as Jay turned, a beat-up red pickup truck barreled past them into the driveway they'd just pulled out of. It barely gave them enough time to get out of the way.

As they drove in silence, Violet tried to tell herself that she was being a baby. That Jay loved her. And *only* her. Not Mike, and not Mike's sister either.

And she believed it. But she was still annoyed that their date had been tarnished by the detour.

She felt the pain in her head subsiding, diminishing a little more with each rotation of the tires, until it was nothing more than an uncomfortable memory.

Jay pulled to a stop in front of her house, and she let him kiss her good-bye. It was a good kiss. And within moments, she was too preoccupied to remember that she was trying to be mad at him, too distracted to care about her grudge, the one he was still annoyingly unaware of.

Dazed by the passionate farewell, she forgot *not* to wave good-bye to him before closing the door behind her.

She may have even lifted her foot demurely as she did so.

CHAPTER 8

VIOLET WAS UNLOCKING HER CAR WHEN THE woman in the crisp white suit appeared.

School was just letting out, and students crowded the parking lot and lined up on the sidewalks in front of the bus lanes, eagerly awaiting their chance to escape. Somewhere behind Violet, a stereo with its bass turned way too high was bumping out a country song that shook the windows of the cars around it.

"Violet? Violet Ambrose?" The woman didn't really seem to be asking the question; she seemed to know *exactly* who Violet was.

But Violet had no idea who *she* was; all she knew was

that the woman was definitely out of place amid the students of White River High, and she looked even less like she belonged to the faculty. Besides, Violet was certain she would have remembered this woman if she had seen her around school. And while the boy who trailed behind her looked barely older than Violet, he too seemed oddly out of place in his faded black T-shirt and ripped jeans. Straight, nearly jet black hair, too long and unkempt, fell sideways across his eyes, adding to the impression that he would be more at home at a skate park than in the parking lot of a small-town school with country music playing in the background.

He kept his hands in his pockets and glared at the asphalt beneath him, never glancing Violet's way.

Violet pulled her key out of the lock.

"Are you Violet Ambrose?" The woman awaited Violet's confirmation.

"Uh-huh." Her curiosity was definitely piqued.

The woman stepped forward, holding out her hand formally. "I'm Sara Priest. I've been trying to reach you."

Sara Priest? That name . . .

Of the FBI? That Sara Priest.

Oh, crap, crap, crap! Violet silently cursed herself.

Violet scrutinized the woman as she absently shook her hand, taking in the details of her meticulous appearance. Not just the pristine suit and the flawlessly sleek ponytail but also her no-nonsense demeanor. She exuded a confidence that Violet knew she would never be able to pull off.

"Can we talk?" FBI Sara asked when it was evident that Violet didn't have anything to say.

"I guess so," Violet conceded, looking around to see if anyone was watching the three of them. She tried to think of some pretense—some reason—*not* to have this conversation right now.

She was suddenly irritated with Jay for having to work today, mad that she'd driven herself to school.

So now here she was. All alone. With FBI Sara Priest.

Crap!

From the sidewalk, near the entrance of the school, Violet saw Mike waiting for his bus. He waved to her, enthusiastic, kind of like a puppy. Guilt over how envious she'd felt toward his new friendship with Jay flooded her, reminding her of how childishly she'd been behaving. Violet lifted her hand and waved back.

Unfortunately, Lissie Adams was standing right behind him, and she saw Violet too.

Lissie was everything Violet wasn't: blonde, trendy, and insanely popular, and it killed her that Jay had chosen Violet over her as his date for the Homecoming Dance. She got her digs in whenever he wasn't around.

And this happened to be one of those moments. Lissie raised a stylishly manicured middle finger and flipped Violet off.

Violet closed her eyes; she was so sick of taking Lissie's crap.

"So who's your friend?" the woman asked, tipping her

head in the direction of the school.

Violet sighed. "She's not my friend."

The woman smiled. "Not her. The boy you waved at."

"You mean Mike?" Violet frowned. "He's just a new kid at school."

FBI Sara pursed her lips, pausing briefly. "What do you know about him?"

"Nothing. Why are you asking?" Violet asked hopefully. "Is *that* why you're here? To talk about Mike?" Suddenly conversations about Mike Russo didn't seem like such a bad idea.

To her credit, Sara Priest didn't miss a beat. "Not at all. I'm here to talk about you, Ms. Ambrose. May we?" She pointed to Violet's car. "So we can speak in private?"

Violet's stomach sank. She was fleetingly aware that she'd never actually been shown a badge, and she knew her parents wouldn't like the idea of her talking to strangers—even if they *were* from the FBI. Still, she had a hard time mustering the courage to do anything but agree.

Her heart skipped nervously as she climbed inside. She thought about *not* letting this Sara person in her car, and instead just locking her doors and taking off. But even as she weighed the option, she knew it was useless at this point. Obviously they knew her name and her phone number. They knew where she went to school and probably where she lived. Did she really think she could *escape* the FBI?

So instead of leaving, she reached across to the passenger side and unlocked the door as she made a hasty scan of the seat to make sure there was nothing there that could make a big, nasty stain. She was afraid that the woman's suit was in danger of being defiled by her dilapidated rust mobile.

Violet wondered if the dark-haired boy would get in too, but he never moved; he just stood there, silently guarding Sara's door.

Strange, Violet thought as she started her car to get the heat going. She hoped that whatever the woman had come to say would be finished before the car actually had a chance to warm up.

"So I'm guessing you want to know why I'm here."

"Uh-huh." Even those two—nearly inarticulate—syllables sounded shaky coming out of her mouth. She hoped she wouldn't be expected to say much.

"Well, it seems that your name has come up during the course of an investigation." The woman beside her brushed invisible lint from her knee before looking up to judge Violet's reaction.

Violet's heart pounded. Hard.

This could go one of two ways. One, she could deal with. The other was bad. Very, very bad.

Maybe they'd found another missing girl's body in the woods somewhere.

She couldn't believe she was hoping for something so terrible.

"Uh-huh . . ." *So far so good on the speaking part,* she thought.

The banging sound that came from the driver's-side

window felt like an explosion to Violet's already raw nerves. She jumped hard and was immediately embarrassed by her reaction as she turned to see who was there.

Chelsea's nose was pressed against the glass, making her normally pretty face look distorted and hideous. Violet could practically see the girl's sinuses from her vantage point; it was more than she'd ever needed to witness.

Violet rolled down her window with the old-fashioned hand crank, and Chelsea jumped back before her face went down with the glass.

"Sorry to interrupt," Chelsea declared, not sounding the least bit repentant. She glanced disrespectfully at the woman in Violet's passenger seat when she said it and then instantly ignored her without waiting for a response. She looked earnestly at Violet. "Do you know where Mike went? I've been looking all over. He wasn't at his locker after class, and I haven't seen what's-her-name, his little sister."

Violet rolled her eyes impatiently. "I just saw him waiting for his bus."

Chelsea sighed. "*Crud!* I was hoping to offer him a ride home." But the way she wiggled her eyebrows implied that "ride home" meant more than a simple car ride. Knowing Chelsea, she was hoping it would.

Violet smirked as a big yellow school bus pulled out of the lot. "I think you just missed your opportunity, Chels."

Now there were only a few straggling vehicles left in the student lot, Violet's and Chelsea's among them, as well as a big black SUV that Violet could only assume belonged to the woman sitting beside her, since it sure as heck didn't belong to anyone at school.

"Fine," Chelsea sighed. "I'll see you tomorrow, I guess."

"Sorry about that," Violet mumbled to the woman once Chelsea was gone.

"I just have a couple of questions for you," FBI Sara continued as if their conversation had never been disrupted at all.

Violet's airway narrowed painfully. *Here goes,* Violet thought, hoping against hope for the familiar questions that she'd already answered a hundred times before.

"First of all, how did you know the body was there?"

Violet stared at her. She wasn't sure how to answer the question. It wasn't clear; FBI Sara hadn't given her enough details to be sure which body she meant.

Violet thought about the first body she'd found last year, discarded and bloated in the shallow waters of the lake. She closed her eyes, trying for the millionth time to purge the image from her mind's eye. But it was too vivid, forever etched into her memory.

"I saw it," she mumbled, hoping that *that* was the body the woman was talking about.

The woman shifted uncomfortably. "You *saw* him?" she asked, eyeing Violet suspiciously. "What do you mean, *you saw him*?"

And that was it. That one clarifying word, and Violet could no longer deny it to herself.

Him, she'd said *him*. Violet had been wrong. Precautions

or not, she hadn't been careful enough. All of the bodies Violet had found last year had been of missing girls.

They knew. The FBI knew. But how in the world was that possible?

She looked at the woman, trying to convey to her that this was all a mistake. It was her only chance. "I—I think you're confused. Maybe you have the wrong person."

"Violet Ambrose? That's you. You placed an emergency call from a pay phone almost two weeks ago." She watched Violet guardedly; her eyes narrowed just enough to look doubtful. "In it, you told the operator that you 'heard something.' You didn't say anything about *seeing* the boy."

It all came crashing down on Violet at once. Her head was spinning. She felt dizzy and sick in an instant.

She closed her eyes, trying to will her head to stop whirling so she could catch hold of her out-of-control thoughts.

She knew she shouldn't have called 911. What had she been thinking?

But she'd used a pay phone. She shouldn't be having this conversation.

"I don't know what you're talking about," she denied, but her voice sounded tinny and hollow, an obvious lie. She thought she was going to be sick. This was some sort of nightmare, almost as bad as her dream about the boy himself.

There was silence, and Violet struggled to keep it together. She needed to find a way out of this, out of her own car, if that's what it took. And away from this woman who had managed to track her down.

"Look, Ms. Ambrose, there's no point denying it. We traced you back using the shipyard's security cameras. We had your license plate. That, coupled with the call you placed, made it easy for us to find you." FBI Sara leaned forward, and Violet thought she might be trying to convey understanding, compassion. Instead she was intimidating.

"It wasn't me," Violet croaked.

"We both know that's not true. I have the recording of that call, if you'd like to listen to it." She pulled a small tape recorder from her jacket pocket.

Violet stared at it, unable to string together another denial.

"I didn't think so." She put the recorder back in her pocket. "We already know you had nothing to do with the boy's disappearance. Or his death. Like I said, cameras. Besides, we have DNA evidence that rules you out.

"So here's the deal. I want to make this easy for you. All I need to do is to ask you some questions. Not now, but soon. It will be quick and dirty, just the facts of how you came to"—her lips pursed again—"'hear' the boy. But for what it's worth—and this is just a hunch on my part—I think there's more to it. I think you didn't *hear* him at all."

Violet blinked once, trying to clear her thoughts as she apprehensively watched the woman in her car. She refused to give even the slightest hint of what was going on inside her head.

Sara continued without waiting for a response. She didn't seem to want one. "In fact, I *know* you didn't hear him, because you called on Sunday. The coroner says that the boy we found had been dead for at least two days before we recovered his body."

Puking became a very real possibility at that point as Violet felt the acids from her stomach swelling dangerously high in the back of her throat. Sweat prickled like icy barbs across her forehead and along the nape of her neck.

Still, she refused to speak. Not so much refused, actually, since she felt like it would be physically impossible now.

Again, FBI Sara continued, undaunted. "And even though we believe you had nothing to do with the boy's death, you were still there. You knew where to find him. So you're going to have to answer some questions, whether you like it or not."

Violet kept her lips tightly sealed.

Something about the look on Violet's face must have clued her in, because FBI Sara finally stopped talking. She scrutinized the girl beside her. "Are you okay?" she asked. The question itself contained little genuine concern.

Violet nodded. "I'm fine—" she started to say, but cut herself off as she choked on her words. Suddenly Chelsea's favorite expression, about throwing up in her own mouth, hit a little too close to home for Violet. She clamped her mouth shut again.

FBI Sara pulled a card from her pocket and handed it to Violet. "You're going to have to talk to me sooner or later. Call the number on the card tomorrow to set up an appointment."

She got out of the car then and walked purposefully toward the black SUV, the boy following right behind her.

Violet looked at the simple business card, absentmindedly running her thumb over the raised gold-foil seal.

She hated the feeling hanging over her, the looming apprehension that prophesized something terrible was about to happen. She hoped it was just worry over having been discovered and being forced to give a statement about something she should never have witnessed in the first place. Something that no normal person would ever have known.

But she knew that wasn't it. There was more to it than just a formal statement. There was something in the way that FBI Sara had worded everything that had Violet concerned.

Whatever the questions Sara planned to ask her, Violet had the strangest feeling that if she were to answer truthfully, Sara might actually *believe* what she revealed about her ability.

But Violet could never confess what she was capable of to Sara Priest. She had no intention of becoming some kind of lab rat for the FBI.

CHAPTER 9

VIOLET ROLLED OVER, CLUTCHING HER PILLOW tightly and wishing that whatever had dragged her awake would simply vanish again, like an unanswered whisper. But unfortunately the impractical chasm between hope and reality was impossible to navigate.

She cursed herself. When did she become the world's lightest sleeper?

A flash of light passed through her window. It came from outside, casting a watery glow around her dark room, and then was gone as quickly as it had come.

That was it. That must have been what woke her.

She groaned, kicking her legs in frustration and throwing

her covers off at the same time. This was ridiculous. She needed to sleep!

The light came again, and this time, with her eyes wide open, she had to squint against the glare.

She sat up, balancing on the edge of her bed, trying to decide what to do. She knew one thing for certain. Someone wanted to get her attention, and she was really too tired, and too irritated, to care why.

She pulled on the sweatshirt that she'd tossed on the end of her bed, zipping it all the way up to her chin. She didn't bother looking out her window; she was in too much of a hurry. She needed to put a stop to this before it woke her parents too.

She rushed down the stairs and unlocked the front door, staring out into the unpleasantly cool night. She strained her eyes, searching for the source of the light, but came up empty.

Nothing but night. And the spiteful cold.

She took one step outside, onto the frigid porch boards in front of her door, meaning to call out to whoever was signaling for her. But something held her back, and she waited instead, holding her breath. The fabric of her flannel pajama bottoms, which had seemed too warm inside, now felt impossibly thin. A gust of frosty air ran up her legs. She shivered, tucking her bare hands into her sleeves, and wished she had more than a pair of cotton socks on her feet.

The nocturnal hush around her was deafening.

And then it came. Again. The flash of intense light that

was so out of place within the midnight shadows that it burned her eyes before vanishing once more.

Violet blinked and leaned backward, her hands searching for the doorknob behind her. Just to make sure it was still there. She clutched it, trying to figure out where the light had come from.

Again she wanted to call out, but her voice had gone too, like the fleeting burst of white light.

Violet was too curious, though, to let it go. Besides, if she couldn't find the source of the flashing and stop it from flaring, again and again, it was bound to keep her awake all night. Or at least for as long as it continued.

She shivered as the arctic night extinguished her reserve of body heat. She decided to concentrate, to wait for the light again, and this time, to pinpoint its location.

She didn't have to wait long. The blaze was like a visual explosion, assaulting her eyes as she forced herself not to blink against it.

That was all she needed. And now she was positive that she'd seen where it was coming from.

She edged forward, hesitantly releasing her grip on the steely cold doorknob as she eased her way toward the blinking light. She cautiously stepped down from the porch and looked around, reassuring herself that she was the only one there.

The flare came again. From the other side of her car.

She moved faster now as she reached the vehicle, rounding the rear of it, and when she saw the flash once more, she froze in place.

It was coming from a box. A plain brown cardboard box sitting beside her driver's-side door. The top flaps hung limply open.

She was confused as she stared at it. Why was the box blinking? And who would put it there, next to her car?

She glanced toward the trees that surrounded her house, wondering—only fleetingly—if she was alone.

And then she faced the box again, taking a step closer, her feet freezing on the frosty surface of the gravel driveway, too numb to feel the sharp rocks beneath them. She leaned over the top of it, afraid that whatever was in there might flash again while she peeked inside.

It didn't. But she wished that it had. She wished she'd been blinded by the searing light, so that she hadn't seen what it was.

Violet felt sad and sick at the same time. And angry.

This box had been placed there deliberately for her to find.

She wondered why she hadn't recognized it before. The draw of the dead, an echo. The sporadic blinking of white light. The cold must have numbed more than her feet. Even her senses had been anesthetized by the glacial chill.

But it explained why only she had been awakened. And why she'd felt compelled to locate it.

She peered at the tiny black cat lying at the bottom of the box. Its head fell sickeningly—unnaturally—to the side. Its lifeless green eyes stared back at her.

It's not Carl. Violet released a grateful breath that it wasn't her own cat. And then shame flooded her for entertaining such an insensitive thought.

The burst of light came again, scorching her retinas, and she had to blink several times to clear the red spots that clouded her vision.

She was no longer afraid that someone else might be around. Her rage went far beyond caring for her own safety now. She wished he *was* here, whoever was responsible for . . . for *this*. She wanted him to show himself. She *dared* him.

Fury filled her icy veins, thawing her uncertainty. She knew what she had to do. And the sooner the better.

She closed the flaps, careful not to disturb the lifeless body any more than was necessary. The poor thing had been disturbed enough already.

Violet whispered beneath her breath, too quietly for anyone else to hear, even if she hadn't been alone. Only the cool air around her mouth seemed to notice, and she could see the misty gusts expelled from her lips.

"Now I lay me down to sleep. . . ." It was the same prayer she'd said for every animal she'd ever buried.

She carried the box, walking purposefully beneath the pale moon, not needing it to find her way around her house, toward the woods.

". . . I pray the Lord my soul to keep. . . ." It was the only prayer she knew.

A burst of light exploded from beneath the flaps of the corrugated box she cradled, tiny glowing slivers filtered from between the gaps.

". . . If I should die before I wake . . ."

She reached the darkened entrance to her graveyard, the one her father had helped her construct when she was just a little girl: Shady Acres. And now, in the dead of night, the name seemed more appropriate than ever before. An omen of sorts.

She wasn't afraid, though. Not here. Never here.

A familiar white noise, the static of so many dead animals who had once called out to Violet to find them, melded together in a peaceful resonance after their bodies were laid to rest.

She stepped inside the chicken-wire fencing meant to keep out scavengers who dared to disturb her lost souls. She knelt in the dirt, beside a spot that had already been dug, a shallow grave waiting to be filled. There was always a space ready in Violet's graveyard.

She shivered as she opened the box, unable to ignore the hostile temperature enveloping her.

". . . I pray the Lord my soul to take."

She tipped the box, letting the small, stiffened corpse drop gently into the soft dirt at the bottom of the grave. She bit her lip, trying not to imagine this poor animal's death. Trying not to cry as another white flash split the night.

She knelt down, reaching for a pile of soil that waited alongside the superficial hole in the earth, and scooped it with her hands, piling it over the lifeless cat within.

Amen. She mouthed the word without sound.

When she was finished, she sat back on her heels. She

could feel the sense of peace washing over her already.

The cat was releasing itself . . . releasing her.

Violet picked up the box and hurried back toward her house without looking around again. She left the empty box outside as she closed the door behind her, making her way back up to her room.

She washed and changed quickly, trying to banish the disturbing sensation that lingered, making her shiver long after the wintry cold had faded. The unsettling awareness that someone had left her a message tonight.

But what was the message supposed to be?

And just who had left it?

WRATH

THE GIRL STOOD THERE, HIDDEN AMONG THE trees, watching Violet. She was glad now that she'd dressed in black—the heavy black coat, the ski mask that covered her face, the dark gloves—not just for warmth but to cloak her from sight.

She really hadn't expected to hide within the natural cover provided by the thick bushes and trees surrounding Violet's house; she'd simply expected to get in and get out.

Drop off her "gift" for Violet and leave.

But Violet had surprised her by coming outside in the middle of the night. And when she had, the girl had stood frozen in place, unable to move . . . or even to think clearly.

She'd been afraid that Violet might see her there. But she hadn't.

Instead, Violet was fixated on something else, giving her time to react, to escape deeper into the shelter of the woods, where she could watch without fear of discovery.

Before Violet's appearance, she'd worried that she was going too far. That the message was too harsh. But seeing Violet, watching her, incensed her all over again. The anger she felt was beyond reason . . . beyond explanation . . . beyond control.

She wasn't sure how Violet had known where to look, but somehow she'd found the box. And when Violet had glanced in her direction, searching the trees, the girl had dropped to the ground, curling into a ball, hugging herself tightly as she waited to be caught.

But Violet never found her.

And, as she lifted her head again, she realized that none of Violet's reactions were what she'd hoped for. Or expected. Instead of the fear, she saw anger. Instead of revulsion over the mutilated animal, Violet seemed . . . calm.

Suddenly, she wished she'd done more. Upped the ante.

She wanted to see Violet scared. Afraid. Terrified.

Maybe next time.

As she watched Violet carry the box around to the back of her house, she thought she saw Violet's lips moving beneath the diffused light cast by the moon high above. But who would she be talking to? Herself? The dead cat?

And then Violet moved around to the back of her house and out of sight.

The girl lingered there, in the woods, wondering what Violet might be doing. Wondering if this was her chance to escape, but too curious to see what Violet did next. And too angry to go just yet.

She hated Violet. More at that moment than ever before.

More, even, than she hated herself.

When Violet came back, she was still carrying the box, but it was empty now. She could tell by the way Violet carried it, no longer embracing it against her chest but rather letting it hang loosely at her side as she walked.

Where had the cat gone? Had Violet dumped it somewhere? Thrown it away? Buried it?

When Violet rushed through the yard to her house, she didn't even look around her.

At that moment, the girl thought about making her presence known. She thought about what it would be like to hurt Violet just for the satisfaction of witnessing the expressions she so longed to see.

She imagined striking Violet with her bare hands. Clawing at her eyes. Ripping her hair from her scalp.

Fear. Terror.

She imagined slashing Violet's face.

Begging. Pleading.

She imagined breaking her neck.

Surrender.

The daydreams were so sweet.

And then Violet closed the door to her house, leaving her with nothing but her fantasies.

CHAPTER 10

"SO WHY DO YOU THINK HE HASN'T ASKED ME out?" Chelsea asked, unwrapping another piece of gum and stuffing it in her mouth. It was her third piece.

"Shhh . . ." Mrs. Hertzog warned, placing a finger to her lips.

Chelsea frowned at the librarian but lowered her voice as she leaned across the table and repeated her question. "Mike Russo? How come he hasn't asked me out yet?"

Violet already knew who "he" was without Chelsea qualifying her question with either a first—*or a last*—name. Mike was all Chelsea wanted to talk about lately, but today, of all days, Violet didn't mind. It kept her from thinking of . . . *other things.*

Violet hadn't told anyone about the cat. Not Jay, not her parents. No one.

Somehow, she felt changed by it. It had become her dirty little secret.

Whenever she thought about standing there, shivering from the cold and looking into the box that entombed a dead cat, Violet realized that her ability to search out the discarded dead had been used against her. And the person responsible probably hadn't even realized it.

Whoever had left that cat couldn't have known that it would wake Violet. And they had no way of knowing that the echo emitted by the cat would also be imprinted on them, a mark they would carry forever. That meant Violet would know who had done this, that they wouldn't be able to hide from her.

And she assumed that whoever had done this was someone she knew. *Why else would someone place a dead cat beside her car?* She was bound to discover who it was sooner or later.

The problem was, she wasn't sure she really wanted to know who had left it. Or why. Sometimes not knowing was better. Easier. And maybe even safer.

But if someone could kill an innocent animal to deliver a message, or a warning, then how far would they be willing to go to convey their true feelings?

She knew she should be afraid for herself. But she was worried for more than just herself now.

She was worried for Carl. For her friends. And for her family.

"I already told you, Chels, give him time," Violet whispered back, managing to stay decibels quieter than Chelsea, who was physically incapable of silence. She and Mrs. Hertzog had a standing feud over the matter. "Has he called you at all?" Violet asked, even though she already knew the answer. Chelsea would have exploded with joy if he had.

"No," Chelsea answered glumly, and then she snapped her gum, earning herself another scowl from the librarian. She ignored the scolding look. "And I don't get it. I've given him my best material, including the *I'm-easy-and-you-can-totally-have-me* bedroom eyes. What's he waiting for?" Chelsea stopped talking and dropped her face into her open history book. "Look out, crazy librarian at nine o'clock."

By the time Mrs. Hertzog reached them, Chelsea was pretending to be interested in her assignment, filling in the dates on her paper as if it were the most fascinating homework in the world. Although Violet was almost certain that the War of 1812 *hadn't* occurred in 1776.

"Miss Morrison, do I need to remind you that you're supposed to be working? Your teacher sent you down here to study, not to socialize." She smiled sweetly at Violet. Chelsea's gaze narrowed as she glared, first at Violet and then at Mrs. Hertzog. But, wisely, she kept her mouth shut. "If you need help finding reference material," Mrs. Hertzog offered, glancing over the answers on Chelsea's paper, "I'd be happy to point you in the right direction. . . ."

Chelsea swallowed, and Violet suspected she'd just swallowed her gum, since gum was a library no-no, before answering. "No, thanks. I think I've got it covered." She smiled, trying for sweet but getting closer to sour. "Unless you have any information on the Russo family?"

"What *Russo family*?" the librarian challenged, as if it were highly unlikely that Chelsea was really interested in "research."

She was, just not the kind of research she could do at the library. And Chelsea wasn't the only one interested in Mike Russo.

Violet thought about her meeting with the lady from the FBI, and wondered what Sara Priest had been fishing for. Violet couldn't help thinking that her interest in Mike hadn't simply been random.

"Never mind, Mrs. Hertzog, don't worry about it. You don't have the information I need." Chelsea smirked at the woman and then pretended to salute her, a dismissal if Violet had ever seen one.

To her credit, Mrs. Hertzog didn't react to Chelsea's lack of respect. Instead she issued a veiled warning: "All right, but if you change your mind, I'll be right over there."

Chelsea's eyes narrowed as she watched the librarian walk away. "Thanks a lot, Violet. Aren't you supposed to have my back or something?"

"For what? The big throw down? Were you planning to fight her? Besides, she likes me. Why should I get on her bad side just because you are?"

"As long as you guys are still tight, right, Vi?" Chelsea drawled. "Seriously, though, I need to figure out a way to get Mike Russo to notice me."

"I'm pretty sure he's noticed you."

"You know what I mean." Chelsea huffed. "By the way, what's up with the uptight lady and the hot dude at your car yesterday? And by 'hot,' I mean dark and dangerous, of course. Please tell me they're some distant relatives come to tell you you've inherited a family fortune or something. I could use some good news." Chelsea crossed her arms over her chest, watching Violet closely.

Violet felt her stomach tighten. It was weird enough that Sara Priest had asked her about Mike. If she hadn't known better, she would have thought Chelsea had just read her mind. Why else would she be asking Violet about Sara and the boy now?

Regardless of why, Violet did not want to talk about her little chat with the FBI.

She decided there was only one way to change the topic.

She sighed. Thankfully, Chelsea's mind had been pretty one-track lately. "So, about Mike. What do you know so far?"

Chelsea perked up, leaning forward as she heard the magic word: *Mike*. "Nothing useful. He has a sister, what's-her-name in the tenth grade."

"Megan," Violet volunteered.

"If you say so. I know they live with their dad, Ed, and that he's a mechanic at Craft's Auto Repair off Highway 410." Chelsea chewed her lip. "I also know that Mike's in AP English *and* history, he only missed two days last year, and he doesn't play any sports. Oh, and they moved around a lot.

Four schools in three different states in the past two years."

Mrs. Hertzog took two steps in their direction, her eyebrows raised in a warning to Chelsea.

Chelsea mouthed, *Okay*, and waved the woman away again.

When the librarian went back to her post near the entrance, Violet stared at Chelsea, not sure if she felt admiration or disgust. "How do you know all that about them? Are you *actually* spying on him now?"

"Not spying *exactly*." Chelsea cleared her throat. "But I *may* have gotten a peek at his school records. Andrew Lauthner's been working in the office during study hall for extra credit. He has a hard time telling me no."

That was an understatement; Andrew Lauthner was the lone member of Chelsea's personal fan club. He'd been waiting for Chelsea to notice him since the third grade.

Violet shook her head as she went back to work on her assignment. "I don't know what to tell you; you already know *way* more than I do."

Chelsea slouched in her chair. "Well, do me a favor and try to find out *something*? I really wanna figure out a way to get him to play tongue tag with me when we all go to the movies this weekend, maybe even get to second base." Chelsea didn't need Violet to say anything; she was on a roll now. "It'd be better if it were just the two of us, since Jay's always hogging Mike's attention, but since I haven't been able to make that happen, can you at least talk to your boyfriend about *not* derailing my plans this time? I really need this date."

"I'll do what I can, Chels," Violet offered reluctantly. "But I'm not making any promises."

Silently, however, Violet agreed with Chelsea, and she hoped as much as Chelsea did that Jay wouldn't monopolize Mike's time this weekend.

Chelsea was something else. Like an unstoppable force of nature. Similar to a hurricane or a tornado. Or a pit bull.

Violet admired that about her.

And, in this instance, Chelsea had proven to be nothing less than formidable.

So when Jay had mentioned earlier in the week that they might be able to go to the movies over the weekend, Chelsea held him to it. A time and a place were chosen. And word spread.

And, somehow, Chelsea managed to unravel it all.

She still wanted the Saturday night plans; she just didn't want the crowd that came with them. She'd decided it should be more of a "double date." With Mike.

Except Mike would never see it coming.

By the time the bell rang at the end of lunch on Friday, everyone had agreed to meet up for the seven o'clock showing the next night. But when they split up to go to their classes, Chelsea set her own plan into motion. She began to separate the others from the pack and, one by one, they all fell.

She started with Andrew Lauthner. Poor Andrew didn't know what hit him.

"Hey, Andy, did you hear?"

From the look on his face, he didn't hear anything, other than that Chelsea—*his Chelsea*—was talking to him. *Out of the blue.* Violet needed to get to class, but she was dying to see what Chelsea had up her sleeve, so she stuck it out instead.

"What?" His huge frozen grin looked like it had been plastered there and dried overnight.

Chelsea's expression was apologetic, something that may have actually been difficult for her to pull off. "The movie's been canceled. Plans are off." She stuck out her lower lip in a disappointed pout.

"But I thought . . ." He seemed confused.

So was Violet.

". . . didn't we just make the plans at lunch?" he asked.

"I know." Chelsea managed to sound as surprised as he did. "But you know how Jay is, always talking out his ass. He *forgot* to mention that he has to work tomorrow night and can't make it." She looked at Violet and said, again apologetically, "Sorry you had to hear that, Vi."

Violet just stood there gaping and thinking that she should deny what Chelsea was saying, but she wasn't even sure where to start. She knew Jules would have done it. *Where was Jules when she needed her?*

"What about everyone else?" Andrew asked, still clinging to hope.

Chelsea shrugged and placed a sympathetic hand on Andrew's arm. "Nope. No one else can make it either. Mike's got family plans. Jules has a date. Claire has to study.

And Violet here is grounded." She draped her arm around Violet's shoulder. "Right, Vi?"

Violet was saved from having to answer, since Andrew didn't seem to need one. Apparently, if Chelsea said it, it was the gospel truth. But the pathetic look on his face made Violet want to hug him right then and there.

"Oh," he finally said. And then, "Well, maybe next time."

"Yeah. Sure. Of course," Chelsea called over her shoulder, already dragging Violet away from the painful scene.

"Geez, Chels, break his heart, why don't you? Why didn't you just say you have some rare disease or something?" Violet made a face at her friend. "Not cool."

Chelsea scoffed. "He'll be fine. Besides, if I said 'disease,' he would have made me some chicken soup and offered to give me a sponge bath or something." She wrinkled her nose. *"Eww."*

The rest of the afternoon went pretty much the same way, with a few escalations: *Family obligations. Big tests to study for. House arrests.* Chelsea made excuses to nearly everyone who'd planned on going, including Claire. She was relentless.

By Saturday night, it was just the four of them . . . Violet, Jay, Chelsea, and, of course, Mike. It was everything Chelsea had dreamed of, everything she'd worked for.

They'd decided to drive together . . . in Jay's car, obviously. When they stopped to pick up Mike, Violet started to get out so she could climb in back with Chelsea, giving

Mike's longer legs the front seat, but Jay reached out and caught her wrist.

"What are you doing? I want you to sit with me." His fingers moved to lace through hers as he drew her back inside. "Mike can sit in back."

Violet felt herself blush with satisfaction.

Mike came out of his house and jumped down the porch without ever touching the steps. Behind the darkened curtains, the television flickered.

"Here he comes!" Chelsea squealed, sounding like a little girl as she bounced up and down in the backseat, shaking the entire car. She clapped her hands with excitement.

Violet pulled her seat as far forward as she could to give Mike some extra room. He'd need it if he was going to be confined back there with Chelsea.

"Heeyyy, Mike." Chelsea managed to drawl the two words into several long syllables as Mike slid into the car. The syrupiness of it sounded so foreign oozing from Chelsea's mouth.

"Hey," Mike said back to her. One word, one syllable.

"So I guess it's just the four of us tonight," she purred.

"Really? I thought we were meeting a buncha people."

"Nope. Just us. Everyone else bailed."

Violet smiled to herself as she listened to Chelsea's account, amazed that her words came out sounding so . . . *sincere.*

But Violet knew better. And she realized from the look Jay flashed her that he knew too.

Mike, on the other hand, was too new to understand the disturbing way that Chelsea's mind worked. There was a brief pause, and then Violet swore she could hear a smile in his voice when he answered, "That's cool."

He might rethink that later, Violet thought, *when Chelsea stops holding back and decides to assault him right in the middle of a crowded movie theater. Unless he's into that kind of thing.* She grinned wickedly to herself.

And then she wondered if Jay would attack *her.*

She hoped so.

CHAPTER 11

THE REAL SHOW OF THE NIGHT HAPPENED WHEN they stopped at Java Hut to kill some time before the movie.

Java Hut had first opened its doors as an internet café before there was a computer in every home. But as the concept became obsolete, Java Hut managed to stay open by becoming the perfect after-school and weekend hangout. Now, instead of just coffee, they served burgers and fries and ice cream, and along with the computers, there were also gaming stations. And that night, like most Saturday nights, it was busy and loud.

When they walked through the front door, Violet wondered if she'd ever get used to the attention Jay drew whenever they were out. Girls—of *all* ages—seemed to be drawn to him, and Violet thought she understood why. There was something about his utter lack of awareness of his charm that was universally appealing.

And women seemed compelled to abandon all good sense just to garner a moment of his notice, even if it was purely utilitarian.

Waitresses fawned over him. Cashiers lingered with his change, drawing out that moment when their hands would brush. And even the female teachers were inclined to give him a little leeway . . . giving him extra time to turn in assignments and neglecting to hand out a tardy slip when he was late.

Jay was oblivious to it, even when Violet pointed out the obvious. He thought they were just "being friendly" or "doing their jobs." But Violet never got free dessert or an open hall pass to roam the school during class time.

So it wasn't a total surprise that Jay would turn a few heads while they were out tonight. She just hadn't anticipated the power of the two of them together. Two good-looking guys more than doubled the attention they drew. Even among people they knew at the Java Hut that night, Violet and Chelsea became instantly invisible.

Girls not only noticed the pair of boys but also giggled behind cupped hands and waved at the two of them.

Jay was either unaware or chose to ignore them altogether. Mike, on the other hand, was not. And did not. Not only did he notice the interest he attracted, he seemed to enjoy it.

Violet recognized it immediately for what it was: Mike

was as much an attention whore as Chelsea.

Violet was fine with that. Chelsea, not so much.

Violet let Jay draw her through the crowds that bottlenecked near the entrance. She liked knowing that he belonged to her while all those envious eyes looked on.

"I guess Chelsea's not the only one who's into Mike," Violet whispered while Jay dragged her over to stand in line at the counter.

Jay glanced back to where Chelsea stood on the outskirts of three girls from school who were animatedly chatting with Mike.

"Yeah, she's not doing too good, is she?" Jay agreed.

"I thought she'd have him eating out of her hand by now." Violet wrinkled her nose, worrying over her friend.

"You mean like you have me doing?"

Violet smiled up at him and then bumped him with her shoulder. "Yes. *Exactly* like that."

Chelsea caught the two of them spying on her, and Violet flashed an apologetic smile. Chelsea rolled her eyes in response. She sulked as she made her way over to join them.

"Get me some fries." The lack of a question in her statement was somewhat reassuring. She was still Chelsea. Disheartened but bossy.

"Giving up already?" Jay asked Chelsea, after the girl behind the counter took his order.

Chelsea shrugged. "Nah, just taking a break. I'll wear him down eventually—it's just gonna take longer than I thought."

"There!" Violet exclaimed, shoving Jay. "Do you see that? That's what I'm talking about!" She pointed at the girl getting his fries. Obviously she didn't realize they were for Chelsea. "You only ordered a small, and she's getting you a large. She probably won't even charge you for it."

Jay shook his head. "She's just confused, that's all. If it makes you feel better, I'll make sure I pay for the large."

"*Ugh!* I give up. That's not even the point! She's only doing it because she thinks you're hot."

"You're crazy." Jay laughed at Violet, and the girl behind the counter laughed along with him as she set down the overflowing basket of fries. There was no way she'd heard what they were talking about.

"Can I get you anything else?" She cocked her head to the side. She looked like she could be a cheerleader, *very peppy*.

At least she wasn't openly suggestive. Perky and flirty, Violet could deal with.

"Nope," Jay answered, handing her a twenty.

She counted out his change and slipped it back to him in slow-mo. And there it was . . . the drawn-out hand brush.

Violet grinned on the inside, keeping her expression perfectly blank. *Predictable.*

"Well, let me know," the girl bubbled hopefully.

Jay handed Chelsea her fries, and Violet reached for his milk shake.

"So is he following you or what?" Chelsea asked, shoving several fries in her mouth at once.

Violet looked to Jay: *Is* who *following him?*

But Jay wasn't listening. In fact, Jay wasn't even there anymore; it was just her and Chelsea. Jay had gone to get Mike, so they could find a table.

Violet gave her friend a baffled look. "You're so weird sometimes. What are you even talking about?"

Chelsea's confused frown mirrored Violet's. Her voice was thick with impatience. "*Hello?* Right front corner table? The guy from the other day."

Violet turned to look. A sea of faces churned around her, moving in and among the tables, but she still didn't see who Chelsea was talking about.

She twisted around to face Chelsea again. *"Who?"*

"When you were talking to that lady after school." And then, exasperated, because it was so obvious to her, she added, "The hot guy who was waiting outside your car."

Violet's mind worked quickly, and when she figured out who Chelsea was describing, alarm seized her stomach. She spun back, this time scanning for someone in particular.

And there he sat, staring back at Violet. Violet could feel his dark blue eyes cutting through her, dissecting her. She felt as if she were crumbling beneath the weight of his penetrating stare.

Violet wasn't sure what to do, wasn't sure how she felt. Was it possible to be burning up and icy cold at the same time? Or was she just numb?

The boy watching her didn't move, didn't do anything. He scarcely acknowledged that Violet had spotted him.

There was just the slightest tightening at the corner of his eyes to give away that moment of recognition.

Violet glanced over to Jay and Mike, who were coming back now, heading right toward her. Dread squeezed her throat, and she winced.

She hadn't told Jay about the FBI. She'd kept it to herself, like so many things lately.

Maybe he would worry. Or tell her parents. Or maybe she still felt guilty about everything they'd been through this past year . . . all because of her.

And now this. *Here.*

She shot Chelsea a warning glance and hoped Chelsea would understand the meaning: *Don't say anything!*

But Chelsea didn't notice her pleading look. Mike was back, and Chelsea was on again. Smiling, flirting, charming.

The real Chelsea was gone. And that was good news for Violet; her friend would be too preoccupied with Mike to blurt out anything about the other day.

"Are you guys ready to go?" Violet asked as she grabbed Jay's arm, steering him toward the exit.

Jay chuckled but shrugged his arm away. "Violet, the movie doesn't even start for an hour. Let's find a place to sit so we can finish eating."

Violet blinked, trying to think of an argument *against* staying, but she couldn't. And before she could protest, Jay, Mike, and Chelsea were already headed for an open table.

Violet sighed, defeated by her crippling inability to think quickly.

Her legs felt unsteady as she gave in and followed the three of them. She stopped once, to glance over her shoulder. But the boy was no longer sitting at the front of the café.

Violet's heart leaped into her throat as her eyes scanned the room. She'd thought it was paralyzing to have him sitting there, watching her. But *this* feeling was worse: *not* knowing where he'd gone, yet knowing he could still be nearby.

She hoped that he'd decided to leave her alone. But somehow she doubted it.

Violet sat silently at the little round table while the others ate and talked and laughed.

Thankfully the numbness, that deadened sensation that had gripped her from the moment she'd first spotted FBI Sara's friend sitting there, had lifted. It had been replaced by something else, something closer to outrage. Violet felt as though her personal space had been invaded, her privacy violated.

She felt clearer now. Too clear, as a heightened sense of awareness infiltrated her mind. Her head reeled with questions and theories, suspicions and doubts. She worried as she scanned the other customers, and as she warily eyed the café's entrance.

She couldn't stop herself from wondering: *Why did he come here? What does he want?*

If Jay noticed, he didn't mention it. He was enjoying himself. He and his friends were having fun, even without her participation.

Violet didn't care. She had other concerns at the moment.

She was relieved when it was time to go, and she led the way out to the parking lot, pushing through the crowd, rushing to get out of the confined space. And, somehow, Jay managed to keep up.

She felt better once she was outside, like she could breathe again. They were already at Jay's car when Mike and Chelsea caught up with them.

Chelsea stopped grinning at Mike long enough to scowl at Jay. "Are you two trying to ditch us or something?"

But it was in that brief moment, while Chelsea wasn't staring at him, that Violet saw the fleeting look cross Mike's face as he glanced down at Chelsea.

It was so quick that unless someone had been looking directly at him, like Violet was, they would have missed it. But it had definitely been there. The corner of his mouth had twitched upward, his eyes crinkling just slightly as he watched her.

And Violet knew: *Mike liked Chelsea.*

As soon as Chelsea's gaze slipped back to him, Mike's cheeks turned pink and he looked away as if she didn't exist. Neither Jay nor Chelsea noticed.

The absurdity of it broke through Violet's apprehensive mood, and she couldn't help grinning to herself. Chelsea had been falling all over herself to get Mike's attention, never realizing that she'd had it all along.

By the time they reached the theater, Violet was feeling much more like herself. She even teased Jay for being so choosy about where he parked his precious car and managed to find her appetite again . . . for popcorn and licorice, at least. She loaded up on both at the concession stand.

When they got to the dim hallway outside the theater, Violet hesitated.

"Here." She handed the tub of popcorn to Jay. "Why don't you give me my ticket stub and I'll meet you guys inside? I've gotta use the bathroom."

She knew it was pointless to ask Chelsea to come with her, because Chelsea had no intention of leaving Mike's side, even for a few short minutes. Instead, Jay handed Violet her stub and she disappeared into the restroom.

Inside, she was all alone, which always bothered Violet. And as usual, she wondered if she were to scream, would anyone actually hear her above the pounding bass from the surrounding theaters? Someday she thought she might try it, just to find out.

No, you won't, she chided herself. *You're such a chickenshit.*

She tried *not* to think about things that might make her scream while she hurried to use the bathroom and wash her hands. And when she was finished, she rushed through the door, nearly running into the person waiting in the hallway.

Violet jumped, startled. And then recognition dawned, and screaming became an all too real possibility.

If only she could find her voice.

"What are you doing here?" Violet glowered at the boy in front of her, lifting her chin. "Are you following me or something? And don't try to tell me it's a coincidence we're both here at the same time. I saw you at the Java Hut."

He shrugged, his hands buried in the pockets of his scruffy jeans. "I just came to deliver a message from Sara Priest."

She blinked. "So *she* sent you?" Violet squared her shoulders. She wouldn't let him see how much Sara Priest's name affected her.

He shook his head, his black hair falling across his eyes. "Not exactly. But I was hoping that maybe you'd be more willing to talk if I came instead of her. You have to return her calls eventually."

Violet's outrage lessened. For days she'd been ignoring the messages from Sara Priest, each of them reminding Violet that this was an urgent matter.

"Just tell her I don't want to talk to her."

She tried to brush past him, but he reached for her sleeve, stopping her. She knew she should jerk her arm back, away from his grip, but instead she let him draw her toward the exit doors at the end of the hallway. It was dark there, private.

He glared down at her, but when he spoke, his voice was quiet. "Come on, Violet, this is serious." Hearing her name on his lips made her pause, and suddenly he had her attention. "You can't just ignore this and hope it goes away. Sara has a job to do, and she's serious about it. And whether you like it or not, it involves you."

"I'm not sure what I can tell her that she doesn't already

know," Violet lied, taking a step back. There was so much that Sara didn't know about her, and that Violet had no intention of confessing.

"The thing is, that's really not for you to decide." His face softened, just a little. "I promise it gets easier." He moved closer to her. "You just need to learn to trust someone."

A door nearby opened softly, like a whisper, but Violet didn't look up. What was he trying to tell her? That he knew what it was like to be . . . *different*? Or that she should confide in him?

Violet was more confused than ever. "I really don't have time for this. I'm here on a date."

The boy frowned as he shoved his hair away from his eyes, and then he handed Violet another one of Sara's business cards while he studied her. "Just call her, Violet. *Please.* You never know, maybe if you help Sara, she can help you." And then he handed her something else, a slip of paper with a phone number and a name—*Rafe*—scrawled in ballpoint pen. "If you're more comfortable, call me instead," he explained, his eyes searching hers. "Believe me, I know how scary this can be."

Violet shoved the card and the phone number into her pocket, not wanting to look at them or to consider the meaning behind his words. She wasn't sure she wanted to know if Rafe truly understood her—or what it was exactly that he did for Sara Priest.

So when he turned to go, Violet stayed where she was, in the dim shadows of the doorway, and watched him leave.

She closed her eyes, wondering what exactly he thought Sara could do to help her. Several seconds passed before she opened them again, just to make sure he was really gone.

She glanced down the hallway and hesitated.

She wasn't alone.

Jay stood there, examining her. Without saying a word.

Violet was unnerved by the accusation she saw in his gaze, and she wondered if it was real or if it was her own guilt she was sensing.

Finally, when Violet had lost track of how long they'd been standing there, he turned and went back inside without waiting for her.

She could feel the tears coming then. Shame and regret flooded her, burning beneath her skin, until she would have preferred the numbness to return.

She escaped to the bathroom once more to splash some water on her face—and to wash away some of the guilt she felt for keeping things from Jay.

Why couldn't she talk to him?

Why was she keeping so many secrets?

Violet slipped into the shadows of the theater and searched for her friends. When she found them, she made her way to where they were sitting, squeezing past feet and knees and trying not to kick over popcorn or drinks.

Jay didn't look up when she stepped over him and sat in the open seat.

But she was surprised, and relieved, when she felt his arm

slip around her shoulder. She knew he was upset with her—she'd seen it on his face when they were in the hallway—so his unexpected touch was comforting, reassuring. It was so Jay.

He leaned in toward her ear, his voice barely a whisper. "You can't keep hiding things forever. Eventually you have to tell me what the hell's going on."

Violet blinked away tears and nodded against his warm lips. He sat back and started watching the movie again.

On the other side of her, Chelsea and Mike were making out.

CHAPTER 12

VIOLET APPROACHED THE POLICE STATION HESItantly. She'd been there dozens, maybe hundreds of times before. Her uncle Stephen was the chief of police in Buckley, so it would have been a tough place for her to avoid. Still, her steps were sluggish.

She walked through the front doors, expecting the place to be empty on a Sunday afternoon. Or *hoping*, anyway.

Instead there was nearly as much activity on a weekend as there was during the week. She was met by several familiar faces and a few equally identifiable echoes—the kind of imprints that those in law enforcement sometimes carried. Among them, the pungent taste of dandelions that she immediately knew was her uncle.

"Hey, Uncle Stephen," Violet said, when she spotted him. "Aunt Kat told me you were here. I hope it's okay that I stopped by."

"Of course. I'll meet you in my office." And even though Violet could hear warmth in his tone, she also recognized the concern.

When he closed the door behind him, his demeanor shifted and his expression became worried. "All right, what's up? You hate coming here." He took his seat behind the desk.

Violet winced. "I don't *hate* it—"

He stopped her. "Don't give me that. You hate it, and you know it. So why are you here?"

She wanted to tell him, to talk to him about everything that had happened . . . the little boy down on the waterfront, the dead cat she'd found in her front yard, the visits from Sara Priest and Rafe. Those were all the reasons she'd come. She needed his help, his advice. But now that she was sitting across from him, looking him in the eye, she couldn't do it.

He was the sheriff, yes, but he was also her father's brother. And because of her, he now carried the imprint of murder, justified or not.

Hadn't she caused her family enough grief already?

Her smile was shaky. "I wanted to see if I could pick up some of those sticker badges you give out to kids. I like to give Jay a hard time about his little man-crush on you."

Her uncle's laugh filled his cramped office. "You're

terrible, Vi. You act more like your aunt Kat every day. Has she been giving you lessons?" But he was already reaching into his desk drawer and pulling out a stack of the foil stickers. He slid them across the desk. "How's he ever gonna stop being so jumpy around me if you don't stop teasing him?"

This time Violet's smile was genuine. "Give him time, Uncle Stephen; he'll relax. He's just grateful, that's all." She slid the stickers into her jacket pocket, feeling like a coward.

She didn't bother telling her uncle—again—that she was just as grateful as Jay was, because he already knew. She could never repay him.

He held her gaze for a moment, studying her.

"Well, thanks for these." She pointed to her pocket, trying to think of something more to say, something to stop her from feeling so awkward. "I guess I'll let you get back to work."

He walked her out and, once on the sidewalk in front of the station, he hugged her. She winced against the bitter taste that saturated her mouth when he did.

He pressed a hard kiss on top of her head. "I love you, kiddo. If you ever need to talk, I'm here."

Violet looked up at him, knowing he suspected she'd come for something more than just the stickers. And feeling bad that she hadn't been able to confide in him.

"Thanks, Uncle Stephen. I love you too."

She closed the door of her car and started the engine before pulling out her cell phone. She scrolled through the missed calls in her call log and hit Enter.

After two rings, the call was answered, and Violet spoke, her voice sounding shaky but resigned. "This is Violet Ambrose," she told the person on the other end. "I guess we need to talk."

Violet stood outside her private graveyard as the first stars pierced the sable sky. The woods beyond had become a collection of shadows, a collage in charcoals and grays. She shivered, but not from the cold. Her coat was plenty warm; it was doubt that wracked her now.

She studied the handmade markers, headstones that littered the ground before her. Why did some bodies—like these, like the girls from last year and the boy from the waterfront—call to her while others let her be? Why did some bodies *need* to be discovered so badly that they caused her physical pain?

Violet had her suspicions—speculation, really—that it had something to do with the brutality of their deaths. About lives unfinished. And it seemed, so far anyway, that human bodies pulled more than animals.

But she had no way to know for sure; there didn't seem to be any hard-and-fast rules. So far all she had were guesses and theories.

She hugged herself, listening to the backdrop of static that the reburied bodies of her cemetery created, the satisfying hum of peace as the echoes blended together. It settled over her as she remained silent, motionless.

She was still angry that she hadn't had the guts to talk to

her uncle today. She should have told him everything; she hated keeping so many secrets. But she'd hate it more if her family—and Jay—had to worry for her the way they had before, when a killer had hunted her. She couldn't bear to cause that sort of pain again.

No, she decided. She would handle this on her own, at least while it was still manageable.

The boy's body had been recovered; there was nothing more she could do for him.

The dead cat was disturbing and threatening, but so far that was the only message she'd received. Maybe it was just some twisted prank.

And Sara Priest was just a woman from the FBI who wanted to talk to Violet. *Talk*. She could do that without her parents holding her hand, couldn't she?

So why did she feel so guilty about not telling them? Why did her secrets feel more like lies?

Then there was Rafe. She knew Jay was still upset with her for not explaining who he was after he'd shown up at the theater the night before; why else wouldn't he have called her while he was at work today? He always called.

She blew on her frozen fingers as she turned away from her graveyard, her feet crunching through the ice-crusted grass.

She hoped that, after tomorrow, she'd have some of the answers she was searching for.

CHAPTER 13

VIOLET'S STOMACH WAS TWISTED IN KNOTS AS SHE got on the elevator in the parking garage. This was the sort of place that could give a girl nightmares. At least, the kind of girl who could sense the imprints of those who had killed.

This was *exactly* the kind of place Violet normally avoided—hospitals, morgues, and police stations. Even stores that specifically catered to hunters.

And FBI field offices.

Not that she'd been given much choice in the matter. Violet got the impression that FBI Sara wasn't planning to drop it.

The elevator ride upset her already queasy stomach, and she fought a new wave of nausea. She leaned her head back against the cool steel wall and took several long, deep breaths, bracing herself against the onslaught of sensory inputs she assumed awaited her, the ones that only she could decipher.

When the doors opened, she was released into a small lobby, complete with metal detectors and armed security.

So far, so good, Violet thought, relaxing only slightly when her senses remained unafflicted. The security guards had obviously never had to gun anyone down in the line of duty. At least no one who'd died.

Violet secretly mocked herself for being such a baby. With any luck, she'd be in and out of here in no time. She could do this.

The downtown building was basically what Violet had imagined. She'd seen enough action movies to have a picture in her mind, and this place pretty much fit the bill. Maybe a little more sterile than she'd expected, and a little more subdued and peaceful, but otherwise very governmental.

Unfortunately none of these observations made Violet feel any more at ease.

Once she'd shown her ID and made it through security, one of the guards called Sara Priest to let her know that Violet had arrived.

Sara's heels clicked on the floor when she came out to meet Violet in the lobby, and again, Violet was struck by how immaculate Sara was—the epitome of what an FBI agent should look like. The only thing missing were the dark shades.

Her greeting was a brief "I'm glad you could make it," and they skipped the small talk as Sara silently led Violet down a corridor past offices and cubicles. The offices would have been like the ones in any other building, quiet and even boring, except that it was making Violet's head pound to be there.

When they entered the small conference room, Sara closed the door behind them and pulled out a chair at the table, offering it to Violet.

"Can I get you something to drink?" Sara asked, her voice suggesting that she was making an effort, at least, to be polite.

But Violet was still mad about being bullied into coming and had decided to take a different approach. Something less than civil. She shook her head, stubbornly crossing her arms in front of her.

Sara took the seat across from Violet's. When she sat down, her jacket draped open and Violet caught a glimpse of her gun's handle, holstered in a leather shoulder strap she wore. Seeing the weapon fractured Violet's resolve.

This wasn't a game, the gun reminded her, and pouting wasn't going to make this any easier. Violet uncrossed her arms.

"Ms. Ambrose, may I be blunt?" Without giving Violet a chance to respond, FBI Sara bulldozed on. "This meeting really has less to do with the murder of a little boy than it has to do with *you*."

And, just like that, she had Violet's interest.

"In fact, your statement is just a formality that will probably be filed away and forgotten." She leaned forward then, narrowing her eyes as she watched Violet closely.

"I, however, am fascinated." She left the words dangling between them.

"Really?" Violet cleared her throat, doing her best to sound indifferent.

Sara nodded and leaned back, crossing her arms casually. "So, tell me. How does it work?"

Violet's heart slammed against her rib cage. What exactly did she think she knew? How could she know anything at all?

She had to be bluffing.

"I don't know what you're talking about." Why was this phrase beginning to sound so familiar? She felt like every time she was with this woman, she was repeating those exact words.

"Come on, Violet." And suddenly they were back on a first-name basis. "You know what I mean. Somehow, when no one else in the country could, you found that little boy. And since you couldn't *see* him, and you damn sure didn't hear him, there must've been something else. Something . . . *special* . . . about you."

Violet wound her fists tightly beneath the table as she leaned forward. She tried to look confused. She wished there were awards for real-life acting performances, because she thought she was doing a pretty good job. "Like what?" she breathed, trying to mimic the blank expressions she'd seen on Claire's face so many times before. Only, Claire's were for real.

Sara paused, and there was an uncomfortable moment during which Violet thought that the woman might be second-guessing herself. Then Violet watched as the uncertainty changed to something else. A new tactic.

"All right. I can see you're not entirely comfortable talking about this." Sara's voice was suddenly smooth, too smooth, and it made Violet even warier. "Clearly we've gotten off on the wrong foot—"

Violet interrupted with a sound that was half laugh, half snort. "Yeah, you think?"

Sara stopped and stared at Violet. And then the corner of her lip ticked up into a smile. A real smile. Sara sighed as she tugged off her jacket, slinging it over the back of her chair. She shook her head, meeting Violet's gaze. "How about we start over? Why don't I tell you a little bit about me?" Her tone was closer to genuine, bordering on sincere. "Are you sure you don't want some water or something?"

"I'm fine," Violet answered again. Even though she felt herself relaxing, she still just wanted to get this over with.

Sara nodded. "I'm a former FBI agent who now acts as a consultant for them. Occasionally with other agencies as well. I'm what they call a profiler, a forensic psychologist. Which basically means that I try to get inside the bad guy's head. In this particular case, I was called in almost immediately to help track down the abductor, the man who had taken the little boy you . . . *discovered*." She crossed the word quickly and kept talking. "It's my job to figure out what kind of person would do something like this—and why. And, hopefully, to prevent it from happening again."

Violet was confused. She understood the words, but there

was something she didn't understand, something important. And she didn't think it was something she could just overlook. "So you don't actually work for the FBI?"

Sara Priest shook her head. "Not always. Right now I do, at least for the moment. But sometimes it's the Seattle PD or another police department. On rare occasions, I even work for private investigators or attorneys. But mostly it's the FBI."

Violet wasn't sure what this meant, but somehow it seemed significant. Sara Priest *wasn't* an FBI agent. That changed everything, didn't it? "So is that why you didn't ask my parents' permission to question me? Does that mean I didn't have to come here in the first place?"

"Smart girl," Sara praised her. "I half-expected you to show up with your uncle." At Violet's surprised look, she raised her eyebrows. "Yes, Violet, I did my homework. I know your uncle is the chief of police. But here's the deal: I'm only questioning you; you're not a suspect in a crime. And you're here of your own volition. I only *asked* you to come. Although rather strenuously, I'll admit."

"And if I want to leave?"

Sara Priest remained unruffled by the threat. "I hope you won't. I hope you'll at least hear me out."

Violet still wasn't sure, but she was already there, and a part of her wanted to know where she'd slipped up, what she'd done to arouse suspicion about her ability.

She shrugged. "Fine, I guess. But can I ask you a question?"

"Sure."

"Why did you ask about my friend Mike Russo that day in the parking lot?"

Sara didn't hesitate, and she didn't need further reminding; she knew what Violet was talking about. "I thought I recognized him. From a case I worked about two years ago, while I was still with the Bureau. I had to look it up when I got back, but I was right. It was him."

Violet leaned forward, her interest secured. "What case?"

"Has Mike mentioned anything . . . about his mother . . . ?"

Violet shook her head.

"Sad, really. Your friend looks different now—older—but I'll never forget him. Just over two years ago, his mother went missing." She frowned, as if the memory was still fresh. "The husband was a mess. He just kind of fell apart after his wife disappeared, poor guy. And those kids . . ." She sighed. "I was surprised to see that they'd moved back to the area. If I were him, I'd want to stay as far away as possible."

"And you never found her?" Violet was sure she already knew the answer. She remembered Chelsea saying that Mike and Megan lived with their father; she never mentioned their mom.

Sara confirmed her doubts. "No. There was a brief investigation, but the husband always believed she just took off. He said she was under a lot of pressure and he didn't think she could cope anymore. I was never completely convinced, though. There was an abusive ex-husband who was still in the picture, showing up at her work, trying to get her back, even all those years after their divorce. I could never get a good read on him, but in the end there wasn't enough evidence, so we could never charge him."

"What did Mike and his sister think?"

Sara shrugged, pursing her lips. "Nothing, as far as I know. They were just kids; there was never a reason to involve them, especially since the investigation into the ex was going nowhere. I questioned them briefly, but I doubt they ever knew I suspected foul play." She glanced at Violet. "Still, I wish I knew for sure."

That crawly feeling was back, the sensation that Sara was asking for some sort of admission from Violet, and Violet felt herself withdrawing, pulling away. She wasn't ready for that. Not yet anyway.

Sara must have realized, and she quickly changed the subject. "As I was saying before, sometimes, as part of my job, I run across people who call in tips for various reasons. Usually these leads go nowhere; people see what they want to see. Mostly they just want to be helpful, but in the process a lot of manpower gets wasted. But your *tip* proved to be very valuable." Sara nodded to Violet. "Thank you, by the way. Sometimes the *not knowing* is the hardest part for families. You gave that boy's family the closure they deserved."

Violet remained silent.

"I know you don't trust me, and that's okay. I haven't given you any reason to, and I apologize for that. But my motivations for tracking you down, for trying to talk to you, are good ones." She leaned forward again; her eyes were eagle sharp now, and she had Violet in her sights.

"I work with certain people, Violet. People with unusual . . . talents, you might say. *Unconventional aptitudes* that might be considered by some to be extreme, maybe even peculiar. Some of my colleagues think it's a bunch of crap, but I've seen it work. I've seen these people in action." She waited a moment before continuing. "I could understand if someone with an *alternative* way of viewing the world might want to keep that to herself, for whatever reasons. Reasons maybe only she understands."

The soft click of the door interrupted them, and Violet was grateful for the intrusion. Her fists were balled tightly in her lap, her palms sweating.

She didn't know why, but she was surprised when she saw who was there.

Rafe poked his head inside as he spoke quietly to Sara. "We're ready whenever you are." If Violet thought he'd seemed out of place on the campus of her school, it was nothing compared to how odd he appeared in the starched world of the FBI field offices.

"Give us a minute," Sara responded, and a silent look passed between them, leaving Violet with the impression that they understood each other easily, with very few words.

He didn't even glance at Violet before he closed the door again.

But Sara was studying her. "Does any of what I've said make sense to you?"

Violet nodded. She understood perfectly—both the

stated and the unstated implications.

Sara was *telling* Violet she knew she was special. That she knew Violet had somehow found that boy in a way that no one else could have. Or at least, from what Sara had just insinuated, that only a very few others could have done.

But Violet was only willing to acknowledge the shallowest significance of Sara's words. Violet felt like she was standing on a narrow precipice, tenuously balancing at the brink of admission. And she refused to make that leap.

"Good. Can you do me one quick favor? It'll just take a minute."

"Okay," Violet agreed.

Sara surprised Violet by standing up to leave.

Violet followed as Sara held the door open. She had reservations about going into the hallway again, where the saturation of imprints seemed to be the strongest. Fortunately they didn't have far to go, and they slipped through another doorway just a few steps away.

Rafe was already there, waiting. His blue eyes met Violet's briefly, delving into her, making her uneasy all over again.

She wondered what it was that she saw in his expression. Concern? Or maybe it was curiosity. Maybe she was an oddity to be examined. Violet glanced away before she had the chance to interpret it, insulating herself from the discomfort his brief gaze caused her.

And then Rafe moved discreetly to the far corner of the room, making himself as unobtrusive as possible. He seemed comfortable there, watching soundlessly, and with everything else that was happening, Violet found herself forgetting his shadowy presence almost immediately.

This room was different from the one they'd just been in, although she recognized it immediately. Not from personal experience but from TV and movies. It was a viewing room. The kind of room with one-way glass that the police used for lineups.

The space that they stood in was small. Smaller than she would have expected. And it was dark. The room on the other side of the glass, which she could see clearly, was larger and well-lit.

Violet's head started to pound again, this time in anticipation. She was afraid of what this meant, her being here in this room. She didn't think she was ready for whatever Sara had in mind. Her chest tightened and her breathing became shallow.

"Wh-wha—" Violet stammered. She couldn't seem to finish what she wanted to ask.

Sara touched her hand. "Try to relax, Violet," she entreated in a voice that was much gentler now. "This will only take a second. We have a person of interest in the murder of the boy on the waterfront. Just look at him. Tell us if you notice . . . *anything* about him."

Violet couldn't. She wouldn't. She shook her head, but she couldn't put her refusal into words.

"Just stay." Sara's plea was whisper soft.

When Violet didn't object—or rather, *couldn't* object—Sara nodded wordlessly toward Rafe.

He left the room and, within seconds, five men were escorted into the brightly lit space on the other side of the glass.

Violet shuddered.

Sara glanced over to watch her, scrutinizing her.

"Take your time, Violet." Quietly.

"I—can't—" It was a broken murmur.

"Look at them," she coaxed.

Violet was frozen, her eyes beating back and forth across the strangers' faces. Several of the men carried imprints, some more than just one. She could see flames licking over one man's skin, heat shimmering above him. The taste of copper pennies filled her mouth, as did something else, something bitter that she couldn't identify. And even through the glass, she could hear several sounds weaving together: a bird's wings beating frantically, the muffled engine of a large truck, a child crying.

She even wondered too if she didn't smell oranges.

The stimuli were too much, and Violet couldn't distinguish one face from the next. Eventually she couldn't filter one imprint from another. They were all distorted, a tangled mess.

"Can you tell me anything?" Sara sounded far away now, as if she were at the end of a tunnel. Violet hoped she wasn't about to pass out.

She shook her head. It felt like it might split from the pressure building behind her brittle skull. Her eyes darted nervously from one face to the next.

Sara gripped Violet's shoulders. The touch was like a jolt

to Violet, jarring her from the blur of imprints that assaulted her and the even blurrier faces before her. She allowed herself to be turned away from the glass.

Violet knew that Sara misunderstood what she was going through. "I know what happened to you last year," Sara comforted her. "And I know you're afraid. But you don't need to be, Violet, I promise. You're completely safe here. They can't see you."

Violet blinked in response. It was all she was capable of.

"Just tell me this . . ." Sara requested, defeat evident in her words. "Is he in there?"

Violet glanced back, not really looking. She was trying to find something through the intertwined collection of sensations. She tried to locate a sound, single and solitary, from among the others.

The melodic vibrations of a harp.

She closed her eyes as she shook her head.

It wasn't there.

Thank God, Violet thought to herself. *It isn't there.*

Violet stayed in the bathroom for longer than she needed to.

The interior was cool, and within its insulated walls she felt safer. Calmer.

She was grateful that she'd made it there in time, before she'd actually thrown up. Sara had left her alone, and even though there were several stalls, she was never disturbed by anyone else.

Violet leaned over the sink and scooped cold water into

her mouth, swishing it around and then spitting it into the porcelain bowl. She splashed more water on her face, pressing her hands against her flushed cheeks and staring at herself in the mirror.

What is wrong with me? she wondered. *Why am I so relieved that he wasn't there, in the lineup?*

Her eyes looked haunted. She *felt* haunted.

She knew why: She wasn't ready to face him. She didn't *want* to know who he was. Or *what* he was.

She waited for as long as she could, past the point of its being weird that she was still in there, before forcing herself to come out again.

Rafe was waiting for her, looking relieved, and Violet had the feeling that he'd been standing there, guarding the door, the entire time.

"Feeling better?" he asked softly, shifting nervously.

Violet looked around the hallway, wondering why they were alone now.

"Sara had to go," Rafe answered before Violet could ask. And then he handed Violet two manila file folders before walking her to the elevators. "She asked me to give you these and to think about what she said."

"I can't—" Violet insisted, trying to refuse them.

But Rafe held them out until she finally took them. "You don't have to do it right away, Violet. Just look them over whenever you feel up to it."

His dark eyes held hers, and Violet felt that same nagging sensation that had bothered her when she'd been alone with him at the theater . . . the feeling that there was some shared secret between them. A secret that neither of them was willing to acknowledge.

A man in a suit brushed past them in the hallway, and Violet watched him go. She knew him from somewhere, but she couldn't quite place it. She ignored the fleeting sense of déjà vu, too fatigued by everything that had happened to give it more than a passing thought.

When they reached the elevator in the lobby, Violet was relieved as she watched Rafe disappear behind the closing doors.

She sighed, leaning heavily against the hand railing, her forehead resting on the steel wall. When she reached her floor, she hurried into the concrete structure of the parking garage, anxious to get to her car and away from everything about this place.

Ahead of her, a group of men was gathered, and Violet overheard brief snippets of their conversation without meaning to.

"What was she thinking . . . ?"

". . . a waste of time . . ."

". . . total bullshit."

The words would have been unremarkable to Violet had they not been surrounded by something else: the unmistakable impressions that hovered around their words, around their voices . . . *around them.*

Imprints.

Colors. Sounds. Sensations . . . twisting around one

another and bound like tangled threads.

Recognizable to her in a way that was still too fresh in her memory to be ignored.

Bird wings. Flames. A child's cry.

She glanced around at their faces as she passed them, reminding herself to stay steady on her feet, trying to concentrate on her steps so she didn't stumble.

Their suits were out of place for her. She re-dressed them in her head. Flannel jackets. T-shirts. Faded blue jeans.

In her mind, she added the man from the hallway, the one she'd run into on her way out.

It was them. The men from the lineup. FBI agents. All of them.

So, what then, had it all been a joke? A trick? *A test?*

She wondered if they recognized her. If *they* knew who *she* was.

She peered back at them once more as she reached her car. They didn't seem to notice her.

Her hands shook as she got in and buckled her seat belt. She started her car and drove from the building without paying any attention to where she was headed. All of the streets downtown looked the same to her.

Had Sara set her up to see if she could really do what she suspected? Had Violet passed the test? Failed it?

Violet clenched her teeth, feeling angry and betrayed, but not really understanding why. She shouldn't care what Sara thought she could—*or couldn't*—do. And she damn sure wasn't some guinea pig to be experimented on.

Her head was spinning again, her stomach churning violently.

She turned a corner and pulled into a crowded parking lot, not caring that there were no open spaces. She shoved the car door open and leaned outside, throwing up on the pavement. She ignored the attendant in the booth who eyed her suspiciously.

She thought about the words she'd overheard in the parking garage.

Waste of time. Bullshit.

It is *bullshit,* she thought furiously. At least they didn't believe any of it. Maybe Sara wouldn't either.

Violet sat up and wiped her mouth on her sleeve, spitting one more time to try to purge the nasty taste clinging to her tongue.

Maybe now they would leave her alone.

Unless . . .

But the thought was almost too much to even consider.

What if she hadn't failed the test at all?

What if she'd just passed?

CHAPTER 14

VIOLET DUG THROUGH THE REFRIGERATOR looking for something to eat as she tried to forget about what had happened at the FBI offices that afternoon.

She tried not to think about the things she'd said and those she hadn't. She struggled to disregard what she'd sensed and what she'd overheard in the parking garage. But most of all, she did her best to ignore the ideas that Sara had planted in her head.

Her mom interrupted her attempt to scavenge together a meal when she appeared behind Violet, peering over her shoulder. She didn't mention the hour, or that Violet hadn't called to say where she was or when she'd be home, something Violet appreciated more than she could possibly express.

"Here, let me." Her mom smiled, brushing her daughter aside.

Violet waited to see where this was going. Her mom wasn't exactly . . . *domestic.* And cooking ranked somewhere near the bottom of her considerably weak household skills. But she surprised Violet, emerging from the fridge with a carton of eggs and a package of bacon. "How about breakfast for dinner?"

Violet smiled in response.

Breakfast for dinner had been one of her favorite meals ever since she was a little girl. Pancakes, eggs, French toast . . . even cereal somehow tasted better when it was served at the opposite end of the day.

"Absolutely," Violet agreed. "Want some help?"

Her mom shooed her away, just like when she was little and always underfoot. "*Pshh.* Go sit down. It's not every day that I get to fix my daughter dinner."

That's an understatement, Violet thought as she pulled out a chair, propping her chin on her hand. "Actually, Mom, it could be. I still live here, you know?"

Her mom cast a chastising look in Violet's direction as she cracked the eggs into a bowl. "Can it, smart-ass. You're lucky I cook at all."

"*Lucky, hmm?* Not exactly the word I would have used."

Her mom threw a hand towel at her and then began searching through the drawers, looking lost in her own kitchen. Violet watched, grinning to herself as her mom grew more and more frustrated, searching the same drawers over and over again. Finally, Violet decided to help her out.

"The whisk is on the counter. In the ceramic caddy . . . the caddy *you* made."

Her mom stopped digging in the drawer and dropped her hands to her sides in defeat. "Thanks," she sighed.

Violet's mother was an amazing artist, an undiscovered talent lost in their obscure little town. Her paintings graced the walls of their home, along with her sketches. But, above all, she had a gift for working with clay, and it showed in the skillfully crafted canisters, vases, and ceramic bowls around their house.

Violet wasn't creative, at least not in the way her mother was.

She had a different skill.

One that, apparently, the FBI had use for . . . or at least a consultant for the FBI did.

She ushered the unwelcome thought away as her mom placed the heaping plate of scrambled eggs, bacon, and toast in front of her. Funny how something as simple as a childhood meal prepared by her mom could make everything feel so . . . so *right* again.

She ate in a hurry, not because she had somewhere to be but because each bite made her stomach feel a little more settled. During her drive home, the nausea had been replaced by the uncomfortable sensation of too much emptiness. Like there was a void where her stomach should have been.

Violet hadn't noticed how lost she'd been in her own thoughts until she heard her mom's voice and realized she'd been sitting right beside her the entire time.

"Everything okay?" her mom asked just as Violet took another bite.

"Perfect," Violet answered, and then chugged her glass of milk. "This's exactly what I needed. Thanks, Mom."

"No problem. But that's not what I meant. I mean is everything *all right*? Are *you* okay? You seem upset." Her mother reached over and touched a strand of Violet's hair, twisting a long curl around her finger and then releasing it. The look on her face was understanding, inviting. It had been forever since Violet had opened up to anyone.

But what did she expect? She should have known her mom would see right through her. Her mom always seemed to know when something was bothering her.

Violet sighed, thinking she would just shrug it off, keep her worries buried. But instead she heard herself asking, "Why has it always been such a secret?" And when she wasn't sure that her question made any sense, she explained, "You know . . . the thing . . . that I do with the bodies? Why have you and Dad always made it so secret?"

"Hmm." Her mom nodded as if she understood completely. "I wondered when you would ask that."

"Really?"

"Really. I'm surprised it hasn't come up sooner. I thought last year—when everything happened—that you'd want to talk about it. But you never did. You've always been so strong, trying to keep your feelings to yourself." She smiled thoughtfully at her daughter. "I'm glad you want to talk now."

Violet wasn't as confident, and talk of feelings—and sharing them—made her feel uncomfortable. She had an overwhelming desire to take her question back, to forget that she'd ever even mentioned it in the first place.

But her mom made the decision for her. "It was never meant to be a secret, Vi. We wanted to protect you, of course, but we also wanted it to be your choice. *Who* you told, how much you told them. And when. It was never *ours* to tell. We decided early on to wait until you could make those decisions for yourself. We're okay with people knowing—or not knowing, if that's what you want." She picked up her teacup, a pretty little antique thing, and took a sip.

Violet thought about that. It wasn't quite what she'd expected to hear. For some reason, she'd always thought she was supposed to keep her secret close to her, guard it.

"Did Grandma ever tell anyone?" She was suddenly curious about how the others who'd come before her had handled this inherited ability. She knew that her grandmother, at least, had shared the same talent.

Her mom's eyebrows rose, and then she laughed. "Your grandmother told everyone who would listen and some who wouldn't. She once told me that when she was a little girl her teacher made her go home for telling stories about finding dead animals. Of course, your grandmother never found a *human* body." She reached out to stroke her daughter's cheek.

"So why do you think that *you* didn't . . . you know, get . . . *it*?"

Her mom shrugged, a playful smile tugging at her lips. "Just my bad luck, I guess."

"Whatever," Violet muttered, scoffing at the idea that somehow she'd been blessed by *good fortune* to be able to locate the discarded prey of others. But then she thought about her bizarre afternoon at the FBI offices. "So would *you* tell anyone, if you were me?"

Her mom got up from the table, clearing away the dishes. "I would think about *why* I was doing it, if there was a purpose in someone else knowing, and then do whatever my heart told me was right," her mom answered as she dumped the dishes into the sink. She winked at Violet. "I know one thing, sweetheart. I know without a doubt that you'll make the right decision, whatever you choose to do."

And then she walked out of the kitchen, leaving Violet with more questions than before. Somehow she'd expected her mother to confirm what she'd always believed: that it was a secret. And that it should remain that way.

Instead her head reeled with new possibilities. About telling someone new. About helping the FBI. About purposefully tracking down killers.

It was a lot for one girl to consider. And for now, at least, it was a task she was too physically and emotionally depleted to worry about.

She turned out the lights as she made her way up to her room.

★ ★ ★

As tired as she was, Violet didn't go to sleep right away. Instead she lay on her bed, stretched out on her stomach, looking at the files Sara had asked Rafe to give her.

She knew what Sara expected, of course, what she thought Violet could do with a stack of photographs and police reports. She thought Violet was some kind of psychic. Sara thought Violet would be able to solve mysteries simply by running her hands over the evidence they'd gathered.

If only it were that simple.

Violet reached for one of the two files, the one from the little boy's case. She glanced inside at a photograph of his face. She ran her fingertip over the picture, tracing the line of his sweet little mouth, wondering how someone could harm a child. Violet felt a dark stab of sorrow deep in her chest. He was so young, so innocent.

She closed the folder and opened the other one instead.

Inside was a photo of a woman. According to the file, her name was Serena Russo—Mike's mom. The picture wasn't current; even two years ago it would have been dated, as if it were pulled from a frame that had been hanging in the family home. It was faded, and the clothing was long out of style, but in it she was smiling. She'd been happy when the picture was taken.

There were two other photos in the folder, both from crimes older than Serena Russo's disappearance. Both taken after her first husband had abused her. In them, her face was bruised, her eyes swollen, her lips bloodied.

Violet turned over the pictures of the injured woman, unable to look for too long.

Goose bumps raked her skin as she glanced at the mug shot of the man responsible. She looked at his name: Roger Hartman. She glanced casually at his address and was startled to see that it was only an hour away from where she lived.

Violet could understand why Sara believed that this man might be responsible for the woman's disappearance, and she wondered what it was that Sara really suspected. Did she think that Mike's mother was dead? That she'd been murdered by her abusive ex-husband?

It seemed unfair that he should be allowed to go on as if nothing had changed, when the Russo family had been torn apart.

Suddenly, Violet was sorry that she couldn't help, sorry she wasn't able to do something to ease the emptiness that Mike and his sister must feel in the wake of their mother's absence. To lighten the burden that their father must bear without his wife.

The not knowing, as Sara had described it.

She closed the file and shoved them both into her backpack.

Violet wished she could help, wished she could do something to give Mike's family a little closure of their own.

GLUTTONY

SHE HATED THE CLINKING SOUND OF A BOTTLE. It was never a good sound, especially in the dead of night.

It was the sound of her father.

Alone, in the darkness of her bedroom, she wanted to scream. She felt as if she would choke on the voice she held inside as her throat ached to set it free.

She listened as his heavy work boots shuffled across the floorboards of the living room, wondering for the millionth time why it had been her mother who'd left instead of him. Why couldn't he have been the one to abandon his family?

Almost worse than the sound of the bottle, though, was the dread that swelled within her during those moments before he came home from work each night, as she waited to see which man he'd be, which father would walk through the door at the end of the day. Because she was convinced now that they were not one and the same, her old father and this new man who filled a place in their house. Her real father had gone—along with her mother—leaving her with this new man, who only in appearance resembled the father he once was.

She'd come to learn that some monsters weren't make-believe.

Yet there was always that fleeting instant, no matter how hard she resisted it, in which she hoped that it wouldn't be him. That, instead, her real dad would walk through the door. That he'd come home at last.

But he never did.

Her real dad was gone. And in his place he'd left someone withdrawn and bitter. And very seldom sober.

She was lonely in ways that no one could ever understand.

She strained to hear, clutching the covers close as she curled into a ball and waited for the sounds in the other room to settle once more. She heard the crack of another bottle top. Soon enough, he'd be sleeping.

With relief came hatred.

She hated her father, the man he'd become.

She hated the woman who'd given her life and then left her behind, abandoning her children when they needed her most.

There were others she hated as well, others who had what she didn't, others who held the things she wanted most in this world. But mostly she hated herself for not being strong enough to save herself. Not yet.

But someday she would be. She wouldn't be here forever; the conviction of those silent thoughts fortified her.

Eventually she would find a way out.

CHAPTER 15

VIOLET WASN'T SURE WHAT SHE WAS DOING OUT here; she only knew that she didn't want to be at home, alone with her thoughts.

She'd been driving around town for over an hour, trying to be swallowed by the night, to get lost in it. It was her favorite time to drive, when the streets were all but forsaken.

The rain splashed against her windshield, blurring the lights outside into reflective pools, adding to her sense of seclusion.

It was good thinking time.

She brought her car to a complete stop at the flashing red light of a four-way intersection, even though there were no other cars waiting. It seemed like even when no one was looking, she was always following the rules, always trying to do the right thing.

She wished she knew what the right thing was for her now, what she should do about Sara's proposal to use her gift to help others. Violet wasn't even sure whether it was an official offer, or just a fishing expedition by an inquisitive observer. The fact that Sara had given her files to look through meant that she was probably serious.

But there were other opinions to consider; she'd heard the agents in the parking garage:

Bullshit, one man had declared.

A waste of time, stated another.

These were men with badges, experienced investigators. And *they* certainly didn't think that the FBI needed Violet's particular brand of assistance.

Maybe they were right.

Violet didn't know. She'd spent so much time hiding what she could do that the idea of exposing it to anyone, other than Jay or her family, went against everything she'd ever believed in.

It was a secret . . . *her secret*. How could she be expected to share that?

Except that it didn't have to be a secret.

Frustration clouded her judgment. She realized that she was still sitting at the flashing stoplight, waiting for something to happen.

But there would be no signs, no easy answers.

She didn't want to keep driving aimlessly; she needed to

go somewhere . . . even if that somewhere was just home.

She sighed, making her first real decision in days.

Her car grumbled in its usual way, reassuring her that it was still alive as she did an illegal three-point turn in the middle of the deserted stretch of road. She kind of liked doing something that she wasn't supposed to, even if it was only a traffic violation. It made her feel like she was breaking the rules for no good reason at all.

She turned down Jay's driveway, killing the lights as she did. She didn't need them; she could have navigated her way with both eyes closed.

Not for the first time tonight, she wondered what she was doing. She wasn't sure why she'd decided to come here, but she knew one thing:

She needed to see Jay.

She cut the engine and stepped out into the rain, sneaking around to the side of his house. She tapped lightly on his bedroom window and waited. After a few long seconds, just as she was about to knock again, his curtains parted.

When he saw her, he smiled.

Immediately, everything felt better. Her tattered edges were soothed. She'd done the right thing, coming here.

Jay opened his window. "Go to the door. I'll let you in." His voice was quiet and still slow with sleep.

"No," she whispered back. "You come out here."

He didn't argue. "Let me get some pants on. I'll be right there."

Violet watched as the curtains fell back into place. The

light never came on inside, but within seconds he was climbing out his window. He grinned at her when his feet hit solid ground.

"What are you doing here?" He wrapped his arms around her as if he could, somehow, shield her from the rain falling down upon them. He didn't complain about the weather.

She pulled loose, just enough so she could gaze up at him. Seeing him made other things seem less . . . *important*. Less troubling.

"Do you want to go somewhere?"

Violet shook her head. "Can we just talk?"

"Sure." He shrugged casually, but Violet could read the concern in his expression.

He followed her to her car, and they got inside.

Violet didn't start the engine; she preferred the quiet. The soft sound of the rain hitting the car created a restful sound track to her mood. Jay reached over and wiped raindrops from her cheek, brushing the saturated tendrils of hair away from her face. Violet grabbed for his hand and held on as she waited for the right words to come.

Jay didn't rush her.

She owed him so many explanations that it seemed silly to worry over childish insecurities. Her voice was soft. "What did you think when I first told you about the animals I found?"

He seemed confused. It obviously wasn't what he'd expected. "Violet, I was seven years old. I thought it was badass. I think I was probably even jealous."

She made a face at him. "Didn't you think it was creepy? Or that I was weird?"

"Yeah," he agreed enthusiastically. "That's why I was so jealous. *I* wanted to be the one finding dead bodies. You were like an animal detective or something. You were only *weird* 'cause you were a girl." He grinned. "But I learned to overlook that since you always took me on such cool adventures."

Violet released a breath, smiling. She knew he was telling the truth, which only made it funnier to hear him saying the words out loud. Of course, what little boy didn't want to go scavenging through the woods and digging in the dirt?

She tried again. "Did you ever tell anyone? Does your mom know?"

He lifted her hand to his mouth and rubbed her knuckles across his lower lip, his gaze locked with hers. "No," he promised. "I swore I wouldn't, not even her. I think she knows something, or at least she thinks you have the worst luck ever, since you found all those dead girls." He lowered his voice. "She was really worried about you after the shooting last year. You're like a daughter to her." He leaned close. "Of course, that makes it kind of creepy when I do things like this."

He kissed her. It was intimate. Not soft or sweet this time, it was deep and passionate, stealing Violet's breath. She laid her hand against his chest, savoring the feel of his heartbeat beneath her palm, and then traced her fingertips up to his neck, into his hair.

He pulled her over the console that separated them, dragging her onto his lap. He ran his hands up her back restlessly, drawing her as close as he could.

It was nearly impossible for her to pull herself away. "Wait," she insisted breathlessly. "Please, wait." She had her hands braced against his shoulders, struggling more against herself than him.

His glazed eyes teased her. "I thought I was the one who was supposed to say no. I'm the girl, right?"

She sighed heavily, leaning her head against his shoulder and trying to recapture her runaway thoughts. She still wanted to talk. She wanted the other things too, but she needed to sort through her thoughts first.

"Sorry, it's just . . . I have a lot of . . ." She shrugged against him. His damp T-shirt was warm and practically paper-thin, tempting her to touch him. She ran her finger down the length of his stomach. She knew it wasn't fair to tease him, but she couldn't help herself. He was too enticing. ". . . I have some stuff I need to work through." It was the best she could do for an explanation.

He caught her hand before she'd reached his waistline, and he held it tightly in his grip. "I'm trying to be patient, Violet, I really am. If there's something you want to tell me . . . Well, I just wish you'd trust me."

"I'll get there," she explained. "I'll figure it all out. I'm just a little confused right now."

He let out a shaky breath and then he kissed the top of

her head, still not releasing her hand. "So, when you do, we'll pick up where we left off."

She nodded against him. She thought she would keep talking; she still had so many doubts about what she should, and shouldn't, be doing.

But instead she just stayed there, curled up on his lap, absorbing him, taking relief from his touch . . . and strength from his presence.

CHAPTER 16

"YOU LOOK LIKE A HOT MESS," CHELSEA TOLD Violet as she slipped into a space beside her in the hallway. "I heard you missed first period; I thought maybe you were taking a sick day."

"Thanks a lot, Chels," Violet answered irritably. "I overslept and practically had to break every speed limit just to get here in time for second."

Chelsea made a face. "*Please*, you drive like my grandma! You didn't break any speed limits."

Violet couldn't lie: "No. I didn't. But I did write my own tardy note."

"Only 'cause your mom said you could. Did you say

you had explosive diarrhea?"

"No, just that I slept in."

"You should have said diarrhea. Or at least menstrual cramps, then you could get out of PE. It's like a twofer."

Violet laughed even though her head was pounding. "Nice. You're such a lady."

Chelsea nudged her then, drawing her attention to Mike, who was heading right toward them. "Speaking of ladies, check this out. Mike's growing a mustache."

Violet squinted to get a better look. Chelsea was right; there was a dark patch of facial hair springing up just above his upper lip.

"Why?" Violet asked, trying not to make it too obvious that she was staring.

"Because I told him I liked them. I wanted to see if I could make him do it."

Violet felt an unexpected stab of discomfort as she glanced at Mike. Knowing what she did, knowing what his family had been through . . . she suddenly felt sorry for him. She was relieved he had no idea that she knew about his mother.

He grinned at Chelsea as he approached, barely noticing that Violet was standing there.

Calling it a "mustache" was a stretch, by any standards. It was definitely noticeable, but it was spotty at best, and the sprigs of clumpy hair looked oddly out of place on his handsome face. Violet was amazed that in less than a week since their movie-night hookup, Chelsea already had him jumping through these kinds of hoops. She was something else.

"Hey, baby," Chelsea said in a voice that bordered on baby talk as Mike bent down to give her a quick kiss. "Miss me?"

Violet almost rolled her eyes.

"I thought about you all period," he answered, his voice husky. "Did you get the note I left in your backpack?"

Violet couldn't hold back any longer; she rolled her eyes. Neither of them noticed.

"I did. You're so sweet." The cooing verged on sickening. "Did anyone say anything about your mustache?"

Mike winced, as if he suddenly remembered the patchy hair on his upper lip. "A coupla' people," he reluctantly responded, and Violet suspected that he'd taken his fair share of ribbing over it.

Chelsea ignored the obvious distress in his voice. "Vi and I gotta run or we'll be late." She stretched up to kiss him and then rubbed her thumb across the hairs above his lip as if she were petting them. "See you after class."

Chelsea tugged at Violet, who was still staring at his unsightly mustache. It was like seeing a car accident . . . hard to look away.

"So do you? Like it, I mean?" Violet asked as she was being dragged down the hallway.

"The mustache?" Chelsea grimaced. "God, no. It's hideous on him."

"Then, why?"

"I told you, to see if he'd actually do it. Don't worry. I'm gonna make him shave it this weekend."

Violet wasn't sure whether to congratulate her friend on her training abilities or reprimand her for being so cruel. In the end, she didn't do either, mostly because she knew it wouldn't make any difference.

Chelsea was Chelsea. Trying to convince her that what she'd done was wrong would be like banging your head against a brick wall. It would be painful to you but accomplish nothing.

Jay sat down across from Chelsea and took both of her hands in his. The oversized lunchroom was buzzing with activity, and he practically had to yell to be heard.

"Chelsea, for the love of everything good and holy, please . . . *please* stop ruining my friend."

Violet bit her lip to stop from laughing at the two of them. She knew what he was talking about before he even explained. It was the new facial hair.

Chelsea jerked her hands out of his. "Oh, relax, drama queen. He's not broken. Besides, I'm gonna fix him this weekend."

Jay seemed relieved. "I wish you'd do it sooner. The poor guy's really taking a ration of crap over that thing."

"He'll be fine. Trust me. It's like a character-building exercise. When this is all over, he'll be a stronger person." She said it like she meant it. She was actually trying to convince someone that this was all for Mike's own good.

Jay wasn't buying it, but he let the subject drop when Mike came up behind Chelsea and planted an enthusiastic kiss on her cheek. Obviously, Mike wasn't suffering too much from Chelsea's little experiment.

Chelsea rubbed the spot where his lips had touched her and made a face that only they could see. "*There's my guy!*" she said. "Jay was just telling me that he doesn't like your 'stache, baby. But I told him he's crazy. I think it's hot."

Mike looked embarrassed that they were talking about it again. Violet realized that it was a sore subject and wondered what Chelsea had done to make him so eager to please her.

But before she could speculate, something strangely familiar drew Violet's attention, just out of the corner of her eye.

It was so faint, and gone so fast, that she wasn't even certain she'd seen it. A blink. A weak flash.

Violet turned in the direction from which it had come, wondering what it could have been.

Students crowded tables and leaned against walls. They moved in and out of doorways, and she could see them drifting idly through the hallways that surrounded the administrative offices at the entrance of the school, just beyond the cafeteria.

It could have been a camera. Or the pulse of a flashlight, although that seemed oddly out of place at school . . . during the day.

It might have been nothing.

But it wasn't. A gentle hum beat through her veins. She knew that it wasn't *nothing.*

She stood up, ignoring the others around her. "I'll be right back," she said to no one in particular as she scanned the area, trying to locate the translucent flicker once more. She couldn't be sure from where, exactly, it had come, but she headed toward the busy hallways. She recognized everyone but no one in particular.

She felt like she were chasing phantoms as she searched each face, looking for something that might distinguish one individual from the rest. Looking for that *certain something* that he wouldn't even realize he carried.

It was the light, the pulsating flashes that had woken her the night the dead cat had been left outside her house. With everything else going on, she'd nearly forgotten about the cat . . . and its killer. And now here it was, the imprint of death.

Even though it was washed out, almost completely blanched by the light of day, she was sure that was what it was.

Icy fingers gripped her heart at the thought of one of her fellow students, someone she knew, someone she was so near every day, having done something so horrendous. And then leaving it for Violet to find.

She tried to locate the flash again, tried to pinpoint it among the faces around her. When she couldn't see it, she started to think that maybe it was gone. Or, possibly, that she'd only imagined it.

And then it came again, just the hint of that diffused, glowing spark. Gone as quickly as it had come. But farther now than it had been before.

Maybe it's coming from outside, Violet thought, looking through the windows.

She shoved her way through the crowd, out the double doors near the office, and into the light of day. She didn't see him, the person who carried the imprint of the dead cat.

She kept walking, searching. Ahead of her, in the parking lot, she could see cars coming and going. Around her, students and some faculty members meandered along the sidewalks that wound around the campus.

Her heart beat a reckless rhythm. She was afraid to discover the truth. And afraid not to.

She slowed, moving carefully, trying to notice everything. But the harder she searched, the more she realized she was too late. Whoever she'd sensed was gone.

She reached the end of the buildings, where the parking lot started, and took a heavy step forward, off the curb, searching around her. There was no one there. No flashing light. She was alone.

It didn't make any sense.

She sighed, disappointment sinking in. She didn't know what to think.

But she was tired, she reminded herself. She'd barely slept, and not just last night but for a long, *long* time. Too long. Maybe her mind had slipped past normal fatigue and into something far more dangerous, far closer to the kind of exhaustion where her thoughts could no longer be trusted.

She shook her head, not wanting to entertain the disturbing notion.

She wasn't crazy. She *had* seen something. It had definitely been there, and even if it hadn't been an imprint, it *had* been real.

She waited for a few minutes and then gave up, going back to the cafeteria.

Tonight, she decided with determination. *Tonight I need to sleep.*

GREED

IT WAS THE STRANGEST THING, SEEING VIOLET GET up from her lunch table and walk right toward her. It was as if Violet had known she was being watched.

But that was impossible.

She'd only meant to spy for a moment, to numb herself just a little. And when she saw Violet heading right toward her, wearing that strange look of recognition on her face, she'd backed away before Violet could discover her . . . hiding there, stealing a glimpse into the life she could never have.

Perfect Violet. With the perfect life.

She slipped out of the building before Violet could reach her, disappearing around the corner. She paused for a moment, frozen—trapped—as she waited for her father to get into his truck. She hated that he'd insisted on coming inside to sign her in, resentful that he'd made her late in the first place as she stayed awake half the night, waiting for him to pass out.

As he pulled away, she circled the building, searching for another way inside, and wondered what would happen if she let Violet catch her.

She toyed with the notion of opening up to Violet, and the idea was oddly appealing.

What if she could *tell someone the truth? What if she could share her burdens?*

And what would she say? That her mother had run off? That her father was a drunk?

Who was she kidding? She wasn't going to tell anyone. There was no one she could trust . . . no one who cared about her pathetic existence.

Especially not Violet Ambrose.

She reached an open doorway and took a relieved breath. She entered the stream of students pouring into the halls before their next class. She moved among them, reassured that she was once again undetectable.

Just the way she liked it.

Anonymous. Faceless in the crowd.

Just another girl.

CHAPTER 17

WHEN VIOLET AND JAY WALKED TOGETHER TO the parking lot after school, Violet couldn't help inspecting everyone around her. Studying them. Searching them.

One of them carried an imprint.

She kept telling herself to just forget it, but she couldn't.

"Hey, it's for you," Jay announced, interrupting her thoughts as he reached for the pink paper that was tucked beneath his windshield wiper. He sniffed it before handing it to her. "Smells good."

Violet laughed at him for smelling the note, then turned it over in her hands.

Her name had been written with purple felt-tip marker in distinctly girly lettering. She sniffed it apprehensively; it smelled like grape. A lacy heart sticker held it closed.

"That's weird." She picked at the corner of the sticker, flashing Jay a sly look. "Maybe I have a secret admirer."

Jay threw his bag in the backseat and climbed inside to start his car.

Violet unfolded the letter and read it. Her heart stopped.

The words inside were written in the same feminine handwriting as her name on the outside. She read them again, thinking that she'd made some sort of mistake the first time.

She hadn't.

She refolded the paper, this time in a hurry, trying to ignore the unnerving sensation that someone was watching her. She shoved it into her backpack and then threw hers in back with Jay's.

"So? Who was the love note from?" he asked absently as she got in the passenger seat.

Violet shook her head, trying to find the words, but they weren't there. She felt like she was stuck in her dream again, the nightmare in which she was trapped, entombed, in the suffocating darkness. Unable to save herself.

"Violet?"

She blinked. "What?" She still hadn't answered his question. "Chelsea," she floundered. "It's just a note from Chelsea."

He looked worried. "You okay?" He touched her cheek, his brow wrinkled.

She nodded. "I'm tired. Really, really tired."

He accepted that, mostly because he knew, probably

better than anyone, that it was true. And it had been.

Up until she'd read that note.

Jay had to work that afternoon, so Violet had planned on going home to take a well-deserved nap. But when she got there, her dad was still at work and her mom was gone for the afternoon, and Violet realized that there was no way she'd be able to sleep. Not yet. Not while her house was empty.

She wandered around, trying to find a way to make herself comfortable. It was crazy that she was afraid there, of all places. Violet had never been afraid in her own home, not even as a little girl.

She'd never believed in the bogeyman or monsters that hid in the shadows beneath her bed or in her closet, in the places where a night-light couldn't reach . . . if she'd been the kind of girl who had actually needed a night-light.

And yet, here she was, terrified in the one place she should feel the most secure.

Thanks to that stupid note.

She pulled it out of her backpack and stared at it again, not sure what she hoped to gain from reading it one more time:

Rosie Is Dead
Violet Is Blue
You Can't See Me . . .
But I'm Watching You

Ever since she was a little girl, she'd heard that nursery rhyme put together a hundred different ways using her name. But it had never felt so threatening, so ominous. Violet understood the implied meaning behind the words.

It was another message from the person who'd left the cat. The same person she'd followed today through her very own school.

He, *or she*, Violet corrected herself as she scrutinized the girlish handwriting, was taunting Violet. Stalking her, openly baiting her.

And that person knew where she lived.

Violet shoved the note into the bottom of her backpack and closed all the blinds in the family room, sitting on the couch in the dark and trying to trick herself into feeling isolated, safe. She wanted to be tired again, enough so she could fall asleep, so she would feel better and be able to think more clearly. But the longer she sat there trying to make herself relax, the more she realized it was impossible.

Finally she decided that she needed to get out of her house. At least for a while. At least until her parents got home. But she needed to do one thing before she left.

She put on her shoes and her jacket and double-checked that Carl was safely inside before slipping through the kitchen door at the back of the house and hurrying across the lawn to her mom's art studio. Inside she rummaged around the messy tabletops until she found a small piece of wood. It was flat and smooth, the perfect size for what she needed. She hoped her mom wasn't saving it for anything special.

She opened a small container of acrylic paint and grabbed a thin paintbrush. The color she'd chosen was a pretty shade of pink.

Violet worked meticulously—respectfully—on her project, making sure to give it the care it deserved. When she was finished, she rinsed the brush and replaced the paint where she'd found it.

She crept quietly around the shed, toward the edge of the woods to where her tiny cemetery bordered the back of their property. She walked around the grave markers and homemade headstones, watching her step, until she found the site she was looking for.

Then she knelt down in front of the fresh grave and set the small painted plaque with the little cat's name on it:

ROSIE

Violet had planned to hit the drive-through and grab a cup of tea, a little something to keep her going for the rest of the evening. Something to keep her alert.

But when she got to Java Hut and saw Chelsea's car in the parking lot, she changed her mind. It wasn't like she had anyplace better to go.

As she locked her car, Violet couldn't help wondering if the person who'd written the note also hung out at the Java Hut. The thought made her suspicious of everyone she passed.

Inside she spotted Chelsea and Jules at a table in the back corner.

Violet ordered a cup of tea at the counter and carried it back to where her friends were sitting. She was surprised that Claire wasn't with them, since Claire hated being left out.

Chelsea made a face at Violet's tea. "Shouldn't you be having a milk shake or something?"

That was Chelsea's way of saying Violet should order a milk shake so Chelsea could "share" without actually paying.

Violet shook her head, ignoring the not-so-subtle hint. "Nope, I'm good." She pulled the plastic top off her cup and stirred in a packet of honey.

"*I'll* split one with you, if you want," Jules volunteered to Chelsea.

"*Aww.* See? Jules gets me." Chelsea's response was meant as a commentary on Violet's intentional snub.

Jules held out her hand, palm up.

Chelsea frowned at it. "I thought *you* were getting it."

Jules smiled and wiggled her fingers. "I said I would *split* it with you. So pony up, sister."

Chelsea glared at Jules as she dropped some change in her hand. "Anything but strawberry."

Jules grabbed the money and headed toward the counter to order their milk shake.

"I thought you loved strawberry," Violet said once Jules was gone.

"I do. It's reverse psychology. She'll get the strawberry." Even when her statements were outrageous, Chelsea always sounded so sure of herself.

Violet just laughed. "Just because you would do the opposite doesn't mean Jules will."

She sipped her tea; it was perfect, hot and sweet. Just the jolt of caffeine Violet needed to ward away the exhaustion for a bit longer.

"So are you and Jay coming to the cabin?" Chelsea asked.

The question was unexpected, and from so far out of left field that Violet thought she'd finally succumbed to the lack of sleep. "What are you talking about, Chels?"

"Oh yeah, that's right, you took off during lunch today. Hey, where'd you go, anyway?"

Violet wasn't about to tell Chelsea that she'd been chasing invisible lights through the school. "I had to take care of something before class started. So, what cabin?"

Chelsea didn't question Violet's nonexplanation; instead she answered, "Mike's family has a hunting cabin up in the mountains. Some of us were thinking of taking an overnight trip up there in a couple of weeks to play in the snow and hang out. You know, snuggle up by the fire and all that good stuff." Chelsea's eyes glittered enthusiastically.

Violet hated to let her down. "I really doubt my parents are going to let me stay the night in a remote cabin with a bunch of boys."

"Oh, please, Snow White, Mike's dad'll be there. He's actually kinda funny . . . you know, in a weird dad kind of way. Don't worry, your purity will remain intact. Scout's honor." She made some sort of gesture with her fingers that Violet assumed was supposed to be an oath, but since Chelsea had never actually *been* a Girl Scout, it ended up looking more like a peace sign. *Or something.* Violet maintained her dubious expression.

But Chelsea wasn't about to be discouraged, and she tried to be the voice of reason. "Come on, I think Jay's checking to see if he can get the time off work. The least you can do is ask your parents. If they say no, then no harm, no foul, right? If they say yes, then we'll have a kick-ass time. We'll go hiking in the snow and hang out in front of the fireplace in the evening. We'll sleep in sleeping bags and maybe even roast some marshmallows. It'll be like we're camping." She beamed a superfake smile at Violet and clasped her hands together like she was begging. "Do it for me. *Ple-eease.*"

Jules came back with their milk shake. It was strawberry, and Chelsea flashed Violet an *I-told-you-so* grin.

Violet finished her tea, mulling over the idea of spending the weekend in a snowy cabin with Jay and Chelsea. Away from town. Away from whoever was leaving her dead animals and creepy notes.

It *did* sound fun, and Violet *did* love the snow. And the woods. And Jay.

She could at least ask.

Like Chelsea said, *No harm, no foul.*

CHAPTER 18

THE EXHAUSTION HAD FINALLY CAUGHT UP WITH her, and that night Violet slept like the dead. For the first time in weeks, she felt completely and totally rested. And by morning, she felt sane again. Clear.

It was a great feeling.

She got up early. Well, maybe not *early*, but not late either, and in time to actually eat something before she had to leave for school. Not bad.

In the rush of the morning, she easily ignored the first hang-up call she received, chalking it up to mistaken dialing. The call log had simply read: *Unknown Caller.*

She shoved her cell phone into the pocket of her hoodie,

and crammed her math book, and the homework assignment she'd been working on over her bowl of cereal, into her backpack.

Inside her jacket, she felt the phone vibrating. She pulled it out to check it.

Unknown Caller again.

"Hello?" She glanced out the window to make sure Jay wasn't there to pick her up yet.

There was a moment in which she thought that the person on the other end might say something, a long, empty pause, but nothing happened. Finally, Violet pulled the phone away from her ear.

The call had ended.

She tucked it away for a second time. Jay would be there any minute.

Violet cleaned up her mess at the table and rinsed her bowl in the sink. She was listening for the sounds of his car when she felt the vibrations in her pocket. *Again.*

Now she was getting annoyed. She dried her hands on a towel and pulled the phone back out. It was the same thing: *Unknown Caller.*

"What?" she answered irritably.

On the other end, there was silence.

She sighed softly. "Hello?" she tried again, this time trying not to sound so sharp. She checked the phone to make sure the call was still connected. It was.

Nothing.

"Is anyone there?"

And then, something. What was it? A breath? A whisper? Violet heard *something* from the other end.

"Hello? *Who is this?*" she asked expectantly, hopefully.

She waited for a moment and then checked the phone. The call was gone, disconnected.

She chewed her lip as she stared at the screen on her cell phone, waiting for it to buzz again. She wondered who it could have been and reassessed her initial assumption that it had been a wrong number . . . who would call and then hang up when she answered three separate times? She could think of only one person.

She looked down at her backpack, lying on the floor by the kitchen table. Inside there was a pretty pink note with a disturbing message written in scrawling purple script.

She heard Jay's car outside in the driveway just as the phone in her pocket vibrated once more. She hesitated, taking the phone out and staring at it. She thought about answering it, about telling whoever was on the other end to go screw themselves and to stop harassing her, but she doubted it would do any good. So she took another approach.

She picked up her backpack, and on her way to the front door scrolled down and hit Ignore on her phone.

If the person on the other end thought they were going to frighten Violet with stupid poems and hang-up calls, they were messing with the wrong girl. Even the dead-animal thing was right up her alley.

Far more terrifying people had come after Violet.

And failed.

★ ★ ★

The plans to go to the cabin came together surprisingly well. Mostly surprising because Violet's parents had actually agreed to let her go.

She was still a little stunned, since it was, after all, a boy-girl sleepover. Which sounded like a little kids' slumber party, but to the parents of teenagers usually conjured up images of illicit sex and illegal alcohol consumption.

Violet had expected her parents to have similar concerns. But apparently they trusted her.

Of course there were several strings attached. Violet's parents insisted on meeting Mike's father before the trip, since he was chaperoning. And they wanted to know the names, the parents' names, and the phone numbers of everyone who would be going on the Saturday night sleepover. They also wanted the address of the cabin. And, of course, an ironclad guarantee from Jay that he would keep an eye on Violet.

That last promise had been easy enough to secure. It was funny how quickly Jay had taken on the role of Violet's protector once they'd started dating. Actually before then, even.

Funnier still how much faith her parents put in him, considering the fact that Jay would officially be younger than Violet in less than a week.

Violet was about to turn seventeen, while Jay would still be sixteen for nearly two full months.

Jay liked that, the whole older-woman thing. He also liked to joke about the fact that Violet would soon be dating a younger man.

One night, when Violet's parents had gone out, he teased her about it, whispering against her throat, "I should probably be dating girls my own age now that you'll be over-the-hill." Jay was stretched out on Violet's bed as she curled against him.

Violet laughed, rising to the bait. "Fine," she challenged, pulling away and leaning up on her elbow. "I'm sure there are plenty of men my own age who would be willing to finish what you've started."

Jay stiffened, and Violet realized that she'd struck a nerve. "What is it?"

He shook his head, and Violet thought he might say, "Nothing," so when he answered, his words caught her off guard. "*Is* there someone else, Vi?"

Violet frowned, baffled by the unfamiliar jealousy she saw on his face. She wondered what in the world he meant as she reached down and smoothed a strand of hair from his forehead. "What are you talking about, Jay?"

His eyes met hers. "I saw you with that guy at the movies, Vi. Who was he?"

Violet closed her eyes. She wasn't ready yet. She didn't want to tell him about the FBI, about Sara and Rafe or what she'd learned about Mike's mother. She wondered briefly if he knew about Mike's mom—if his friend had ever confided in him. But somehow she doubted it. Jay wasn't like her; he didn't keep secrets.

"It's not like that," she explained, hoping that would be enough.

Jay got up and went to the window, pushing the curtain aside. Every muscle in his body was rigid. "Like what, Vi? What's going on? Something's been bothering you lately. Why can't you tell me?"

He was right. She owed it to him to at least try. "I don't know how to explain, but I just feel like everything's changed between us—"

"Of course it's changed, Violet, what'd you expect?"

Violet tried to ignore the bitterness in his voice, telling herself she had no right to be hurt. "It used to be that I would never keep secrets from you. You were my *best friend*. But now that we're dating, it's just . . . *different*. I feel like I have to watch what I say, or you get all worried. Sometimes I just want you to be the old Jay again, so I can talk to you." Violet crept behind him, wrapping her arms around his waist and resting her cheek against his back.

It wasn't exactly a confession but it was progress, she decided. And soon, *very soon*, she hoped she'd feel comfortable enough to open up completely.

She felt him relax, and his voice softened. "Is that what this is all about? You feel like you can't talk to me anymore? *We* haven't changed; we're still the same people."

She slipped her hands beneath the front of his shirt, slowly running her fingertips over his chest and back down to his waist. He turned in her arms and smiled, but his grin was filled with mocking suspicion. "Are you trying to distract me, Violet Ambrose?"

"I guess you're smarter than you look," she teased as

he pushed her backward so that they both fell on her bed.

"And *you* are not as funny as you think you are." His mouth hovered over hers, his arms tightening, crushing her against him. Violet giggled and tried to squirm free, but Jay wouldn't let her. He kissed her throat, his lips teasing her until it wasn't his grip that made it hard for Violet to breathe.

"Oh, and Violet," he whispered against her ear, his breath tickling her cheek, "I'm *still* your best friend. Don't ever forget it." His words were fervent and touching.

Violet tried to think of a response that made sense, something appropriate, but all she could manage was: "*Please.* Don't stop."

She didn't mind begging if it meant getting her way.

Apparently that was enough to satisfy Jay, and he kissed her possessively. Thoroughly. Deeply.

He eased her back until she was lying against the pillows, and she waited for him to stop, to tell her that they'd gone far enough for tonight. But she didn't want him to. She wanted him to keep going. She wanted him to touch her, to kiss her, to explore her. Her body ached for it. She reached for him, clinging so tightly that her fingers hurt. Everything inside of her hurt.

Jay settled over her, covering her with his body, reacting to her. Violet wrapped her legs around him, pulling his hips closer, telling him with her every movement that she wanted *him*, that she wanted *this. Now.*

"Are you sure?" Jay asked into the warm breath between them, barely lifting his mouth from hers.

She nodded, but when she tried to speak, her voice trembled. She hoped he didn't read it wrong. "Of course I am." She was nervous and terrified and thrilled all at the same time.

He smiled against her mouth, still kissing her, and she melted into him, unable to stop her heart from thundering.

He reached around for his wallet. "I have a condom." His voice was rough.

Violet smiled. She'd been waiting for this moment for far too long *not* to be prepared, but she was happy to hear that he'd been considering it seriously also. "Me too," she told him, reaching into her nightstand drawer and pulling out a handful of them. "I knew you'd give in."

He groaned, his lips moving to her neck as he tugged at his shirt and pulled it over his head.

Violet thought he was beautiful. He was right for her; he always had been.

And as he slowly slid *her* shirt up, his fingertips stroking her bare skin and making goose bumps prickle in the wake of his touch, she wondered why it had taken them so long to get to this place.

Nothing had changed in that moment when Violet and Jay had finally decided to have sex. Nothing—and everything.

Violet was amazed by what they'd done. Amazed that they'd shared themselves with each other, *like that.* It was wonderful, and beautiful, and not anything that Violet had expected it to be.

The pain had been more intense than she could have imagined, and she'd done her best not to cry out. But, of course, Jay had noticed as her body tensed, and then she shuddered. Tears dampened her lashes, yet she'd refused to let them fall.

Jay had insisted that they stop, but Violet wouldn't let him. Instead they'd waited, with Jay holding her, stroking her hair, her shoulders, her face, until the pain subsided, becoming something . . . *less.*

Later, when she was lying in his arms, she shuddered again.

Jay hugged her tight. "What's wrong? You're not sorry, are you?" The tenderness of his words made her heart twist.

"Of course not. How could I be sorry for *that*?"

He kissed her eyes, gently. "Then why are you shivering? I didn't mean to hurt you, Vi."

She shook her head, clumsily bumping his chin. "I don't know why." She ran her fingertips over his arm, memorizing the feel of his coarse hairs, his skin, the muscles beneath it all. "It's just . . . it's a lot. You know?"

Jay smiled. It was a satisfied smile. "Yeah." He leaned back and pulled her to him, tucking her against his shoulder. "It *was* a lot. A *really* good lot."

She wanted to shove him, to banter, to play, but she was too exhausted.

When Jay finally got up to leave, Violet leaned up on her elbow and watched as he buttoned his jeans. She wished they could stay like that—together—for longer. Forever.

She already missed the feel of him beside her, and the scent of him around her. She sat up to give him back the T-shirt she was wearing.

His lazy smile was far too beautiful to be real. "Keep it," he insisted. "I like it better on you anyway." The way he stared at her made her stomach flip. It was a look brimming with tenderness. They were a part of something more now; they belonged to each other.

He tugged his hoodie over his bare chest, and then he leaned down to kiss her one last time, his lips lingering.

His thumb traced the line of her cheek. "I love you, Violet Marie. I'll always love you."

And then he left.

And, once again, Violet slept deeply, soundly, wrapped in Jay's shirt.

He was the perfect remedy to all her worries.

Jay had to work the next day, but he called frequently. Checking in to make sure Violet was feeling all right, that she hadn't changed her mind about their decision, and that she missed him. Violet called him just to hear the sound of his voice. And to make unfairly suggestive comments, taunting him across the phone lines.

Violet loved this new game. Jay would groan uncomfortably from the other end, but he never cut her off.

Violet continued to ignore all of the calls that weren't from Jay. Not just the ones from the anonymous caller but also those from Sara Priest.

Sara had left another voice mail for Violet, and even though she was no longer calling from the FBI field offices, Violet felt no less threatened by the subject matter. She just wasn't ready to deal with that part of her life, especially while she was still getting used to this new twist in her relationship with Jay.

But by afternoon, Violet was lonely and bored. She sat in her bedroom, trying to concentrate on her homework, as memories of their night together continued to distract her. She could practically *feel* Jay's skin against hers, his lips glancing over her body in previously undiscovered locations. Even thinking about it made her feel flushed and dizzy.

She couldn't stop herself from stealing a look out her bedroom window. The wind was blowing, harder than before, and the tall trees around her house rocked, thrashed about by the strong gusts.

Violet loved the wind.

She tried to stay focused on her reading assignment, but the noises outside her window beckoned her. She closed the book, setting it aside. She couldn't just sit inside on such a great afternoon.

In no time, she had changed and was making her way along the same path she'd run hundreds of times before. She skipped her iPod in favor of the sounds of the wind rushing past her, whipping strands of her own hair against her face, gathering leaves and debris and rustling them along the ground.

For the first time in weeks, Violet allowed her mind to empty as she ran with complete abandon. The air that blew around her was brisk; she could smell the chill, and she inhaled it deeply. But as long as she kept moving, she stayed warm. Only the exposed skin of her cheeks tingled from the icy drafts.

Overhead, branches creaked in protest as they were bent too far by sudden gusts. Violet looked up and watched the treetops rocking wildly above her. The gales were getting stronger as the sun moved lower against the sky.

She continued to run, appreciating the power of the mounting storm.

Somewhere nearby, a branch snapped, and Violet slowed, realizing just how hard the wind was blowing. The sky grew dusky as twilight descended, casting a shadowy hue across the forest as the trees above her shivered and waved.

She was no longer certain she was safe beneath the canopy of evergreens. They were no match against the sheer force of the escalating wind. She knew where she was, and she knew that the fastest way out of the woods was to move off trail and to head toward the road.

She stepped through the brush, moving as quickly as she could. She passed rotting stumps and climbed across fallen trees. She wasn't far, and as long as there was still light, she could find her way easily.

The hem of her running pants snagged on a gnarled branch that tangled through the undergrowth, and Violet tugged her leg. The wind continued to pound her, whipping her face as she leaned into it now, keeping her head low.

As she bent to free her pant leg, she saw something

flicker. Strange that she noticed it at all, and she turned her head toward it, squinting. After a moment, the same white light seemed to come out of nowhere. A blink.

Whatever it was, it had Violet's attention and she moved in that direction, away from the main road. She could see where it was coming from, flashing from between the trees, and as darkness fell, it became clearer, easier to locate. But as she neared it, she questioned what it was she thought she'd seen.

Ahead of her, Violet approached the back of a house. She walked slowly, watchfully, until she was practically standing in a backyard.

Night seemed to drop in suddenly, leaching all of the remaining light until she felt as if she were inside a void, looking out. The house was bleak and weary-looking, even from behind, and she realized, after just a moment of studying it, that she'd seen this house before.

Inside the lights were off but, behind the glass, from between the curtains of a single window, the flickering continued, sending broken fragments of light into the blackness that encircled Violet. She blinked, recognizing what the sputtering light reminded her of, and she wondered if there was a television on somewhere inside the house.

The wind blistered her back, blasting her and tangling its icy fingers through her hair. Another branch, this one practically right above Violet, cracked loudly. She jolted, feeling suddenly dizzy, but her eyes never left the window.

And then Violet realized why it couldn't be the light

from a TV that she was witnessing. She scanned the property, looking beyond it to the street on the other side.

There was blackness for as far as she could see. No streetlights, no signals in the distance. *Nothing.*

The electricity was out. The windstorm had taken out all the power to the area.

And inside the house the white flash burst again.

Violet knew what it was. She recognized it from the night she'd woken in her house. In the dark it was almost unmistakable. It was the imprint that matched the dead cat.

Whoever had killed the animal was in there.

She stumbled backward, trying to create some distance as she made her way toward the road . . . and away from Mike's house.

By the time Violet got home, she'd had time to think. More than enough time.

She'd been cautious along the darkened streets, where the wind wasn't filtered, where she wasn't protected by the layers of trees and brush, and some of the gusts had nearly knocked her off her feet. Small trees and branches littered the roadways like an obstacle course, and they'd continued to fall as she picked her way among them toward her house.

The power was out all the way home, and the blackness was oppressive. Just one more obstacle forcing her to pay extra care to every step she took.

Yet she couldn't stop thinking about what she'd just seen. The lone bursts of light amid a canvas of shadows, flickering from that one window and reminding Violet that someone had been stalking her. Leaving her messages . . . and worse.

And now she knew who that person was.

She'd known immediately, *without question*, that it wasn't Mike. She'd seen him too many times since the cat had been left for her; she would have recognized the imprint on him easily. And she would never forget the feminine handwriting on the note, the pink paper and the scented pen.

She also remembered seeing Mike's little sister flirting with Jay the only other time she'd been at Mike's house, when Megan hadn't realized that Violet was waiting in the car, watching them.

The very thought of the pretty girl killing that poor little cat made Violet's skin crawl. She couldn't imagine what kind of twisted human being could wrap their fingers around an animal's neck and snap it, for any reason . . . let alone to send some sort of sick message.

And just what was that message supposed to be? What had Violet done to make the girl hate her so much? Why did Violet deserve to be despised?

It didn't matter, though, did it? Whatever her reason, whatever she thought Violet had done, she was sick, and someone had to stop her. Before she hurt something, *or someone*, again.

Violet knew it was time to stop keeping secrets. She had to tell Jay.

★ ★ ★

Her dad had been waiting for her on the front porch, holding a flashlight and pacing. He rushed to meet her at the road. Violet was trembling, both from the cold of the cutting wind and from the disturbing discovery she'd made in the woods.

"Violet," her father scolded, taking off his coat and throwing it around her shoulders. "What were you thinking, going out on a night like this? Your mother was about to call in the National Guard." He squeezed her tightly as he led her up the steps. Violet leaned into him, her teeth chattering. "Come on, there's a fire in the woodstove, and I bet you could talk your mom into making you some hot cocoa."

He was right, of course. Her mom was so relieved that she forgot to lecture Violet for taking off in the middle of a windstorm. Violet sat as close as she could to the woodstove without actually burning herself, until the warmth began to find its way into her numb fingertips and toes, and the chill was chased away.

The wind howled as it continued to pummel the house, and the sound of branches and treetops cracking intermittently filled the night. Inside they lit candles and used flashlights to get around.

Violet knew that if the power stayed out, her father would go out to the garage and set up the generator. But generally, in storms like these, the power was back on in hours rather than days, so until then they would just wait it out.

Violet wanted to call Jay, to tell him what she'd learned, to tell him everything, but not with her parents so nearby. They had gathered together, staying close to the fire to keep warm while the temperatures outside continued to plummet.

Violet's mom handed her a mug of steaming hot chocolate, and Violet wrapped her still icy fingers around it, inhaling the rich scent. "Thanks," she breathed.

Her mom sat cross-legged on the floor beside her. She patted Violet's leg. "So I know you didn't want to make a big deal of it," she started, "but I invited Uncle Stephen and Aunt Kat and the kids over for your birthday." Before Violet could protest, she held up her hand. "It won't be a party. Just dinner. And a cake." She looked pleased with herself as she added, "And presents."

"Yeah? And it's not a party?" Violet complained.

Her mom grinned. "Come on. We just want to wish you a happy birthday. Jay and his mom are coming too. It'll be fun."

Violet rolled her eyes. She knew there was no point arguing; she'd already lost this particular battle. She realized even before the conversation had started that her mom was going to throw her a party, regardless of what she wanted. "Fine," Violet finally conceded. "But no hats. And no streamers or balloons. Seriously, it's just a birthday *dinner.* Okay?"

"Agreed. No streamers," her mom promised.

"Or balloons."

Her mom sighed as if Violet was ruining everything. "Fine, no balloons either."

Violet smiled, lifting her mug and taking a sip of the

steamy chocolate inside. It felt good going down. "And, Mom . . ." she added quietly.

"Hmm?" her mom answered, lost in her own thoughts, probably dreaming of ways to get around the no-balloon rule.

"Thank you," Violet whispered.

CHAPTER 19

WHEN VIOLET AWOKE, THE POWER WAS BACK ON. All the switches must have been in the on position, because where it had once been black, light now radiated into every corner, every crevice. She was certain that was what had awakened her.

She and her mom had fallen asleep at opposite ends of the same couch, and their legs were tucked beneath the heavy blanket they shared. Outside, Violet could still hear the wind whistling low and deep as it danced around the house, but it was so much quieter than the unremitting pounding she'd fallen asleep to.

The overhead light turned off, and Violet sat up to peer

at her dad. "What time is it?" she whispered, trying not to disturb her mom.

He glanced at his watch. "Just after midnight. Power just came on, so the house should be warm in a few minutes, if you want to go up to bed."

Violet stretched as she untangled her legs from her mom's; her neck ached from leaning crookedly against the armrest. Her dad went back to closing up the house, checking windows and doors and turning off light switches.

Violet went to her bedroom, working out the kinks in her neck along the way. But as she left the warmth of the woodstove behind, she realized that her dad was right about the heat. It was still freezing, although she could hear the old furnace working now, and she knew the heat would kick in soon.

She tugged on a sweatshirt and climbed beneath her blankets, covering her head before dialing Jay's number on her cell phone.

He answered on the second ring. "I've been trying to call you for hours. You okay?"

"Yeah, the power just came back on. Yours?"

"It's only been on for about ten minutes." And then his voice took on a completely different quality. "I was kind of hoping you'd need someone to keep you warm."

Violet smiled, curling into a ball against the chill and letting the heat from his words creep through her. "You wish. You know, that's all you seem to think about lately," she teased. She heard him laugh, and she smiled, enjoying the moment. And then she sighed, ruining it. "Jay, we need to talk."

"Sounds serious." His tone was still mischievous. Violet wished she could play along.

"It is."

There was a pause, and then, "Do you want me to come over?"

"No." Violet hesitated. It seemed so much harder now. She'd been thinking about this all evening, replaying the words in her head, in conversation after conversation. And in every one, she'd felt so confident, so sure. Now, not so much.

She sighed again.

"Okay, you're starting to freak me out, Vi. What's wrong?"

She shook her head against the handset. "I saw something tonight." Again she felt so *un*sure. *Crap! Why was this so hard?* "I went for a run before it was too windy, and while I was out there I saw an echo. An imprint, actually, of an echo that I've seen before."

His voice was playful once more. "You've seen *a lot* of echoes, Vi."

He still didn't get it.

"You know I haven't been entirely honest lately, that something's been bothering me." She was sitting up now, no longer cold. She let out a breath. "I don't even know where to start."

"The truth would be good." There was nothing playful

about his tone now, but there was no going back.

She took another breath. "A couple of weeks ago someone left a dead cat at my house. It was the middle of the night, but I know it was meant for me, because whoever put it there left the box next to my car."

There was a brief silence on the other end, and Violet worried that she'd made a mistake confiding in him. "Jesus, Violet, why didn't you tell me? Why wouldn't you tell me something like that?" She could practically hear him raking his hand through his hair, just as he always did when he was stressed.

And that was exactly why she hadn't said anything. That, and his next unambiguous words.

"What did your uncle say?"

She didn't know how to answer. She knew Jay would be upset when he heard her response. She braced herself. "I haven't told anyone else. You're the only one who knows."

"Why would you keep this to yourself? What if someone's after you again? What if whoever did this decides that a dead cat isn't threatening enough? Was it that guy from the movies last week?" He sounded breathless, and she knew he was pacing. "I'm coming over," he insisted. "We have to tell your uncle."

"Wait, Jay. *Please*, just . . . *wait*," Violet cut him off. "Just let me finish. It wasn't the guy from last week."

She heard him exhale. "Okay. Fine. Go ahead. . . ."

"I do know who left it, though," she continued before she could change her mind again. "The imprint I saw tonight—the one from the cat—it was coming from inside Mike's house."

At first Violet thought the line might have gone dead; Jay said nothing.

Her voice, when she spoke again, was like a dry whisper, barely a breath. "Hello?"

"I'm here." But there was an edge now that Violet hadn't heard before, one that had nothing to do with concerns for her safety. She could feel her heart plummeting. "So what are you saying, Vi? You think Mike left the dead cat? You think *Mike* did that?"

"No, not at all." She leaned forward, needing him to understand. "There were other things that happened. A note, the one that was left on your car; it wasn't from Chelsea. I didn't know who put it there, but it was from a girl. And there were some hang-up calls." Her heart was hammering as she got closer to it, hovering near the threshold of her accusation, and when she finally made it, her voice came out reedy and weak. "I think it was Mike's sister."

She wasn't sure what she'd expected from him in that moment, but it certainly wasn't anything like the response she got.

"Megan?" he countered, his voice incredulous. "Why would she do that?"

"I don't know, Jay. But I think it's safe to say she's messed up." Frustration flared, setting her cheeks on fire. Violet recalled the way the girl had flirted with Jay the night they'd stopped at her house to drop off Mike's wallet. "Maybe she likes you. Maybe she doesn't like that we're together, and she wishes that *she* was your girlfriend."

And then he laughed. Softly. Just beneath his breath.

But that was all it took. Violet bristled, her back stiffening as resentment overshadowed reason. "What the hell, Jay? This is definitely not funny. Whatever her problem is, it's serious. She killed a cat. And for some twisted reason, she left it at my house as some sort of *message*. And then there was the note. She's a psycho, Jay. She needs help."

Violet waited. She wanted him to say something, *anything*, to let her know that he understood. She squeezed a handful of her quilt in her fist, balling it tightly and then releasing it as she waited for his response.

"I think you're wrong, Violet."

Violet squeezed her eyes shut.

"They've been through so much this year. Mike's mom isn't around, and his dad is barely hanging on. Mike's sister is pretty much all he has left."

The last thing she wanted right now was to feel sorry for Megan. "It doesn't change what I saw."

"Maybe you were confused. It was dark, maybe it wasn't an echo at all. We both know you've been wrong before. Remember Mrs. Webber?"

But Violet didn't need Jay to remind her of her first-grade teacher. That was entirely different; Violet had only been six when her teacher had come to school carrying the shadowy aura that she hadn't worn the day before. The dark air that clung to her skin like heavy black smoke had terrified Violet, and she'd run from the classroom, forcing the school nurse to call her parents.

By the time her mother had finished picking up Violet's class work from Mrs. Webber, the teacher had confided to her that she'd run over a raccoon on her way to school that morning.

And Violet had learned to be careful in making assumptions.

But this time she wasn't confused. She felt the sting behind her lids as she blinked furiously to ward away the tears.

Hadn't Jay just assured her he was still her best friend? Hadn't they just spent the night in each other's arms, making promises and whispered pledges? Hadn't she given herself to him completely? How could he question her? Especially now. Over this.

"I'm not wrong," she insisted quietly. It pissed her off that her voice betrayed her, making her sound weak instead of determined. "You're wrong, Jay. This time, you're wrong."

She hung up the phone, no longer fighting the tears. She leaned down, curling around her pillow and sobbing, using it to muffle her frustrated cries. She didn't try to stop herself, didn't try to tell herself that everything would be okay; she just let the tears come. She let herself *feel* everything.

For the first time in months, she let herself feel angry, betrayed, afraid, alone. Everything that she'd so carefully tucked away.

She cried until her eyes were raw and her face was swollen. She felt drained and empty. Hollow. It felt good, the nothingness. And when she finally felt nothing at last, she slept.

Her phone was ringing—or vibrating, in this case—from beneath her pillow. Violet dug it out and squinted at the small screen.

Her eyes felt like they'd been scraped with steel wool. She tried to rub away the grittiness, but it was hard to see through the watery haze. The LED screen glowed in the darkness.

The clock on her nightstand told her it was 2:03.

The caller ID on her phone said: *Unknown Caller.*

Her breath lodged in her throat, and her pulse quivered as she hauled herself up. She thought about ignoring the call. But she had to make a decision fast, or she would miss it. She closed her eyes and hit Answer.

She cleared her throat. "Hello?" Her voice was still scratchy.

Like before, there was nothing from the other end. Violet strained to hear, listening for something, anything that would confirm the girl's identity. She cupped her hand over her other ear.

"Hello?" Violet repeated, her voice barely a whisper.

Silence was the only response.

Violet was nervous, but when she spoke, she tried to sound confident. "I know who you are," she stated quietly.

And there it was.

She'd heard it that time. Without a doubt, something—*someone*—on the other end. She was sure now that the girl was listening. Violet had her attention.

She heard a brief rustling, as if the phone were moved, being repositioned.

She waited a moment and then tried again. "I know what you did," Violet said as calmly as she could. Her heart was trying to pound its way out of her chest, slamming violently against her aching ribs. "I know you killed that cat."

The stillness around her was unbearable. The quiet in the house was matched only by the silence from the caller. Violet suddenly had second thoughts about her accusations; somehow, saying them out loud to the person she suspected of committing them made them sound strangely absurd. She had a fleeting insight into what Jay must have felt.

Not that it mattered; he should have trusted her.

She took a breath, deciding that she didn't care how it sounded. She wasn't wrong. "I know it's you, Megan." Her voice dropped even lower, if that were even possible, until she could barely hear herself. "And so does Jay."

On the other end, there was a barely audible sound. Violet thought it might have been a breath, a sigh, or maybe the whisper of a moan. She couldn't be certain. But after that moment, after that brief lapse, there was nothing but a deafening hush.

Nothing.

Megan had hung up on her.

CHAPTER 20

VIOLET STUDIED HERSELF IN THE MIRROR AND understood why her mom hadn't given her a hard time about staying home from school. She looked like a train wreck. Her skin was pale and sickly, her eyes red and puffy. She winced as she wiped her nose, which was raw and sore.

She blamed Jay for the dismal image that stared back at her.

And Megan, of course.

Violet made her way back to bed. She had been tired before, but never like this. She felt defeated, stripped of all rational thought. She was certain she'd be incapable of making it through a single class, let alone an entire day.

She tried *not* to think about Jay. Whenever she did, she felt her heart collapsing in on itself.

She told herself that she should be concerned about Megan, a girl who'd been capable of some pretty terrifying stuff, but she couldn't make her mind stay there. Jay's refusal to stand by her when she needed him was more than Violet could bear. She squeezed her eyes shut, forcing the thought away.

She was too weary to play this game again. But it was too late; he'd already found his way back in, and she could feel the tears, despite her best efforts to hold them back.

God, how was it possible that she even had any tears left?

She hated this. She hated feeling so frail, so miserable. She should be angry, or afraid, but instead here she was, lying on her bed, unable to function. All because of Jay.

And what did it all mean? That he was choosing Megan over her? Or that he was simply unable to accept that Megan was capable of that type of violence?

Did it matter?

Either way, Jay hadn't supported her.

He'd tried calling Violet, and when she didn't answer, he'd sent her a single text message, asking if he could come over. Asking if they could talk.

Violet typed out her response, pausing for just a moment before hitting Send.

I don't want to see you.

It felt so permanent, so final. So painful.

She covered her mouth with the palm of her hand,

drawing her knees up to her chest as she choked on her sobs. But the worst pain came from a place she couldn't physically reach. Her heart felt as if it had been crushed—it was lonely and miserable.

Violet worried for it. She wondered if she could trust it to keep beating.

She felt as if it had given up.

She felt like giving up.

She tried to tell herself to stop being so dramatic, but it didn't *feel* dramatic.

She'd lost Jay. And more than just losing the one person she'd fallen so wholly in love with, the person she'd given herself to *completely*, she'd also just lost her very best friend in the entire world.

She didn't know how long she lay there, balanced at the edge of sleep and wake. It was a tenuous place for Violet to be, with her subconscious permitted to contribute to the images that gathered there.

At one point, Violet put her iPod on, to block out her thoughts, to block out everything, but nothing could stop the corrupted dreams that lingered whenever she dozed, or the torment that attacked when she woke.

So she tossed and turned, trying not to think and not to feel.

It was almost dark when she felt the side of her bed sink, and she opened her eyes. Chelsea gazed down at her.

"What are you doing here?" Violet asked, scooting up

on her pillow. Her throat burned.

Chelsea shrugged. "I was worried about you." Her face scrunched up. "You okay?"

She wasn't okay. She wasn't even close.

Violet wanted to tell her friend that she was fine, that she was sick and that was why she hadn't been at school, but she just shook her head. Her voice was hoarse. "We broke up. Jay and me, we broke up."

"Aww crap, Vi." Chelsea took Violet's hand and squeezed it. "It'll be all right. I'm sure it's just a fight. It's *you and Jay.* Everything'll be fine, I know it will. Do you want me to talk to him?"

Violet shook her head again. "Please don't, Chels."

Chelsea looked pained, worried, confused—too many emotions that were unfamiliar to her—all at once. Finally she sighed. "Scoot over."

Violet didn't argue. Instead she made room for her friend.

Chelsea climbed in beside Violet. She lay on her back so they were both staring up at the ceiling. "Well, if he's stupid enough to let you go, then he doesn't deserve you," Chelsea clucked, reassuring Violet in her own way, nudging her beneath the covers. "Besides, you'll always have me, and I'm *way* more fun than Jay could ever be."

Violet managed a watery laugh through her tears. She didn't know how to tell Chelsea how grateful she was that she'd come by tonight without sounding corny, like some cheesy greeting card. But she couldn't imagine anything better than having her friend beside her, whispering encouragement as darkness fell.

Violet knew that her mom had come in to check on her after Chelsea had gone, because she'd felt her mother's cool hand brushing over her cheek and lying against her forehead.

She doubted that her mom really thought she was sick, but she never said a word. She just slipped in silently to make sure that Violet was all right and slipped out again. For that, at least, Violet was thankful.

During that endless night Violet came to a conclusion: She was damaged, sure, but she was stronger than that. She wasn't broken. She would survive this. She had to. And she didn't want Jay to know how badly he'd hurt her.

She wanted him, but she didn't *need* him.

She closed her eyes, feeling no real peace. The best she could hope for at this point was for a little of the numbness to find her at last, and to dull the ache in her heart.

But sleep was all she actually got.

Violet stayed home from school again the next morning, not because she was exhausted, although she was. Or heartbroken, which she also was. Instead she stayed home because it was her birthday.

Happy freaking seventeenth to her!

She wandered out of her room, relieved that the house was empty at the moment. And even though she wasn't hungry, she poured herself a bowl of cereal. It wouldn't do any good to starve herself.

The note on the counter said that her mom had gone out to run some errands, which Violet interpreted as shopping for the *nonparty birthday dinner* that she had planned for Violet. Just thinking about it, about spending an entire evening with her family—her parents and her aunt and uncle—celebrating her birthday, made her stomach twist into painful knots. The fact that Jay wouldn't be there made it almost unbearable.

She was carrying her half-eaten bowl of cereal to the sink when she glanced at the clock. It was still only nine fifteen. Suddenly spending an entire day cooped up in the house again sounded worse than being at school. Violet needed to get out, and there was only one person she could think to call.

She hurried, hoping to be out of there before her mom came home. She threw on some jeans and a T-shirt and pulled her hair back in a ponytail that looked nothing like the ones she'd seen on the pristine Sara Priest. Violet's hair was wild and unruly, even on a good day.

She did a last-minute mirror check to assess the damage. It wasn't *so* bad. At least not once she got past the dark circles and the sallow skin. And that vacant look behind her still swollen eyes.

She decided it was probably better *not* to look in the mirror for too long.

She scribbled a quick note, letting her parents know she'd be back in time for dinner, and she rushed out the door, feeling better the moment her car's engine sputtered to life.

That was when she pulled out her cell phone to arrange a meeting she wouldn't have predicted in a million years. With the last person she'd ever expected to call.

Rafe was already inside, looking at ease for the first time since Violet had met him. She spotted him before he noticed her, and she watched him through the glass, with his inky black hair falling in front of his face. He leaned back in the wobbly-looking bistro chair, his arms folded across his chest, his chin down. He was someone who was accustomed to going unnoticed. He seemed to prefer it that way.

She'd recognized it the moment she'd met him. It was that indefinable quality she couldn't quite put her finger on. He was . . . *different*. It was as if he didn't belong. As if he was a boy who couldn't quite find his place in the world.

Like her.

The thought made her instantly uncomfortable. She didn't like the possibility that she didn't belong, even though she'd considered that very thing more times than she could count.

He had picked the meeting place, a coffee shop in the city. A dark little café tucked within the crowded streets and redbrick buildings of Pioneer Square, an area of Seattle rich with art galleries, restaurants, and antique stores. It was also a popular gathering area for the local homeless.

Violet stepped through the doorway, the raw wooden planks thumping hollowly beneath her feet. The smell of coffee was dark and rich.

Rafe glanced up and saw her there. When he didn't smile, didn't respond at all, Violet was surprised by her disappointment. She wondered what she'd expected.

And she worried that she'd made a mistake, calling Rafe.

"Hi," she said, suddenly nervous as she pulled out the chair across from him.

He lifted his chin in a brief nod and continued to watch her guardedly. He'd ordered before she'd arrived, and steam rose from the coffee sitting between them.

"Thanks for meeting me. I know I didn't give you much notice."

He shrugged as he cleared his throat. As always, his voice was hushed. "I was sorta surprised you called."

Violet felt *exactly* the same way. "You're the one who gave me your number." She challenged him with a look, but she wasn't sure what else to say. Now that she was sitting here, she felt so . . . awkward. "I was just hoping we could talk . . . maybe you could, I don't know, answer some questions for me."

He looked down, as if he were having trouble holding her gaze. "You're right, I did give you my number. It's just . . . I'm not really good at talking. Sara's much better at it." His eyes shifted up then, finding hers, and she was struck again by how intense they were. "I'm not really sure I'm the one you should have called."

Violet shook her head but couldn't find the words to argue. She could practically *see* the walls he had up, the defenses he had no intention of letting down.

"If you want, I can call Sara and set something up between you two, but I just don't think I can do"—he pointed from her to him, shrugging, his face apologetic—"this."

Violet didn't answer; she suddenly felt like a jackass for thinking that she might be able to talk to Rafe in the first place. *What have I been smoking?* she chastised herself. Her eyes burned, stinging, and she blinked hard. She couldn't believe she'd been foolish enough to think they might have some sort of *connection*. But after everything she'd been through, the tears were still too close to the surface, and she was afraid that if she started crying now, in front of him, she might actually die from humiliation.

She shoved away from the table, nearly toppling her chair in her haste to leave.

But Rafe reached for her, grabbing her wrist and stopping her before she could turn away.

Violet flinched at his touch, as electricity sparked between them, shooting all the way up her arm. She jerked her hand back, clutching it tightly to her pounding heart.

"Sorry," he mumbled, looking just as confused by the strange current as she was. He flexed and unflexed his fist, and Violet could see that his fingernails had been filled in with Sharpie. His eyes lifted to hers. "Look, Violet, I didn't mean to hurt your feelings. *Please* . . . don't go. Not yet."

She hesitated, trying to decide, but she couldn't ignore the sincerity she heard in his voice. Finally she pulled her chair back to the table and sat down. But now she was the one with the mistrustful look in her eyes.

He smiled then; it was a sly, wicked sort of smile. It suited him. "I told you I was bad at this."

Violet winced, not yet ready to let him off the hook. "That's kind of an understatement."

"Can we try this again? What did you want to *talk* about?"

Violet exhaled noisily as she propped her elbows on the table and tried to explain. "I don't know why I called you, really. I just . . . I didn't want to be alone anymore. And that doesn't mean I think we have to be *friends* or anything." She made a face at him. "It's just that you're the only one who knows about Sara Priest. And that I found that little boy. At least, the only person I can talk to." She thought about Jay, about how she should have been able to tell him.

So why hadn't she? Why hadn't she told him about her meeting at the FBI?

It didn't really matter now; Jay wouldn't be around anymore.

"I guess I just don't know what to do, and you seem to have some of the answers."

Rafe's eyebrows rose teasingly. "You think *I* have the answers?"

Violet shrugged. "Well, you and Sara."

"And you don't want to talk to her." It wasn't a question this time. Rafe leaned back as he crossed his feet lazily at the ankles, but he wasn't fooling Violet; she knew she had his attention.

She also knew she'd have to tread carefully; Rafe didn't seem like the *sharing* type.

But they did have something in common, whether either of them was willing to admit it or not. Sara Priest was proof of that. "Look, I get it. *You* don't want to talk about *you*, and *I* don't want to talk about *me*. So where does that leave us exactly?" She cocked her head to the side.

Rafe lifted his shoulder. "Right back where we started, I guess."

"That's a bunch of crap," Violet insisted, narrowing her eyes at him. "You know *way* more than you're letting on. Like, why is Sara so interested in me? What is it that she thinks she knows?"

Rafe leaned forward, no longer feigning indifference. "You tell me, Violet. Obviously there's . . . *something*. Otherwise neither of us would be here in the first place. You'd be safe at home in your cozy little farm town and I'd still be in bed." His face was expressionless, but Violet saw the taunting gleam in his indigo eyes. "If you want to swap secrets, then you go first."

Violet squeezed her lips together, worrying and biting them until she tasted her own blood. She considered what he was telling her, and recognized the corner she'd let him back her into. He had her. Of course, he knew that. Violet wasn't going to reveal what she could do . . . to tell him of her talent for seeking out bodies. And he damn sure wasn't about to confide in her.

She exhaled, releasing the breath she'd been holding as

she'd waited for him to disclose something . . . *anything.* "So do you work for her? Is that the deal with you two?"

Rafe laughed. It was the first time Violet had ever heard him laugh. The sound was quiet and low, just like his voice. "I work *with* her. Big difference." He reached in his pocket and handed her another business card, just like the others. "If you have any other questions about Sara, I think you need to call *her.*"

Violet glared at him, but she knew enough to realize that they'd reached an impasse.

Rafe reached forward then and pushed the coffee across the table. "I got this for you. Double-shot vanilla latte. But it's probably getting cold by now."

Violet wrinkled her brow. "How'd you know what to order?" She picked up the cup. It was still warm.

He shrugged. "Just a hunch. Most girls like vanilla."

Violet looked at him dubiously. That was pretty much the faultiest logic she'd ever heard. Most girls liked *a lot* of different things: chocolate, caramel, nonfat milk, *whole* milk, whipped cream, iced coffees . . . the options were endless. How could he possibly have pegged her for a vanilla-latte kind of girl?

Lucky guess, she supposed as she took a sip. She got up to leave, recognizing that their conversation was over.

But Rafe reached out to stop her, careful this time to touch her jacket instead of her skin. "Oh, and Violet?" This time he was smiling, kind of. "Happy birthday."

CHAPTER 21

WHEN VIOLET WALKED THROUGH THE FRONT door, the house was filled with the smells of food. *Real food*, the kind that didn't have anything to do with the freezer section of the grocery store. That could mean only one thing . . . that someone other than her mom had prepared her birthday dinner.

Violet didn't care about the who; it was the *what* that had her mouth watering as she closed the door behind her.

The delicate scent of rosemary mingled with the heady aroma of garlic and lemons. She knew immediately that her dad had been cooking, because it was Violet's favorite—at least of the homemade variety—*lemon chicken*.

Suddenly she was famished. And even the deterrent of an evening with her family—or anyone, for that matter—wasn't enough to keep her appetite at bay.

She could hear laughter coming from the kitchen, and she knew that she was already late for her own party. Thankfully she was able to slip quietly upstairs to change and freshen up. She felt like crap after driving all the way to the city and back, trying to get information from Rafe. And she knew she probably looked it too. She pinched her cheeks, to give the illusion that there was still blood pumping somewhere within her body, and quickly brushed her teeth.

When she decided it was the best she could do on short notice, she headed back downstairs, where her mom was waiting at the bottom of the staircase.

"Happy birthday, Vi!" She grabbed Violet, wrapping her arms around her.

"Mom, have you been drinking?" she scolded, only half-joking as she struggled to break free. She could hear the others in the kitchen, chairs scraping and voices coming out to greet her.

"No," her mom scoffed, as if the suggestion was absurd. "I'm just—" She started to say something, but then changed her mind.

Worried, Violet thought, finishing the sentence in her head. And she wondered what her parents must have thought over the past couple of days, with Violet skipping school and hiding in her bedroom, barely eating, and then disappearing this morning.

She didn't ask though, mostly because she didn't want to know the answers.

"Happy birthday," her dad interrupted the awkward hush. He embraced her too but more gently, thoughtfully.

Violet smiled at him.

Her aunt and uncle were there too, along with her two little cousins, Joshua and Cassidy. Cassidy reached her arms up for Violet, and Violet lifted the little blonde-haired girl, commenting about how heavy she'd gotten, even though she was as light as a feather.

"So what are you now," Violet teased the little girl wiggling in her arms, "like twelve, thirteen years old?"

"No!" Cassidy giggled, but that was all the answer she gave.

Joshua, who was just barely five years old himself, was already serious like Violet's dad, a little accountant in the making. She had to force herself *not* to notice the similarities between him and the picture of the little boy from the waterfront. "She's not even three yet. Her birthday is April sixth," he stated precisely.

"Hmm," Violet responded skeptically, looking at him like she didn't quite believe it. "I would've guessed older than that."

Joshua shrugged as if it didn't matter to him. And then he asked, "What's wrong with you? Are you sick or something?"

"Joshy! That's rude!" Her aunt Kat glanced apologetically at Violet. "Say you're sorry right now."

Violet set Cassidy down. The little girl grabbed hold of Violet's leg and held on tight.

"It's okay," Violet told her aunt. And then to Joshua, she shrugged lazily. "I'm something, all right. I just don't know what."

The awkward hush was back. And Violet was aware that they all knew, or at least had their suspicions, about what was wrong with her. Probably that she and Jay were fighting, maybe even broken up.

She was glad when her dad linked his arm through hers and drew her toward the kitchen. "Come on. There's enough food for an army. Let's eat."

Violet didn't have to be asked twice. Food, at least, was something she could agree on. And he was right: There was more than enough.

Violet found a spot at the table and pretended to be interested in the conversations going on around her. She didn't want anyone to ask her what was wrong. She didn't want to answer questions that were too tough even to consider.

Her dad finished fixing dinner, and the chicken was served with garlic mashed potatoes and a Caesar salad. Thankfully the conversation steered away from anything to do with Violet—at least where Jay was concerned—and there were very few lapses. And even though it was Violet's birthday, Violet was hardly required to participate.

She found herself chatting with the little kids—her cousins—more often than not, mostly because they didn't need anything real, anything deep, from her in return. They were risk-free, and Violet preferred it that way.

Her mom had gotten around the no-balloons-or-streamers rule on a technicality. Obviously, Violet had not been clear enough, and she realized that she should have been broader in her statement, making it a *no-decorations* rule instead. But since she hadn't, and since her mom had taken her at her word, the table—and the room—was overflowing with flowers and candles.

The result was dramatic. And even though Violet wanted to protest, to claim that her wishes had been ignored, that the spirit—if not the letter—of her request had been violated, she couldn't.

Maybe it was just the effects of the first real food she'd eaten in days, or maybe it was the lack of sleep, but even *she* had to admit that it was beautiful. It made Violet feel better to be surrounded by it, and by her family, on her birthday.

"Thank you," she said, almost to herself, as she kept her eyes down, concentrating on her plate.

The only reason she knew they'd heard her at all was the brief lull in the conversation.

That, and Joshy's unaffected, knee-jerk response. "You're welcome."

Violet smiled as she took another bite of her mashed potatoes.

The conversation continued. There was cake and there were presents. Violet did her best to stay in the moment, to remain focused on the here and now, instead of letting her mind wander to other places.

But it was hard, and she found herself distracted far too often, which was what made it so much worse when they heard a knock at the front door.

Violet's stomach tightened anxiously. There was no one she wanted to see right now, at least no one who wasn't already there in her house.

She hated the tangle of sensations, the expectation and the dread. She felt traitorous to herself for even hoping it might be Jay when she'd spent so much time convincing herself that he was the last person she wanted to see. *Especially tonight.*

Violet glanced around the table, at her mother and father and her aunt and uncle and even at her two little cousins. Everyone seemed as paralyzed as she was.

"I'll get it." Her uncle Stephen finally stood up and left the room.

Violet held her breath.

She knew. She already knew it was him. She was afraid to see him, afraid of what it might do to her fragile resolve.

But when her uncle came back into the kitchen, he was alone. And maybe only she noticed it, but she felt herself slump into her chair. She choked on the bitter disappointment that she'd been mistaken and was frustrated with herself for feeling that way.

And then he said the words that Violet had both anticipated and feared. "It's Jay. He wants to talk to you."

The air felt black and oily, suffocating her as she sat there. No one spoke as they all remained still, watching her.

She frowned as she looked at her uncle pleadingly and shook her head, unable to give him her answer out loud.

"Are you sure?" he asked calmly, and even though his voice was quiet, it was far too loud in the stark silence of the kitchen. Even the kids had stopped squirming in their seats.

Violet nodded, begging him to understand. But she didn't need to worry. *He* didn't question or second-guess her when she needed him.

When he left the kitchen, her mom and her aunt made polite small talk rather than pretend that they weren't listening, trying to hear what was going on out at the front door.

But Violet couldn't sit there and pretend any longer. As soon as she heard the front door close, she excused herself without explanation. "I'm going up to my room," she said flatly, unapologetically.

Nobody tried to stop her or ask her if she was okay. Her parents would tell her aunt and uncle good-bye for her, and later—much later—when she was feeling more like herself again, she would apologize.

But right now she didn't have it in her to be polite or to make nice with well-meaning family members. For now, she just wanted to be alone.

She was finished with her birthday.

Violet waited until the house was silent before going downstairs again.

She'd stayed in her room, trying to slip back into that

state, the stupor in which she'd dully existed until Jay had arrived at her party, crashing through her poorly constructed composure. But no matter how hard she tried, the feelings were just too strong, and too close to the surface to stuff back down.

So instead she wanted cake. Maybe a good sugar fix could take the edge off.

She crept quietly toward the kitchen, and when she got there, she smiled. Her dad must have known she'd be back down.

On the counter, which had been cleared and cleaned after the party, sat a plate covered in plastic wrap. And beneath the transparent wrap was a gigantic piece of her birthday cake.

Violet felt a rush of emotion, but in a good way. *In the very best way.*

Next to the plate was a small pink gift bag stuffed with pretty tissue paper. Violet ignored the bag, only briefly eyeing it before going to the fridge to get the milk.

Only when she sat back down in front of the plate and unwrapped the cake did she wonder about the gift sitting beside it.

She thought she'd already opened all her presents, the ones from her parents and from her aunt and uncle, but she must've left the party before they'd had the chance to give her this one.

She lifted one bare foot onto the stool and propped her chin against her knee as she took a bite of the cake. It was perfect, exactly what she needed right now. How was it possible that something as simple as a slice of birthday cake could make her feel so much better?

She reached over and fingered the delicate tissue of the present; the iridescent sheen of it sparkled slightly in the faint glow from the light above the stove. Violet smiled again, wondering if the sugar was already hitting her system or if she was just that shallow, if receiving a present wrapped in such a pretty package could really make her this happy.

Shallow, no. But she was still a girl, after all.

She let the paper slip from her fingers long enough to take a gulp of the cold milk, washing down the rich frosting just so she could start all over again. She wasn't in a hurry. She didn't have any better place to be at the moment.

After she swallowed, she took another bite, licking the frosting from the tines of her fork before finally setting it down on the plate. She pulled the bag toward her and peeked inside.

Whatever was in there was wrapped in the same pretty tissue paper.

She pulled out something small but solid. It fit in the palm of her hand. She removed the shimmering paper, unwrapping it, and inside was a bifold photo frame.

Violet wondered who it was from, admiring the delicate filigree work around the frame's borders as she opened it. But when she saw the photographs that were already framed inside, she froze.

It was from Jay.

The gift. The photos. He must have left the present with

her uncle when he'd stopped by earlier.

Her stomach lurched. She hated him for making her feel so confused, so conflicted.

The pictures inside were from the second grade, each of their school photos from that year. That particular picture of Jay had always been one of Violet's favorites, mostly because she'd been the one responsible for his hair.

It was the year that the photographer had passed out those little black combs to all the kids as they stood in line, and Violet had decided to "fix" Jay's hair. She'd led him over to the water fountain and doused his hair and then slicked it down around the crazy, crooked part she'd made with the free comb. She'd thought he looked perfect.

And now, looking at the picture, with his goofy hair and his brand-new oversized grown-up teeth in the front of his mouth, she saw that he did.

In a completely ridiculous way.

It didn't matter though. The gift would have been thoughtful and sweet at any other time. But not now.

His gift didn't change anything.

He didn't trust her. He didn't believe her. And that was all that mattered now. He couldn't take that back by dropping off a present . . . not even an adorable one.

It was the worst possible gift he could have given her at a time like this. And it was exactly the kind of ending Violet should have expected from the worst birthday of her life.

She shoved the frame and the tissue back inside the bag,

and she left it, along with the rest of her uneaten cake, on the counter as she stalked back up the stairs.

Stupid, stupid Jay.

Just when she was starting to feel a little bit better, he had to come along and ruin it again.

SLOTH

SILENCE GATHERED, HERALDING HER FAVORITE time of night.

She crept from her room as noiselessly as she could, the old floorboards creaking on occasion, but she had learned the best places to step to keep them from protesting too loudly. The house was dark, just the way she liked it. And calm.

The living room was cluttered with dirty dishes, and newspapers were spread over nearly every surface. Laundry—dirty and clean—littered the floors, and bottles covered the coffee table in front of the television.

She worked quickly, gathering the newspapers. She carried plates and empty bottles to the kitchen, picking up garbage and folding laundry. She tried not to breathe the sour odor of cheap whiskey that mingled sickeningly with the scent of cigarettes that clung to everything her father touched—his clothing, his skin, his breath. She cringed at the idea of those odors—his odors—touching her.

She told herself to ignore them; the sooner she finished, the sooner she could get back to bed.

She heard a door open down the shadowed hallway, and her breath lodged in her throat. Her heart forgot to beat.

Footsteps padded over the floorboards, obviously not as careful as hers had been, and she winced with every creak she heard.

"What are you doing?" her brother muttered, bleary-eyed, and at last she found her breath. "You can do this in the morning."

She shook her head. She didn't want to tell him the truth, that she much preferred to do her chores when their father wasn't around. That in the morning there was still a chance he'd be there. That she might have to see him, to talk to him. "I couldn't sleep," she lied.

"At least let me help," he offered, clearing the countertops and carrying the rest of the dishes to the sink.

She thought about opening up to her brother, about asking him how he could stand this useless version of their father. How he could stand any of it.

But she knew how: He was stronger than she was; he always had been. Even when they were little, she was the one who stumbled and fell, who needed someone to pick her up and brush her off. She was the one who'd needed their mother.

He had always been so independent, so determined to do things on his own. He was smart, social, resilient. Everything she wasn't.

Sometimes she wondered if he'd even noticed that their mother was gone. That their father was no longer the same man. And that she was damaged . . . broken.

She wanted to talk to him, but she wouldn't, because she didn't want him to see how weak she was.

So, instead of talking, she finished the dishes in silence.

As she dried her hands, her brother tied off the kitchen trash bag. "Go on and go to bed." His smile was genuine, maybe even sweet. "I'll finish up and turn out the lights."

She didn't argue; she just nodded, making her way back down the hallway, watching each step she took, carefully calculating where her foot should fall so as not to wake her father.

CHAPTER 22

VIOLET WENT BACK TO SCHOOL THE NEXT DAY, mostly because she knew staying home again wouldn't make her return any easier. She had to get it over with eventually. But being there, under the same roof as Jay, was something along the lines of a carefully choreographed dance. And it wasn't just Jay she needed to avoid.

Violet didn't expect it to be difficult to steer clear of Megan. They were in different classes—different grades—and it had never been a problem before. But now Violet was acutely aware that it was always a possibility, that at some point, and when she least expected it, there was a chance they could cross paths.

Jay, however, was a different story. It would have been

impossible to avoid him altogether, especially since they shared some of the same classes. But Violet did everything in her power to stay as far away from him as she could.

She arrived to her classes early and asked other students if she could switch seats with them, earning her a strange look or two, but no one actually complained—at least not out loud anyway.

But even with those precautions, Violet still felt uncomfortable. She could feel Jay's eyes on her, beseeching her to look his way, daring her to ignore him.

And it was hard. Violet *wanted* to peek, to sneak a glance in his direction, just to see him for a moment. But she couldn't take the chance. She knew that he'd be waiting, watching for her to slip.

Between classes it was more difficult, and after fourth period Jay was waiting for her in the hallway. It was tough to see him there, face-to-face, hard to remain detached when he seemed so earnest, so sincere. His eyes were tired and red, and he looked defeated even before he spoke.

She tried to brush past him, but he stopped her, grabbing her hand and pulling her back. His touch was like liquid fire against her skin, and Violet cringed at the tingling awareness she felt as his fingers scalded her.

"Violet, please . . . just talk to me."

But if seeing him had been difficult, hearing his voice was worse. It was raw and full of emotion. He sounded so . . . *so miserable.*

Like her.

But she couldn't let him do this to her. She had to be stronger. "Jay, don't. I don't want to talk to you. Just leave me alone." She wanted to say *please*, to beg him to walk away in case she wasn't able to, but she was afraid of that word. It was too soft, and she worried that it might reveal too much of what she felt in that moment, seeing him in person.

She pulled her hand out of his grip. And again she was mad at him for letting her go, despite her words and her actions. She didn't turn back; she just left him standing there. But she knew he was watching her the same way she knew she wanted to turn around and take it all back.

She wanted to tell him that it didn't matter, that she didn't care what he thought, or believed, because she loved him. And she needed him.

But she couldn't. Because it did matter.

At lunch, Violet sat alone in her car so she wouldn't risk running into Jay again.

She checked her phone for the thousandth time, to see if Sara Priest had called, and realized she was disappointed when there weren't any new messages.

There was a part of her, and she wasn't sure how small that part was anymore, that hoped Sara hadn't given up on her just yet.

Recently, Violet had time to think about everything that had happened, including how Sara Priest had come into her life . . . through her discovery of the boy. And suddenly things seemed a little clearer, which should have been frightening, disturbing even, considering that the rest of her life was such a mess. Instead it made perfect sense to Violet.

The way she'd reacted the past several months: withdrawing, keeping Jay—and everyone else around her—at arm's length, afraid to let them get too close.

She'd been so afraid of letting anyone else get hurt because of her.

But now she knew; now she understood it wasn't her fault. None of it. She couldn't help what she did, what she was capable of, any more than if she'd been born *without* the ability to find the dead. It was just a part of who she was.

And Violet didn't want to ignore that part of her anymore. There was nothing wrong with it . . . *with her.* In fact, it might even be useful. It *had* been useful.

And she remembered how she'd felt before, when she'd searched for a serial killer. Like she had a purpose.

She'd felt good. Valuable. Alive.

She wanted *that* again. She wanted to find a way to recapture those feelings, to have a reason for her "gift."

She didn't want to hide anymore or to have secrets, at least not from those she trusted.

Maybe Rafe was right; maybe Sara Priest could be that solution.

Unless Sara wasn't interested in Violet any longer. Unless Sara Priest had grown tired of waiting for her to decide.

But Violet couldn't worry about that yet. She had other things to figure out first.

Like, just who *were* those she could trust?

* * *

Violet waited in her last class for as long as she could before venturing out into the nearly deserted hallways, and then outside, to the parking lot. The grounds were quiet—eerily so—but Violet preferred it that way.

The very idea of bumping into Megan, or just seeing her in passing, made Violet's skin crawl.

So when Violet heard a voice calling her name, *a girl's voice*, her legs suddenly felt weak. Until she recognized the abrasive tone.

Without turning, she smiled to herself as she waited for Chelsea to catch up.

"Hey, didn't you hear me? *God*, where's the freaking fire?" Chelsea complained with exaggerated breathlessness. And then she immediately forgot she was upset. "Hey, you don't mind if I catch a ride, do you? I rode with Jules this morning, but she's staying after with Claire to work on their science paper, and I really don't want to hang out with them in the library. Plus, you know Mrs. Hertzog hates me. She'll just spend the whole time shushing me."

"No," Violet drawled sarcastically, walking toward her car and trying to keep a straight face. "Not you, Chels. You're as quiet as a mouse."

"I know, right? She's crazy." She stuffed her hands in her pockets, shrugging indifferently as she kept pace with Violet. And then her eyes widened. "Oh, I almost forgot." She pulled out a folded piece of notebook paper from her right-hand pocket. She held it out to Violet. "Jay asked me to give this to you."

Violet saw her name written in Jay's handwriting on the outside of the note, and her heart squeezed. She didn't want to take it, but ignoring it, leaving it in Chelsea's hand, wasn't really an option either. She grabbed it and shoved it in her pocket.

Chelsea's usual flippant expression faded and she leaned in close to Violet, almost as if she were afraid someone might see this side of her. "If it makes you feel any better, he's been all *sad doll* lately too."

"What are you talking about, Chels?"

Chelsea stopped walking and stared at Violet.

"Jay. I'm talking about Jay, Vi. I thought you might want to know that you're not the only one who's hurting. He's been moping around school, making it hard to even look at him. He's messed up . . . bad." Just like the other night in Violet's bedroom, something close to . . . *sympathy* crossed Chelsea's face.

Violet wasn't sure how to respond.

Fortunately sympathetic Chelsea didn't stick around for long. She seemed to get a grip on herself, and like a switch had been flipped, the awkward moment was over and her friend was back, Chelsea-style: "I swear, every time I see him, I'm halfway afraid he's gonna start crying like a girl or ask to borrow a tampon or something. Seriously, Violet, it's disgusting. Really. Only you can make it stop. *Please* make it stop."

Violet didn't want to, but she couldn't help smiling at

the absurd picture that Chelsea painted of Jay. And even though she knew it wasn't very mature to feel smug at a time like this, especially over the delusional image concocted by her mentally unhinged friend, she couldn't help herself; she laughed anyway.

Still, she didn't want to talk about it with Chelsea. Not even the kinder, more sensitive Chelsea. "I'm sure he's fine, Chels. And if he's not, he'll get over it."

Chelsea just shook her head. "All I'm saying is . . . I'm here if you want to tell me about it. . . ." She left the offer hanging there.

And Violet felt guilty for not taking her up on it. She wished she *could* talk about what had happened. She wished she could tell Chelsea everything, to explain what she and Jay were fighting about, to tell her about Megan, and what she'd seen at Mike's house that night. But she couldn't. It was too tangled together with her ability.

So she said nothing, and tried to ignore the disappointment on Chelsea's face.

When Chelsea realized that she wasn't getting anywhere with Violet, she changed the subject, but Violet found the new topic even more painful than discussing Jay. "I got the cutest jacket to wear up to the cabin next weekend," Chelsea gushed. "You know, warm but not *too* warm, so maybe Mike will have to use some of his body heat to keep me from getting hypothermia."

But Violet had stopped listening. All she could hear was the rush of blood coursing through her ears.

Her friends were still planning to go to the cabin. Of course they were. How could Violet have expected otherwise?

They reached her car, and Violet clumsily got inside, reaching over to unlock the door for Chelsea. She tried to concentrate on what Chelsea was saying. She wanted to interrupt Chelsea long enough to ask the questions that she knew she would never dare utter: *Was Jay still going? Was he planning to go without her?*

And: *Was Megan?*

Violet's fingers tingled as she gripped the steering wheel. She struggled to remember what she was supposed to do next, and then it came to her. She wrapped her fingers around the key and twisted it. Her car rumbled to life.

Chelsea was unaware of the punishing emptiness that crept over Violet, stealing her resolve and tackling her spirit. Violet stopped listening as Chelsea prattled on, and the words buzzed in the air until they reached Chelsea's house.

Violet remembered to say good-bye, but it sounded bleak and empty in her throat, leaving a caustic trail over her tongue.

She felt as if she were vanishing, like a shadow sitting behind the wheel of her own car, and she wondered how her friend couldn't notice that. How she could just ignore it.

It wasn't until Chelsea stopped at her front door and gave Violet a strange look that Violet realized she was still sitting there, staring at nothing.

Chelsea waved awkwardly.

Violet blinked, reminding herself that it was time to

leave. She put her car into gear and drove away, not bothering to wave back.

If she had, Chelsea wouldn't have seen her anyway.

Violet had become invisible.

Violet stopped at the Java Hut on her way home, desperately needing *not* to be by herself right now. She had hoped that the chaos of the after-school hangout might help. That somehow the noise might penetrate, even obliterate, the nothingness that was smothering her.

But when she stopped her car and looked out the windshield at the crowded parking lot, she hesitated.

She knew she wouldn't run into Chelsea, who she'd just dropped off at home. Or Jules or Claire, who were still at school working on their science project. Or Jay.

It was Wednesday, and Jay worked on Wednesdays.

So why was she suddenly so uncertain? What was her problem?

She didn't know, but now that she was there, seeing her classmates coming and going from the busy café, it was the last place in the world she wanted to be. The problem was, she couldn't seem to do anything about it. So she just sat and watched them go about their lives.

She didn't know how much time had passed, or how long she'd been staring at the entrance, but she recognized the moment that her heart started to beat again. It was the instant she saw the girl walking through the front door of the Java Hut.

Megan was pretty. Small and fragile-looking, and for a split second, for just the briefest of moments, Violet could understand why Jay would have a hard time believing that this delicate wisp of a girl could ever be capable of doing the things Violet had accused her of.

She exited the café, followed by two of her friends, who, by comparison, made Megan appear pixielike. That contrast made Megan's stilted movements seem even more oddly out of place. She gave the impression that she would move gracefully, fluidly, like a dancer, but instead she came across as guarded and cautious. She kept her head low, her arms drawn in tightly, protectively, around her. She appeared frightened. Like a hunted animal.

But that wasn't what stole Violet's breath, making her lean forward to get a better view.

And it wasn't the sudden appearance of a flashing white light that clung to Megan's alabaster skin. Because it wasn't there. The light. The imprint.

It wasn't there.

Violet blinked, thinking that she'd seen wrong. She was tired, exhausted, and maybe her eyes were playing some sort of trick on her. But they weren't.

Megan wasn't the one.

No matter how many times Violet blinked, or how hard she tried to tell herself that she knew what she'd seen that night in the woods, she couldn't make herself see it now—*here*—if it didn't exist.

She tried to make sense of it, of what it could have been.

Could someone else have been in Megan's house the night the power had gone out? Someone who *had* been responsible for the cat's death? Or maybe Jay had been right all along. Maybe she hadn't seen an echo at all, maybe it had been something else altogether. A flashlight. The flicker of candlelight.

Violet didn't know. But she was certain of one thing now.

Megan hadn't killed that cat. She didn't carry the imprint on her. Violet had been wrong. And the truth stung. Knowing that she'd accused this girl of something so unspeakable. And that she'd fought with Jay because of it . . .

Jay.

How was she going to fix this? How was she ever going to explain it to him?

What if he wouldn't listen?

Violet watched numbly as Megan got into a car with her friends, and she realized that she needed to stop her from leaving. Maybe none of it had been Megan—the cat, the phone calls, the note—but Violet had accused her, and now she needed to apologize. Even if the other girl didn't understand why.

Violet's fingers fumbled with the door handle, feeling clumsy and unsure. But she was already too late; the other car was pulling out of the parking space, and Violet stared helplessly as it drove away.

Violet hesitated outside the auto-parts store. She didn't want to interrupt Jay at work, but from where she stood she could see he was alone in there, and she couldn't go one more second without talking to him.

She needed to tell him that she'd been wrong.

As she pushed the door open, Jay looked up from behind the counter and saw her. Her heart lodged in her throat, making it impossible to breathe.

Her face crumpled, and the speech she'd practiced was lost on a whimper the moment she saw him racing around the counter to reach her. He didn't say anything right away, just gathered her in his arms, squeezing her to him. It was his way of saying he was relieved she'd come.

She buried her face in his jacket, inhaling his familiar scent. She clung to him, unable to stop herself, even though she didn't deserve it, didn't deserve him.

"God, Violet, I'm so sorry. I'm so, *so* sorry. . . ." He pressed his face against the top of her head, and she realized then that he needed her as much as she needed him.

She moved closer, molding her body against his, afraid that if they parted, somehow the moment might crumble. His arms tightened as if he knew what she was thinking, and she could *feel* his heartbeat thrumming beneath her own skin, bringing her back to life.

She tried to tell him, to explain, but her voice failed her, coming out on a strangled sigh.

Jay must have misunderstood the sound, and his grip tightened, pinning her against him.

"Don't, Violet. Please, just listen to me. I can't take it anymore. You win. I was wrong. I should never have doubted you. I do trust you. I love you, and I can't do this anymore. I don't want to be . . ." He struggled to find the right words. ". . . *without* you." And then, finally, his arms slackened, releasing her, giving her the choice again. She felt his shoulders slump, and his heart shudder. "Please . . ."

Violet didn't want him to be sorry, but she couldn't speak just yet. She shook her head, rubbing her cheek against his chest, trying to make him understand. She moved her arms around him, beneath his jacket, and clutched his shirt in her hands, refusing to let him go.

That was all the encouragement he needed, and his hands were on her, touching, reassuring. He held her. He kissed the top of her head. And her cheeks.

He waited for her to be ready.

And when her heart rate returned to normal, she tried again. "I'm the one who's sorry, Jay," Violet finally insisted, and this time her voice didn't falter. "I was wrong . . . about everything. I shouldn't have been so quick to jump to conclusions, or to force you to admit that I was right. I shouldn't have pushed you away." She trembled, and Jay pressed her against him again, lending her his calm.

"Shhh . . ." he whispered into her dark curls.

"No, let me finish." She cleared her throat, tipping her head back so she could look at him.

She felt bad for what she saw there. His eyes were bloodshot, and Chelsea was right: He seemed worn down. It was the same way Violet felt.

But when he smiled at her, all lopsided and sweet,

everything felt better. He was beautiful. And he was hers. Still, she needed him to understand.

"Jay, it wasn't Megan." The words felt hot against her throat, like poison.

The smile vanished, and Violet's stomach tightened as she searched for the right words.

"What are you saying?" Jay asked, confused.

"It wasn't Megan who killed the cat. Either it wasn't *her* who I saw at the house that night, or it wasn't an imprint at all. I saw her today. She didn't kill anything. I was wrong. *I'm sorry.*" She was pleading with him, hoping he understood.

He didn't say anything right away, but Violet knew that something was wrong. She could *feel* it. His body stiffened, and she felt him move away from her, slightly—barely—but enough. The gap felt vast.

She was suddenly aware of where they were standing. That they were still in the auto-parts store. Somehow, surrounded by Jay's arms, Violet had forgotten where they were.

"Jay, don't," Violet begged.

Maybe she hadn't said it right. Maybe her explanation had fallen short and he *didn't* understand. She needed to try again.

"Please, I can't be without you either. I don't want to be apart anymore. I was trying to tell you I was wrong—"

But she didn't get a chance to finish, because Jay pulled her back, squeezing her against him, this time leaving no space at all. He leaned over her, wrapping his arms, and his body, around her, and she could feel him shaking his head.

She struggled to move, and to breathe, beneath him, and when she heard his words, she understood.

"No, *I* was wrong. I wasn't thinking about this the right way. It would have been better if it was Megan. It's worse now. It means you aren't safe, because *someone* left that cat." He loosened his hold only enough so that Violet could breathe. "Shit! *Shit*, Vi, someone left you a dead cat. Someone who's still out there. You have to tell your parents. And your uncle. We need to find this guy."

Violet thought about the note she'd received, the pink paper with the flowing script and the disturbing poem inside.

She tipped her head back and stared at Jay, realizing that he was right. "Or girl," she corrected absently.

CHAPTER 23

VIOLET DIDN'T TELL HER PARENTS, OR EVEN her uncle, right away. In fact, she didn't plan on telling them at all. Instead, Violet proposed a different solution. An alternative.

Jay wasn't crazy about her idea at first. Or at all, really. He would have preferred to go to her uncle. Someone he knew. Someone he trusted.

But Violet was adamant, insisting that they keep her family out of it this time. She didn't want to worry them. And selfishly, she didn't want them crowding her, smothering her with concern. Justified or otherwise.

She wanted to try a different approach first.

Jay reluctantly agreed, but only for the short term.

Meaning that he was putting her plan on the clock. If her *proposed solution* didn't work out within the week, he was calling it off and going to her family himself. He wanted Violet safe, no matter what.

Violet grudgingly accepted his terms, believing that her way was better and that it would work. Right up to the point of execution.

Now that she was sitting in her car carrying it out, she had her doubts. Serious ones.

She glanced down nervously at the scrap of paper in her hand and then up at the dilapidated-looking building again. It was the right address. She checked the street sign on the corner one more time—maybe she'd misread it and was on the wrong block.

Nope. Right street, right block. *Damn!*

She tried to ignore the prickling reservations about being here by herself after dark as she rubbed the hairs on the back of her neck to stop them from tingling.

It wasn't exactly what she'd imagined, the location.

Violet had told Jay all about Sara and how she might be able to help, but she'd expected it to be a day or two before she could actually get an appointment. She was surprised, then, when Sara had agreed to meet with her that evening. And even more surprised that they would be meeting at this new place.

She called Jay at work, knowing he'd want to go with her, but explained that things were moving quickly and she needed to go. He offered to leave work, but they both knew the offer was empty; he'd never leave the store unattended.

So here she was, all alone.

Violet stuffed the piece of paper into her purse, trading it for her small can of pepper spray as she shoved her car door open. She positioned her finger on the canister's trigger. Just in case.

The fact that no one was around should have made Violet feel safer, but it didn't. It made her feel like bait.

Young, helpless bait armed with a tiny can of pepper spray.

She hurried up the steps to the lit doorway and pressed the chipped button. She heard it buzz from somewhere inside. Her finger remained in ready position on the trigger in her hand.

She jumped when a voice blared from beside her. "Can I help you?"

Violet glared at the black plastic intercom. She already felt like a worm on a hook—the woman's voice was like slipping a colorful lure around her neck. Definitely baitlike.

"I'm here to see Sara Priest." She said it as quietly as she could and hoped she could still be heard.

There was a click on the other end, like the machine had gone dead. And then nothing.

Crap! Violet silently cursed. Maybe she'd written the address down wrong after all. Maybe she *was* in the wrong place.

She thought about pressing the button again, but her

sense of self-preservation, and her fear of the woman's way-too-loud voice, kept her from going near it. Instead she just stood there, growing more and more anxious by the second.

Violet didn't realize that she'd pressed herself so tightly against the door until it opened from the inside and she stumbled backward.

She fell awkwardly, trying to catch herself as her feet slipped and first she banged her elbow, and then her shoulder—*hard*—against the doorjamb. She heard her can of pepper spray hit the concrete step at her feet as she flailed to find something to grab hold of.

Her back crashed into something solid. Or rather, *someone.* And from behind, she felt strong, unseen arms catch her before she hit the ground. But she was too stunned to react right away.

"You think I can let you go now?" A low voice chuckled in her ear.

Violet was mortified as she glanced clumsily over her shoulder to see who had just saved her from falling.

"Rafe!" she gasped, when she realized she was face-to-face with his deep blue eyes. She jumped up, feeling unexpectedly light-headed as she shrugged out of his grip. Without thinking, and with his name still burning on her lips, she added, "Umm, thanks, I guess." And then, considering that he *had* just stopped her from landing flat on her butt, she gave it another try. "No . . . yeah, thanks, I mean."

Flustered, she bent down, trying to avoid his eyes as she

grabbed the pepper spray that had slipped from her fingers. She cursed herself for being so clumsy and wondered why she cared that *he* had been the one to catch her. Or why she cared that he was here at all.

She stood up to face him, feeling more composed again, and quickly hid the evidence of her paranoia—the tiny canister—in her purse. She hoped he hadn't noticed it.

He watched her silently, and she saw the hint of a smile tugging at his lips. Violet waited for him to say something or to move aside to let her in. His gaze stripped away her defenses, making her feel even more exposed than when she had been standing alone in the empty street.

She shifted restlessly and finally sighed impatiently. "I have an appointment," she announced, lifting her eyebrows. "With Sara."

Her words had the desired effect, and Rafe shrugged, still studying her as he stepped out of her way. But he held the door so she could enter. She brushed past him, stepping into the hallway, as she tried to ignore the fact that she was suddenly sweltering inside her own coat.

She told herself it was just the furnace, though, and had nothing to do with her humiliation over falling. Or with the presence of the brooding dark-haired boy.

When they reached the end of the long hallway, Rafe pulled out a thick plastic card from his back pocket. As he held it in front of the black pad mounted on the wall beside a door, a small red light flickered to green and the door clicked. He pushed it open and led the way through.

Security, Violet thought. *Whatever it is they do here, they need security.*

Violet glanced up and saw a small camera mounted in the corner above the door. If she were Chelsea, she would have flashed the peace sign—*or worse*—a message for whoever was watching on the other end.

But she was Violet, so instead she hurried after Rafe before the door closed and she was locked out.

The room she walked into was like nothing she'd expected, especially after her brief tour of the unremarkable outer hallway. Beyond the secured door, and the camera, was a mammoth space, probably three stories high. Most likely a warehouse that had been converted. But converted in a *big* way.

There was nothing "warehouse" about it now. It was more like a cushy business center. It resembled Violet's image of what a corporate advertising agency might look like. Spacious, airy, comfortable.

Rather than being portioned off into separate work areas, the room was left as one big, wide-open floor plan, filled with computer stations spread out on long tables. There were individual desks, conference tables, and sitting areas. There was even a large break area, complete with what appeared to be a fully stocked kitchen and vending machines.

And there were cameras. Lots of them.

The only thing missing were windows; there were just a few skylights in the ceiling to allow for natural lighting.

Violet was overwhelmed by the vastness of it.

She didn't have much time to take it all in before she saw Sara, the agent-who-wasn't-really-an-agent, sweeping toward her in her starched suit.

Violet tried to muster some enthusiasm. She reminded herself that *she* was the one who had called for this meeting.

"It's good to see you again, Violet. I'm glad you decided to come. Do you want the tour?"

Violet was worried that there was a sales pitch coming, that Sara had misunderstood her reason for being there. She shook her head. "No, thanks. I was hoping we could just talk." She was suddenly *very* nervous.

Sara nodded. "Of course." And then she tipped her head at Rafe, who was still beside them. He took the hint, excusing himself without a word.

Violet watched him go to the kitchen area and grab a can of Coke before dropping onto one of the couches. He practically disappeared into the cushions as he slouched down.

He picked up a remote and flipped through the channels on one of several flat-screen TVs mounted on the walls. Violet was surprised when he stopped at the national news channels, surfing through CNN, MSNBC, FOX News. She'd expected something less . . . *serious*, she supposed. He propped his sneakered feet on the table, making himself at home.

"So what do you think?" Sara asked.

Sara's voice grabbed Violet's attention, and Violet realized that she'd been staring at Rafe. Embarrassed, she glanced away, pretending to study the rehabilitated warehouse instead.

Violet had only seen one other person in the building, a girl not much older than her and Rafe, who worked quietly at one of the computers. She never looked up, as though Violet's presence was unremarkable. The woman—the one with the too-loud voice from the speaker outside—was nowhere to be seen.

"It's . . ." Violet wasn't sure exactly *what* to say. "It's big. And impressive."

Somehow she'd expected something more like a tiny bookkeeper's office, a place where Sara could run her *unusual* operation in relative obscurity. She hadn't expected this kind of oasis, especially not out here, in the middle of the industrial section of the city.

"We get that a lot," Sara explained, sounding less formal now. "It's easier to come and go down here without being noticed. And it's important that we draw as little attention as possible. That's how our clients prefer it. Discretion, complete and total discretion." She led Violet away from Rafe and the girl, to where they couldn't be overheard. "Have a seat."

Violet sat down on a couch and tried her best not to sink in too deep. The cushions were thick and squishy, and Violet struggled to lean forward so she could be taken seriously.

Sara perched on the edge of an adjacent chair, somehow managing to look as stiff and formal as ever, even within the casual setting.

"You know, we do some amazing things here, Violet. My team is one of the best around. Many of them feel a sense of responsibility to use their *talents* to help others." She was still smiling, all sales-pitchy, and Violet felt uneasy again. "Which begs the question, did you ever get a chance to look over those files I gave you?"

Violet felt her palms start to sweat.

She'd looked at the files, yes, but that was all she could do. She nodded.

Sara waited for something more and then filled in the blanks herself. "But nothing?"

Violet half-shrugged, half-nodded, not sure of the right way to respond. She realized that she was dangerously close to crossing that line, to admitting more than she wanted to, but she also needed help. And Sara was her best bet right now.

"That's okay. I want you to know you can trust me, Violet. Whatever you came to discuss stays right here between the two of us."

This was it, Violet decided. "I need your help," she blurted out. "Or at least I was hoping I could ask for it."

Violet watched Sara, wondering at her lack of reaction. Either she really wasn't surprised that Violet had come to ask for a favor or she had a great poker face. Violet was putting her money on the poker face.

"What is it you think I can help you with?"

Violet shifted closer to the edge of the couch. "I have a problem. At home. Well, not really at home. But with someone who doesn't seem to like me, I guess you could say." Words suddenly seemed inadequate. "Someone has been leaving me messages. And hang-up calls." She paused briefly before confessing the last part. "And a dead cat."

The poker face cracked, just slightly.

"Are you sure it was left for you? How do you know that you didn't just happen across it?"

"It was left in a box, next to my car. Whoever put it there did it in the middle of the night so I would find it in the morning." Violet reached into her purse and pulled out the folded pink paper. "And later, there was a note left for me at school."

"May I?" Sara asked, stretching out her hand.

Violet was already handing it to her, and she waited while Sara read it. Violet chewed nervously on her lip.

"What do you think?" Violet finally asked.

Sara refolded the paper but didn't hand it back to Violet. "It's definitely a warning. And you think Rosie was supposed to be the cat, right?"

Violet nodded.

"Right," Sara agreed. "What about the calls?"

"Hang-ups mostly, usually right when I answer them. But sometimes whoever it is stays on the line a little longer. I've talked to them, but they never answer me. I thought I knew who it was," Violet admitted. "But it turns out I was wrong."

Sara eyed Violet carefully as she asked her next question. "How can you be so sure you were wrong?"

Violet decided to be vague; the last thing she wanted to do was to drag Megan's name into this. She'd been through enough already. "I just know. It wasn't her."

Sara weighed Violet's words as she scrutinized her, not suspiciously but inquisitively. Violet felt as though she were being interrogated without a single word being uttered.

"So you think it was a girl then?" Sara finally asked. "Or, rather, you *thought* it was a girl?"

Violet shrugged. "Well, yeah. The note. And the handwriting . . ." It didn't seem like a whole lot of evidence. But then the other part of her suspicion—the imprint she *thought* she'd seen—had proven to be mistaken. It hadn't actually been Megan. She supposed that a boy *could* have forged the note.

"It is decidedly feminine in nature," Sara agreed. "Even the tone of it. However, killing an animal is generally *not* female behavior. Not to say that it's impossible, mind you. Anything's possible, and I've seen some terrible, and extremely contradictory, things in my job. May I keep the note?"

Violet nodded eagerly. Hopefully. "So you'll help me?"

Sara leaned forward, her elbows on her knees. "Of course I will, Violet. I'll do everything I can to figure out who would do this. Do you have any other leads or suspicions about who it might be? Have you made any enemies recently?"

Violet had gone over this again and again. She couldn't think of anyone obvious.

She shook her head but then paused. There was someone who hated her, someone who had been hell-bent on making sure Violet *knew* how much she resented her.

"Lissie Adams. *Elisabeth* Adams," Violet answered. "She goes to my school."

Violet tried to recall the last time she'd seen Lissie at school. She couldn't remember exactly, but it could have been before the cat had been left at her house.

Sara scribbled Lissie's name on a notepad she'd pulled from her pocket. "Can I ask you one more question, before you go?"

Violet nodded again, this time a little more hesitantly.

"I understand that you're not comfortable talking about this, and I respect that. I hope that in time you'll feel you can confide in me." Sara placed a hand on Violet's knee. It was meant as an encouraging gesture, but to Violet it was terrifying. It meant that Sara was asking Violet to share her secrets. "I know you won't tell me what it is that you can do, but can you answer me this?" She didn't wait to see if Violet was willing or not; she just asked her question. "You *can* do something, can't you?"

CHAPTER 24

VIOLET HAD DRIVEN HOME IN COMPLETE silence, without even the radio to replace the buzzing that filled her head. She preferred the stillness; it gave her the opportunity to sort out what had just happened.

How had Sara gotten her to admit that she had a secret?

She hated the way she'd left things after that moment when she'd simply nodded her head. She'd felt dizzy almost immediately, regret pummeling her. She'd wanted to take it back . . . that slight, almost imperceptible bob of her chin. But it was too late. It was out there. And Sara had seen it.

Too late.

Violet had told Sara she had to go. She'd allowed the woman to walk her outside, but only because she was too afraid to go out there alone again, among the darkened warehouses.

But she'd realized sometime during the ride home that, despite being distressed over her confession, something else had changed too. Something she hadn't anticipated.

She felt like a burden had been lifted.

She was sure she must be imagining it. Probably some sort of latent insanity finally rearing its ugly head. That sounded about right. She was crazy. It explained everything, really. The echoes, and dead cats, and serial killers. Insanity, all of it.

But she wasn't about to question it, because whatever it was—her confession to Sara, or the realization that Megan wasn't the one who'd been stalking her, or making up with Jay—she felt better. And that was a far nicer place to be than where she'd been before, wallowing in self-pity and loathing and fear.

She wasn't about to second-guess it. Insanity might not be so bad after all.

Plus she'd slept a deep, dreamless sleep that night, and in the morning, when Jay arrived to drive her to school, she felt alive again. And happy.

Unfortunately, Jay wasn't sharing her optimistic views on madness.

"Good morning," Violet said cheerfully as Jay stomped into the kitchen without knocking.

He frowned at her, his eyes narrowing. "Not really," he grumbled in response.

Violet laughed as she grabbed her backpack. She wasn't surprised that he was still pouting; this was pretty much how he'd looked yesterday, after he'd reluctantly agreed to let Violet handle things her way.

"Actually it is," she insisted, stepping closer and kissing him on the cheek, demanding that he notice her for a moment. She wanted him to pay attention to what she had to say.

Luckily it didn't take much to get Jay's attention. He slipped his arm around her waist and held her there, gently pressing his lips to hers. It wasn't exactly what she'd had in mind, but she wasn't complaining. She let her backpack fall to the floor.

She'd missed the feel of his lips. And the warmth of his touch.

She reacted quickly, getting lost, first in one kiss, and then another. She wanted to stay there, giving herself over to him. He kissed her until her lips felt bruised and swollen, and still they yearned for more. Her head swam, and her heart was whole.

Yet she knew there was something she wanted to tell him, something important.

After a moment, she remembered what it was.

She pulled her head back, smiling at his frustration. Playfully she planted one last peck on his lips. "She's gonna help," she stated smugly.

Jay looked fuzzy, but then his expression cleared. And the scowl was back. "Are you sure? What did she say?"

"You don't need to worry about anything. It was a good meeting. I explained everything, and I gave her the note." Violet tilted her head and smiled. "She said she'd take care of it."

She watched as his jaw flexed, and she knew this was hard for him, letting her handle things her way. But then he sighed, and even though it sounded more like he was choking, Violet was sure that he was exercising a level of restraint that was practically painful for him. It made her want to giggle. She was sure that must be another symptom of her newly arrived lunacy, but she managed *not* to laugh. Instead she cocked her head and somehow maintained a straight face.

When he didn't say anything, didn't, in fact, move, Violet raised her eyebrow inquisitively. "Are we good?" She almost lost it when she heard her voice and realized that she sounded like a schoolteacher scolding an errant child.

Jay frowned as if he were trying to decide, and Violet took that moment to soften her stance.

She lifted her backpack from the floor and, with her other hand, hooked her arm through his. "Come on. Let's get to school so we don't have to stop at the office and explain why we're late." She squeezed him reassuringly. "It'll be fine," she whispered. "Trust me."

"Aww! Look, Jules, they're all kissed and made up. Isn't that the sweetest thing you've ever seen?" Chelsea mocked as she dropped her lunch tray onto the table. But even with her voice dripping sarcasm, she winked at Violet when she thought Jay wasn't looking.

Chelsea was interrupted when Mike came up behind her and put his hands over her eyes. Thankfully the attempted mustache was gone; his lip was smooth and clean-shaven.

"Guess who?" he asked, and Violet smirked. If Chelsea had caught Jay playing such a childish game with Violet, she would have verbally crucified him for being lame. But with Mike, she totally played along.

"I don't know, but I hope my boyfriend doesn't see us together." This time her honey-sweet voice *wasn't* laced with arsenic.

They were kissing before Mike had even taken his seat beside her.

It was almost embarrassing to witness.

But that wasn't why Violet felt herself squirming.

She wondered what Mike would think if he knew the things she'd said about his sister.

She had to remind herself that he *didn't* know. The only person who knew was Jay, and he would never tell.

When Claire joined them, her face lit up. "Violet! You're back!" she announced, drawing unwanted attention to Violet.

Violet glanced nervously at Mike, who just noticed she was sitting there. "Hey, welcome back," he said. "Chelsea said you were really sick."

Chelsea winked at Violet again, this time a little less subtly.

Violet smiled at her. "I'm better now."

"Good," Chelsea declared, brightening. "Then you won't be ditching us this weekend."

Violet stared at her blankly.

"This weekend . . ." Chelsea prompted. "The cabin. We're all still going, right?" She smiled dazzlingly up at Mike, who seemed powerless to resist her.

He grinned back. "Of course."

This weekend! God, is it really so soon? That's, what, just two days from today?

Violet looked to Jay for help. "I don't know . . ." she wavered. "I'm not sure I should." She kept thinking about Mike and his family. About spending a weekend up there, in a small, snowbound cabin in the mountains with them. With her—*Megan*. Violet just didn't think she could do it.

As usual, Jay understood Violet's reluctance. "Maybe Violet's right. She's just getting better. She should probably take it easy this weekend."

"I'm still going," Claire interjected, in case Chelsea was taking a head count.

Chelsea glanced impatiently at Claire and then ignored her. "Oh, come on!" Chelsea complained to Violet. "Seriously? We had it all planned. You can't bail on us now. You have to come. Please, Vi, I never ask for anything."

"Umm, yeah, you do," Violet pointed out.

Chelsea didn't bother arguing. "Okay, yeah, but come on. This is important." She was whining now, pleading with Violet. And then she turned on Jay. "You're not thinking of crapping out too, are you?" She glared at him.

"Dude, no!" Mike practically shouted, finally realizing the implication of Violet staying home. It meant losing Jay for the weekend too. "You guys gotta come. My dad'll hardly be around, so we'll pretty much have the place to ourselves."

Jay shook his head, and even though she knew he'd been looking forward to the trip, Violet heard him say, "Sorry, man, I don't want her to get sick again." He squeezed her hand beneath the table.

Violet suddenly felt guilty. Obviously their plans were hinging on her. If she didn't go, Mike would be stuck up there with a group of girls and his dad. Besides, Chelsea would never forgive her for such a flagrant friend foul.

But an entire weekend with Megan.

Who did nothing, Violet reminded herself again. And who knew nothing about what Violet had suspected.

There really wasn't a good reason *not* to go.

She tilted her head up to Jay, ignoring the daggerlike glares being shot at her by Chelsea—and probably by Mike too.

"You want to go, don't you?" She lifted her eyebrows, knowing that the others could hear.

Jay grinned back at her, leaning closer, but not bothering to keep his voice down either. "I don't want to do anything you're not ready for, Vi. I'll do whatever *you* want. Don't let Chels bully you."

"I can hear you," Chelsea complained.

Jay chuckled but never looked away from Violet. "Why don't you think about it, and we'll talk later?"

She smiled back at him. How did she get so lucky?

In the background, she heard Chelsea gloating. "They're going. They're *totally* going."

ENVY

SHE STOOD NEAR THE EDGE OF THE CAFETERIA, hiding. Watching.

She hated the way Mike and his friends laughed, the way he seemed to fit seamlessly into their group.

She wanted that too. To belong somewhere. Anywhere.

She'd thought maybe it would be different here. That this town, this school, might be special. That this time she would have real friends.

It was foolish, she knew that now, a child's dream. And she wasn't a child. She hadn't been for a long time.

She fingered the hall pass in her hand, rubbing the paper between her thumb and forefinger, willing it to give her the strength she didn't seem to possess on her own. She wanted to reach out to someone, to ask for help, but apparently she just wasn't brave enough.

How many times would she request the office pass, only to change her mind before getting there? How many times could one person disappoint herself?

She stared enviously at Mike, keeping close to the pillar that hid her from view.

He didn't belong either; he just didn't realize it. He was no better than she was—worse, in fact. He was her brother; he was supposed to protect her, to look out for her. And yet he was oblivious to her suffering.

He looked up then, and Megan drew back, slipping all the way around the column so he couldn't see her hiding there. Her hand tightened into a ball around the scrap of paper.

Her heart beat too fast as she waited. She didn't want him to notice her; she didn't want to face him while she was feeling like this.

Despair infected her.

She had friends too. Maybe not the kind of friends she'd dreamed of, but there were people she hung out with so that she didn't stand out as some sort of freak.

But it wasn't supposed to be like that. It was going to be different here.

On that first day, she'd had hope.

She was going to try; she was going to reach out, to let someone in. And she had, more than ever before, when she'd met him. . . .

Jay.

He was everything she could have hoped for, going out of his way to make them—her—feel welcome. He'd smiled when he'd introduced himself, and she'd actually felt something. He was telling her with that smile that he would be her friend. And maybe, someday, something more.

But she also recalled that other moment, could taste it like bitter bile. It was the moment she'd realized that he already had a friend. A girlfriend.

It was the moment that Megan had stopped feeling special.

Only that wasn't entirely true, because Jay didn't stop smiling at her. He didn't stop inviting her to join him, and he even went so far as to use her brother to get closer to her. So, obviously, the girl—his girl—*didn't mean that much to him after all.*

She was just the girl standing in Megan's way.

Megan pounded her fist against the solid concrete of the column and peered around it once again. She pressed her cheek against the cool surface as she stared at her brother's table.

Jay was still there. And so was Violet.

Why couldn't Jay see Violet for the obstacle she really was? Why couldn't he brush her aside so he could—finally—*be with Megan?*

Tears blinded her and she blinked hard, wiping her nose with the back of her hand.

Why couldn't he love her*?*

Well, it didn't matter now. She was done trying to frighten Violet. It hadn't worked anyway. Had she really expected that Violet would be so afraid that she'd . . . what, dump Jay? Stop coming to school? Or, better yet, leave town? All because of some stupid phone calls and a note?

Or a dead cat in a box?

It seemed to work for a while—Violet's absence from school, her separation from Jay—but now they were closer than ever.

It turned out to be more childish fantasies on her part. More foolish daydreams.

She'd had to stop anyway. Violet suspected her. Violet had said her name, that night on the phone.

Of course, there was no way Violet could really know it was Megan. She'd only been guessing. But it wasn't worth the risk.

Megan wouldn't call her again. There would be no more "messages."

Megan smoothed out the crumpled hall pass and read it one last time before dropping it into the garbage on her way back to her class.

Who was she kidding anyway?

She was never going to the guidance counselor's office. She was never going to admit that her father was a drunk. That she was lonely and frightened and angry.

She was just going to shrivel up . . . and fade away.

CHAPTER 25

AFTER SCHOOL, VIOLET THUMBED THROUGH THE files that Rafe had given her when she'd gone to the FBI offices. Well, just the one actually . . . Serena Russo's file.

Violet had made a decision after seeing Mike at lunch that afternoon. She needed to do something for him—and for his sister—to try to make up for everything she'd thought and for the horrible things she'd accused Megan of doing.

She had this ability. This gift. Why not use it, as Sara pointed out? Why not try to help someone?

And in this case, someone Violet felt she had wronged.

She dialed the phone quickly, before she lost her nerve.

After a moment, she spoke. "If I give you an address, can you meet me?"

Violet smiled as she listened to the response on the other end and then repeated the address of Serena Russo's ex-husband, who lived less than an hour from her.

Tonight she was going to try to make a difference.

She'd hoped to get there before dark, but by the time Violet made her way down I-5 through rush-hour traffic, the one-hour drive had stretched to nearly two. Dusk was already blanketing the sky.

Her stomach felt dangerously unsettled, and she tried to tell herself that she didn't have to do this, that she could still turn back.

But she was determined—she was definitely going. She owed it to Mike's family, and she owed it to herself to see if she could make her ability useful once more. Besides, it wasn't like she was going alone, she reminded herself.

She turned off the main roads as she followed the directions she'd printed from her computer. She hadn't expected them to take her so far outside the city, for the location to be so . . . *isolated.* Why couldn't someone, just once, live in a nice little subdivision? A peaceful—yet *populated*—neighborhood?

She slowed her car, watching the mailboxes along the side of the road, trying to spot the address she was searching for. When she finally saw it, her pulse kicked up a notch. She took a deep breath as she pulled off to the side of the road, her car bouncing over the uneven surface. She exhaled noisily.

There were no other cars in sight, which probably meant she'd arrived ahead of the person she was meeting. She thought about waiting but decided against it; she had no idea how much longer that might be.

"This is it," she told herself, her version of a pep talk. "It's now or never."

No one answered, and the corner of her mouth quirked up as she bit her lip and got out. She'd decided to park on the street, hoping that—*just maybe*—she'd be able to glimpse an imprint from a distance, without Roger Hartman ever knowing that she'd been there at all.

Parking her car in his driveway would've been a dead giveaway.

She hoped that his imprint—if he carried one—would be something she could sense from a distance and not something that required her to be in close proximity, like Jay's mom's imprint was. Violet could only sense the campfire smoke if she was standing right beside, or touching, Ann Heaton.

She did not want to touch Roger Hartman to find out if he'd murdered Serena Russo.

Violet pocketed her keys as she made her way down the wooded driveway.

She kept close to the tree line, hoping to remain hidden by the cover of foliage as the evening dusk worked its way toward night. The light from the moon couldn't penetrate the branches overhead, and there weren't any street lamps to illuminate her path.

She navigated cautiously through the oppressive darkness, stumbling several times over rocks and dips in the ground. She moved slowly, carefully, listening for anything that would indicate she wasn't alone. But all she could hear were the sounds of her own footsteps and the forest around her.

Ahead, a dim glow signaled the end of her journey, a small trailer set haphazardly amid the jumble of trees and overgrown blackberry bushes. The pale light coming from inside told her that someone definitely lived there.

Violet stopped, her mind racing, trying to decide what she should do next. It wasn't the ideal plan, she supposed, only now considering the realities of being here . . . on his property, all alone as night fell.

At best, he didn't carry an imprint at all, and he wasn't a killer.

At worst, he was. And Violet had very possibly made a fatal error in coming here.

Her pulse thrummed nervously within her throat, and she tried to swallow around it. She waited for something to happen.

There was no movement from inside the trailer. No sounds. No nothing. Just the light, lone and unwavering. There was no car in the driveway, and Violet began to wonder if Roger Hartman was even home, or if she'd come while he was away.

Suddenly she hoped that was the case.

She listened to the night, paying extra attention to sounds that might come from the direction of the trailer.

And then she heard it. Softly at first. A delicate rhythmic pattering.

Raindrops.

She glanced up, holding out her palm, waiting for the first wet drops to find her. But she knew they weren't coming.

There was no rain.

It was an echo. And it was calling for her.

She looked around at the daunting blackness, wondering what she should do as she gathered the neck of her jacket closed in both hands, clutching it as if it could shield her from the sound, from the darkness, from the danger.

But it wasn't the echo she feared, not *this* echo. She knew it was a body by the draw that beckoned her, reaching into her and gently tugging. Yet it was different somehow.

And then she realized why.

This body had been buried. This body was settled, already at peace. Like the ones in Violet's graveyard, or those at the cemetery she'd visited while looking for clues to catch a serial killer. Violet could sense the echo, but it didn't *demand* to be found.

She stepped forward again, away from the trees and the cover they provided as she followed the noise.

The sputtering of the raindrops—*the echo*—came not from above, as rain would have done, but from *ahead* of

Violet. It was the sound of so many fat drops plunking against broad autumn leaves. Violet had to keep reminding herself that it was illusory, an imaginary downpour that only *she* could sense, as she ducked her head, instinctively drawing away from the shower.

She glanced cautiously in the direction of the trailer as she passed it, worried that at any moment Roger Hartman would come crashing through the door.

But the entrance remained still, the home silent.

She knew when she was close, because the sound swelled, becoming increasingly steady, even if only in her own ears. A damp chill settled over her, creeping beneath her skin and into her bones, making her joints ache.

It was more difficult with these types of echoes, the ones that weren't distinctly visual, to pinpoint an exact location. So as Violet approached, she had to gauge the intensity of the acoustics, had to judge the drop in temperature that caused her to shiver.

She circled a spot out back, behind the trailer, near the base of a knotty-looking pine tree. In the shadows of the night, the old pine stood guard over the grave that Violet believed lay beneath its spiny branches.

She glanced again toward the light filtering from the ramshackle structure before she fell to her knees. The sound of rain was all around her, and the cool chill of the downpour was inside her.

It was here.

The ground was black, and Violet brushed her hand over

its surface, trying to decide where she should dig. There was a part of her that wanted to stop, that told her this was enough, that she should call Sara Priest and let her handle it from here. But she knew she wouldn't. She wasn't even sure what she'd tracked to this location. It could simply be a squirrel or a field mouse left for dead.

She wanted to investigate further, to be certain before calling for help.

The moment her fingers sank into the loose layer of soil, so different from the compacted dirt that surrounded it, Violet knew that she'd found the burial site she'd been searching for.

She scooped a handful of the soft ground, still shivering against the echo that showered around her. She used her fingers to locate an edge and followed it with her hands, crawling through the gloom on all fours. When she realized how large the grave was, she trembled.

A body could fit in there. A *human* body.

She wasn't sure why she reached in again, why she kept working to shovel the earth with her fingers, clawing at it. She should stop, she told herself more than once, and yet she didn't. And all the while, the haunting rain continued to fill the night's air with its poignant storm. The chill it carried was more than real to Violet.

When her hand brushed against something smooth, something that crackled beneath her fingertips, Violet stilled. Whatever she'd just felt was unnatural, man-made.

She prodded it again, listening to the synthetic sound as

her finger glanced over something firmer beneath, something grotesquely familiar in feel.

It was a body.

Wrapped in plastic tarpaulin.

Violet clumsily shot to her feet, inhaling sharply as she clasped her fingers to her chest.

When she felt someone grab her from behind, strong fingers gripping her shoulders, she gasped, choking on her own breath. Her heart pounded viciously, violently. How could she have been so foolish? Why hadn't she waited?

And then a soft voice silenced her, causing her to whimper. *"Shhh . . ."* Breath warmed her cheek. "It's okay, it's just me."

Rafe!

She turned quickly, wrapping her arms around him as relief and gratitude intertwined in a twist of emotions. "Thank God it's you! I'm so glad you came." She clung to him. She was no longer alone; she was safe.

Her fingertips brushed the exposed skin at the nape of his neck, just below his hair, and that static spark, the one she'd felt before, when they'd touched at the café, jolted through her. Jolted them both. Rafe stiffened, and Violet was suddenly all too aware of his nearness, of the warmth of him beneath her, of his sinewy strength, and his scent.

She dropped her arms away. "Sorry," she insisted, her eyes too wide. She was desperate to have this moment forgotten. The pattering of rain continued to beat down around her, and she glanced toward the grave. "I found something . . .

someone, right there." She pointed. "I don't know who it is, but it's definitely a body."

"We need to get out of here." Rafe grabbed the sleeve of her jacket and pulled her away. "We need to call Sara and tell her what you found."

Violet let him drag her past the trailer and down the driveway. And even as she moved away from the sensory rainstorm, the icy dread remained, refusing to release her. She was terrified that whoever had left the light on inside would come back, would find them there, with her covered in the dirt from a shallow grave. She was afraid that they would end up buried too . . . wrapped in tarps of their own.

When they reached the end of the driveway, Violet wiped her hands on her jeans and felt inside her pocket for her keys. Her hands were shaking.

"Can you drive?" Rafe asked in a voice that seemed far too calm under the circumstances.

Violet saw the big black SUV parked behind her car, and she knew that Rafe had driven Sara's car to meet her.

She nodded. "I'm fine." It was a lie. She was certain she could drive, but she wasn't "fine."

"There was a gas station down the street, on the corner. Follow me. We'll stop there and then we can call Sara."

Violet took a shaky breath as she started her engine, waiting for Rafe to pull out in front of her. She worked to get her quivering nerves under control.

Somewhere back there in the darkness, buried beneath

an old pine tree, was a body wrapped in a tarp. And for some strange reason, it felt at peace.

Violet followed Rafe as he turned into the gas station, one with a crowded parking lot and *lots* of lights. She still wasn't sure her heart would ever beat normally again.

He didn't head for a designated space, he just parked off to the side of the lot, and Violet pulled up behind him and waited.

Rafe tapped on the passenger-side door, and Violet reached over to unlock it. He nodded at her as he climbed in. "You sure you're okay? You're kind of a mess."

Violet looked down at her hands, at the dirt crusted beneath her fingernails, and then at her jacket, which was smeared with grime. Her fingers were still trembling, but she ignored his concern. "Do you want to call or should I?"

He pulled out his cell phone and dialed.

Violet was grateful to just sit there and listen. The conversation was brief, and again Violet had the feeling that very few words were needed between the two of them.

"She found a body at the Hartman place; it's out back, under a tree." He paused to listen. "You'll see it; she was digging for it when I got there." Another brief pause, and then Rafe shot her a sideways glance, as if searching for confirmation. "Yeah, she says she's fine." After he listened for a few seconds, he hung up, no good-bye, nothing more from his end. And then he looked to Violet, really looked at her this time. "I mean it. Are you gonna be okay driving yourself home? It's a long way."

She inhaled, and even her breath was shaky, but she nodded anyway. "I just want to go home and shower."

Rafe studied her for a few long moments, and then seemed satisfied with her well-being. But before he could leave, Violet stopped him. "I really am glad you came, Rafe. Thank you."

He smiled in his sly way and slid out of the car. Like with Sara, he gave her no other response. She supposed he wasn't much of a talker.

Once she was alone again, she had time to think. She was nervous about what—or rather, *who*—Sara would find when she got there. She was afraid that it would be Mike's mom—Serena Russo. And that Violet might be the reason that his family discovered that she didn't actually run away all those years ago, but that she was dead, buried at the base of an old pine tree.

But there was another part of her, a part that felt good about what she'd just done. Accomplished even, for the first time in a long time. A part of her that felt like maybe she'd helped.

She needed to get home. She needed to wait for Sara to call back, to tell her if what she suspected was true.

And she needed to deal with the fact that maybe Sara had been right after all, that maybe Violet could give people the answers they were looking for . . . even if they weren't the ones they wanted to hear.

CHAPTER 26

VIOLET POURED HERSELF A CUP OF COFFEE AS she waited for Jay to pick her up for school.

Her mom frowned at her as she carried a box of cereal to the table. "Rough night?"

"Something like that," Violet answered vaguely.

Rough was an understatement. Violet had lain awake half the night, anxiously wondering when Sara—or Rafe—might call about her discovery behind Roger Hartman's house.

Fortunately, since this body, for whatever reason, felt settled and at peace, Violet wasn't plagued by the lingering discomfort she normally felt when she left a body behind.

She was beginning to wonder if she'd ever *fully* understand her strange ability.

She pulled the cell phone from her pocket and checked it again. Still no messages.

"Well, you'll be happy to know that your friend's dad is stopping by today with all of the contact information for the cabin." Her mom offered Violet the cereal. "You look like you could use a getaway right about now."

Violet waved the box away as her stomach sank. With everything that had happened yesterday, she'd nearly overlooked the fact that they were supposed to leave tomorrow.

So much for that plan, she thought sourly. After what she'd discovered at Roger Hartman's place, the last thing Mike and Megan's family would need was a vacation.

On top of everything else, guilt now weighed her down. But until she heard from Sara, she decided it was best to keep up the pretense that everything was going ahead as scheduled.

She managed a weak smile, fake at best, as she downed the rest of her coffee. "I think I hear Jay," she lied, giving her mom a quick kiss on the cheek and picking up her backpack. "I'll see you after school."

Violet hurried out the door and waited the last few minutes out in the driveway, letting the crisp winter air fill her lungs. And numb her thoughts.

Sometime during her third-period class, Violet felt her phone vibrating in her pocket. When she checked, she saw that she'd just missed a call from Sara. She told the teacher that she wasn't feeling well and took a pass for the nurse's office as she slipped into the quiet of the hallway.

She waited nervously for Sara to pick up on the other end, and when she did Sara got right to the point. "I'm sorry, Violet, it wasn't what you thought. It was just a dog."

And with those words, the chill from the echo was back. Violet wasn't sure what to say. "Wh-what do you mean it was a dog?"

"I took a team to the Hartman place, and we found the body inside the tarp. It was a dog, a German shepherd. We haven't been able to reach Roger Hartman yet, but I'm guessing he had something to do with it."

Violet's head was spinning; she was speechless. It was a dog buried beneath the tree?

Not Serena Russo . . .

Oh God, Violet moaned internally. She'd sent Sara, and who knew how many other people, out to Roger Hartman's home looking for a body . . . a *person's* body. Humiliation rushed over her. All of her good intentions were gone in an instant, all of her hopes of doing something positive shattered.

Violet took a deep breath. "Why do you think he had something to do with it?"

Sara didn't hesitate to answer. "The dog didn't die of natural causes. Its neck had been broken."

Violet had her back pressed against the wall, and she leaned forward, one hand on her knee, the other gripping the phone to her ear. She just needed a moment to catch her breath, to gather her thoughts.

In her head, Violet pictured the little black cat lying in the box beside her car, its tiny neck broken.

She heard herself saying good-bye, her voice sounding detached, like it belonged to someone else. She waited there, alone in the silence of the hallway, until she felt the wooziness pass, until she felt steady enough to walk.

Violet thought she understood now why the body she'd discovered hadn't called to her, insisting to be found. Someone—maybe Roger Hartman, even—had buried the dog.

Someone had given it a sense of closure.

She realized also that despite her embarrassment about sending Sara and the others on a wild-goose chase, there was a positive side to all of this.

Mike and Megan's mother might still be alive.

Maybe she *had* just run away. That would be better, wouldn't it? For them? That there was still a chance they could be reunited?

Violet put her phone away, since she was supposed to be at the nurse's office and not making phone calls, before she headed back to class.

Maybe her mom had been right this morning. Maybe she really did need a getaway after all.

CHAPTER 27

THE NEXT MORNING CAME QUICKLY, AND, AS usual, Chelsea had been right. Violet *was* going to the cabin with her friends.

Although she was still having doubts, second-guessing her decision, the wheels were already set in motion, and Jay would be there soon to pick her up, along with Chelsea, Mike, and Claire.

Jules had opted out of this particular trip, declaring that she'd rather jump into a shark-infested pool wearing only a meat bikini than subject herself to a weekend of watching Chelsea gush over Mike. That, and Jules didn't really like the snow . . . unless there was a board attached to her feet and she was hurtling down a mountain at Mach speed. Snowmen and hot cocoa weren't exactly her *thing.*

But they were definitely Claire's, and she was already choosing teams for the big snowball fight she had planned.

Mike's dad, Ed Russo, had stopped by while Violet was at school on Friday to introduce himself and give all the necessary information to her mom, including the phone number to the convenience store that was just a few miles away, since there was no phone service—or cell coverage—where they would be staying.

And even though the number was actually to a pay phone, he'd explained that there was a corkboard where the owners would pin messages; he assured her mother that he would make regular stops at the store, just in case.

Her parents were fine with the arrangement, it was only one night, after all—something Violet continued to remind herself of over and over again.

She could handle anything for one night.

"So what do you guys want to do first?" Claire asked excitedly from the backseat.

"Oh my God, Claire. I don't know, but maybe you should ask us *again* in five minutes. We haven't had enough time to think about it since the last time you asked." Chelsea's mood had gone downhill quickly during the car ride into the mountains, and she had lost her patience for everyone—*including* Claire—who was usually safe from her temper.

"*Effin'-A*, Chels, I was just asking." Claire's lips drew together tightly as she crossed her arms in front of her. It was as close to swearing as Claire ever got. Claire must have really been tired of Chelsea's snippy tone.

Chelsea didn't apologize; instead she closed her eyes and took another deep breath, leaning her head back against her seat.

"Do you want me to pull over again?" Jay asked, glancing anxiously at Chelsea in his rearview mirror. He shot a nervous look at Violet, and Violet knew exactly what he was thinking.

He didn't want Chelsea to puke . . . *in his car.*

Chelsea sighed with annoyance. "Why, Jay? So I can walk around in the cold again, talking about how fucking—yeah, that's right, Claire, I said *fucking*—sick I feel? No, thank you. Just keep driving. The sooner we get there, the sooner I get out of this hellhole."

"No offense taken. Right, Jay?" Mike laughed, hitting Jay's headrest playfully. Apparently he thought *he* was safe from Chelsea's caustic remarks.

He wasn't.

"That's too bad," Chelsea shot back without opening her eyes. "Maybe someone *should* take offense. Maybe it's not the car making me sick, maybe it's the driving."

Violet started to laugh but caught herself, just barely, in time to stop the sound from actually escaping her lips. She covered her mouth with her hand so that only those with their eyes open could see her.

Ha-ha, Jay mouthed, when she glanced sideways in his direction, making it even harder to contain herself.

Sorry, she mouthed back to him, when she finally felt like she had enough control not to laugh.

Violet thought Chelsea might feel better if she were to sit up front, but she didn't offer to trade places with her friend again. She'd tried that already, when they'd stopped to let Chelsea get some air, and Chelsea had snapped at her that she was fine, that she didn't need to change seats.

Violet was convinced that Chelsea had only refused because she didn't want to lose her seat beside Mike, but after having her head chewed off once, Violet wasn't about to make that proposal again. So instead she sat quietly, pretending that it wasn't at all uncomfortable, as they tried to comply with Chelsea's imaginary wall of silence.

At first, Violet tried to ignore the faint sensation that crept over her, the strange quivering that began at her core and gently rippled outward in short, shuddering bursts. But the car was moving at a steady pace, despite the increasing snow on the ground as they moved higher and higher in elevation, and it wasn't long before the quivering became vibrating, and then turned to something more tangible.

A warm wave of fragrant air washed over Violet, bringing with it the sweet summer scent of Popsicles and sticky sunscreen and chlorine that filled the interior of the car. The temperature unexpectedly skyrocketed around her.

"Can you turn down the heat?" Violet whispered to Jay as she tore the hat from her head and tugged at her scarf.

And just as she said it, she heard Claire's horrified gasp.

Violet turned to look out the window.

On the side of the road was a deer, lying unnaturally prone, broken and abandoned against a dirty drift of plowed snow on the shoulder of the highway. Blood seeped into the slushy pile where its face was awkwardly pinned. Its mouth was open, its tongue frozen against its mangled jaw.

Jay reached over and squeezed Violet's knee as they passed, and suddenly the inhospitable temperature and the summer smells made perfect sense to Violet. It was the deer's echo.

Violet and Jay used to play that game when they were little. While other kids played car games involving state license plates or finding the letters of the alphabet in road signs, Violet would point out dead animals on the sides of the highway. Sometimes visible and sometimes not. Some discernible only by the echoes they'd left behind.

She would sense them, sometimes as far back as several hundred yards, and she would describe their unique echo to Jay in as much detail as she could while he would try to spot the corpse that had been left behind.

Road Kill, they called it.

It was sick, sure, but they were just kids . . . with a morbid fascination for all things dead. And she was a girl who could seek them out.

Now the echo felt intrusive, and Jay's presence soothing.

"We're getting close," Mike announced from the back. "Up ahead is the store where we can stop to get some snacks and anything else we need. Last stop. If you need to make a phone call, now's the time to do it," he added.

Violet pulled her phone from her purse and checked to see if she had service. Mike was right; there was no signal up here.

"Oh, thank God. Violet, will you get me some crackers? And see if they have some 7UP or Sprite? I feel like shit."

Violet turned around to look at Chelsea, who still had her head back and refused to open her eyes, but it was Jay who answered. "Are you sure you don't want to get out and maybe stretch your legs a little?"

"Don't worry, Captain Concern, I won't ruin your precious leather," she snarled. "But if you're so worried, leave me a bag or something."

Violet saw Mike lean down and whisper something in Chelsea's ear, his face etched with concern. Chelsea grimaced and turned her head away from him. She didn't even make an effort to be polite about it.

She must really be sick, Violet thought, *to turn on Mike like that.*

The outside of the convenience store was rustic and charming; the exterior walls were rough-hewn logs, giving it the illusion of being a quaint country store. The inside was cluttered and disorganized. The owners—probably out of necessity and in an effort to stock as many items as possible—somehow managed to fill every inch of shelf, floor, and countertop. Even the walls were crammed with items for sale. And where there weren't actual wares, there were signs with products that could be ordered.

It was almost as cold inside the store as it was outside. Violet was glad she'd worn her snow boots and her heavy winter coat on the ride up, and that she'd put her hat and scarf back on before getting out of the car.

It was easy to fill Chelsea's requests, and then it just took a few more minutes for the rest of them to stock up on chips, beef jerky, pop, and an assortment of snacks, including the pack of Oreos that Jay bought for Violet.

Violet thought briefly about calling her parents, just to let them know that they'd made it up the mountain safely. She'd seen the pay phone lodged tightly into an open space between the ice cooler and a shelf piled high with motor oil and propane tanks. Just above the phone, there was a small corkboard littered with colorful sticky notes and scraps of paper.

But she dismissed the idea almost immediately. Her parents weren't expecting her to call unless there was a problem, and Violet was trying to be more independent, to prove to them that they could trust her to be safe on her own. Calling them to "check in" felt like it would defeat that purpose.

So she passed by the phone without a second glance on her way to the cashier.

If she would have stopped, she would have noticed the message pinned there.

Addressed to her.

* * *

Jay had decided to park his car down by the road rather than to risk the steep and winding driveway leading up to the cabin. He was afraid it would get trapped in the thick layers of snow there.

And even though Mike's dad's truck was gone, it was apparent that he'd already been there, by the newly plowed tracks he'd left. But Violet agreed with Jay that it wasn't worth taking the chance. Jay's car wasn't equipped, even with the snow chains, to make it up such a treacherous grade. Not in this weather.

So they'd been forced to carry their things up the hill to the cabin. It wouldn't have been that difficult had it not been for the nearly two feet of snow they had to wade through. Fortunately, they were able to walk in the tracks of Mike's dad's truck.

It seemed that the crackers and Sprite had worked their magic on Chelsea's upset stomach, because she was back to herself again by the time they'd arrived. Violet even heard her apologizing to Mike for being so "grumpy," a word she'd never heard Chelsea use before. Especially not in that octave.

Mike's family "cabin" was less the picturesque mountain lodge that Violet had imagined and more a shelter-from-the-elements kind of structure. Like a shack, sort of. With plumbing.

But what it lacked in electricity, phone lines, and heat, it made up for in sparse furnishings, a tiny kitchen, and a generally musty odor. Its saving grace was an oversized fireplace, with a fire already blazing when they arrived, filling the space with warmth that Violet could feel inviting her inside even before they'd stepped over the threshold.

"Wow," Jay breathed appreciatively, and Violet recognized immediately that *rustic* was his kind of place. "*This is so cool.* How long have you guys had it?"

Mike shrugged, dropping his worn duffel bag on the floor, and Violet could have sworn she saw a puff of dust rising around it. "I think it used to belong to my grandparents, and when they died, my parents got it."

"So where's your mom? You never talk about her. Is she coming too?" Claire asked as she prissily brushed her hand across the seat of a wooden dining chair before setting her expensive suitcase on it. Leave it to Claire to bring a designer bag into the woods.

Chelsea glared disapprovingly at Claire, answering for Mike. "Mike's mom doesn't live with them anymore. And he doesn't like to talk about it."

But Mike just shrugged and added, "It's okay. She took off a while back, and we don't hear from her." And then he put his finger up. "Hold on a sec." He glanced toward the short hallway at the corner of the large living space. "Megan?" he yelled.

It took a moment, but a door that had been closed finally cracked open. The small voice on the other side sounded annoyed. "What?"

"I just wanted to let you know that we're here. Did Dad say what time he was coming back?"

After several long seconds, Violet glanced over to see if the door might have closed again. She thought that maybe his sister had decided to ignore the question, but then, sounding just as bothered as before, she answered him at last. "Does he ever?"

CHAPTER 28

VIOLET'S BREATH CAUGHT IN HER THROAT AS she felt herself being hauled up from behind and lifted into the air.

She knew immediately that it was Jay, because she heard the gravelly sound of his laughter mingled with the warmth of his breath against her ear as they landed sideways in a drift of soft snow. She heard him gasp as her shoulder smashed into him when they hit the ground. Still, he was smiling when she peeked at him.

"Are you okay?" she asked, laughing at the grin on his face. She wondered if she'd ever get tired of that stupid, overconfident look. She hoped not.

"Come here and I'll show you." He beckoned, flicking a lazy snowflake away from Violet's eyelashes with the fingertip of his glove.

It had begun snowing lightly by the time they'd finally gotten all of their things unloaded and decided to go outside. Mike had invited his sister to come along with them, but she'd ignored the request, not even bothering to answer. So they'd bundled up and ventured out to explore, just the five of them.

Despite Violet's misgivings about the actual structure of the building, the location of the cabin was spectacular. It was secluded, sitting high in the mountains amid a serene backdrop of trees that, coupled with the glistening layers of snow, was nothing less than breathtaking.

They had been out in the woods for over an hour, yet no one complained about the temperature. It was just too beautiful, and the snow too captivating, to grumble over the chill.

Claire had tried to organize teams for her snowball fight, girls against guys, but it quickly turned into a free-for-all, and before long Jay was defending Violet from Chelsea, and Chelsea was protecting Mike against Jay. Claire became neutral, like Switzerland, trying to make up rules to keep a full-scale war from erupting. But eventually she gave up and found a quiet place out of the way, where she could make snow angels.

By the time Chelsea and Violet had joined her, they'd unanimously decided that Chelsea's "angels" weren't really angelic at all and had to be renamed. Thus, "snow devils" were born. They even made little horns on them, to complete the effect.

But now that it was just her and Jay, stealing a few minutes for themselves, Violet was happy to submit to the quiet calm of the ice-covered forest surrounding them.

Jay's lips touched hers. It was like igniting a fire.

Violet closed her eyes and got lost in the warmth that radiated from the pit of her stomach as his mouth settled over hers. She drew herself against him, straining to get closer beneath the thick layers of clothing.

It was the frozen explosion of a snowball overhead that interrupted the moment. Icy debris rained down over them.

Jay wrapped his arms around Violet's head and covered her while he glanced up to see who had broken the temporary cease-fire.

And then he whispered so that only Violet could hear him, "I'll be right back." He gathered a handful of snow, compacting it tightly, eagerly, between his gloves as he stood and hurried away, leaving her alone beneath the shelter of the trees.

Violet heard Chelsea and Claire bickering in the distance over the snowman they were working on.

She lay there, on her back, staring up into the white-capped branches that crisscrossed above her, filtering the falling snow and diffusing the already tenuous light that tried to penetrate the thick gray sky. It wasn't yet twilight, and already darkness was descending as the low cloud cover deepened, threatening to mask the remaining daylight from view.

Violet blinked as fragile snowflakes battered her face, and she breathed in the cold, crisp air deeply. She listened as, farther away, Jay and Mike attacked each other with snowballs, their laughter booming loudly in the otherwise calm of the day.

It almost would have been easy to disregard the tugging she felt coming from the opposite direction. And she tried, closing her eyes and pretending for a moment that she hadn't noticed it at all. But it was visceral, the pull, finding its way beneath her skin and slithering there until she itched with it, until she could no longer ignore its enigmatic lure.

The song of the dead.

And it was calling her.

She eased herself up slowly, still trying to decide—as if she'd ever had a choice in the matter—and brushed the snow from her back as she rose. She glanced around to make sure no one was watching. She didn't want anyone to see her as she slipped between the trees, into the woods, to seek out whatever wanted—no, *needed*—to be found.

She felt the glimmer of cold pain dawning at the base of her neck, and she shivered against it, rolling her shoulders forward, trying to draw warmth from herself.

It was darker there, underneath the shadowy layer of branches, away from the more open field where she'd played with her friends, and she worried briefly about losing her way as she moved deeper and deeper beneath their cover.

These weren't *her* woods; this wasn't *her* land to navigate. Here, if she got lost, if no one knew where to find her, she could wander aimlessly for hours and hours, and there would be no familiar landmarks to guide her back again.

But there was the snow.

And as long as the branches continued to catch the newly tumbling flakes, her tracks would lead her back out once more.

She clung to that hope as she abandoned all other reason in pursuit of a baser desire. To find the echo within the woods.

It was hard work, walking through the thick drifts that had built up, even beneath the shelter of the snow-crusted foliage. The heavy white layers made it difficult to move forward, tugging at her boots and making her legs burn. And before long, even Violet's head ached from the effort.

The skin around her cheeks felt hollow and dry, and her eyes burned against the frigid air that seemed colder here, denser somehow, and harder to breathe. Violet strained to keep moving, and with each step, the pain became more and more intense. Yet beneath her skull she could feel the tremulous vibrations of the echo pulling her onward.

She blinked heavily, squinting against the imaginary blades that slashed through her scalp, her forehead, her eyes.

That is the echo, she realized, the excruciating ache that ravaged her, nearly blinding her at the same time she was compelled to locate it. And she was helpless to stop herself from seeking it out.

To Violet's way of thinking it was the very definition of insanity. But there was nothing she could do about it now. Whatever was out there needed her to come.

And she would.

She gave no more thought to the cold, her body feeling numb in comparison to the pain in her head. She wasn't even sure she would know if she *was* cold anymore, which could be dangerous at best. Life threatening at worst.

And then a sudden awareness seeped through her discomfort, and all at once Violet was certain that she'd found the source of the echo. The body she'd been searching for. It was buried beneath the very spot on which she stood. She was besieged by a sense of relief like nothing she'd ever experienced before. It was as if the torturous grip on her was abruptly loosened by her proximity to the dead thing below her.

She could breathe again. Freely. Almost euphorically.

She dropped to her knees and sighed, enjoying the dizzying sensation that swept over her.

But she didn't waste any time. She reached out and dug her gloves into the soft upper layers of snow, scooping quickly and creating a fresh mound beside her. Her hands broke through deeper sheets of thin ice, cracking them apart easily and shoveling that snow aside as well.

She worked diligently, efficiently, and the effort warmed her, distracting her from the lingering headache that buzzed dully in the backdrop of her brain, fogging her thoughts and keeping them from becoming completely lucid.

She felt like she was stoned. Drugged by the echo itself.

The disorienting, narcotic sensation kept her focused on her task as she kept digging.

When her gloved hands reached solid ground, Violet belatedly realized that it had all been an effort in futility. The ground wasn't soft, the soil not loose enough to dig in. And it wasn't just hard; it was frozen into an icy barrier. Solid.

It was no use. There was no way to reach whatever lay below.

That was how Jay found her, kneeling in the snow, trying to think what she should do next through the haze of her cloudy mind. Trying to decide how to solve this puzzle.

"*Crap, Violet.* Didn't you hear us yelling for you? You scared the hell outta me." Jay scolded her at the same time he stretched his hand out for her.

Violet stared at it, momentarily confused by the gesture. *What does he want me to do?* she wondered dreamily.

"Do you want up?" he asked, bending down this time and grasping both of her hands in his. He pulled her to her feet, guiding her until she was standing.

The ringing in her head intensified.

Jay looked around Violet's feet, glancing from her puzzled expression to the piles of snow on the ground and back to her face again.

Understanding finally forced his brows together. "Did you sense something out here?" he asked, keeping his voice low now.

Violet nodded. That much she knew. That much was clear to her still.

"We can't stay here, Vi. Everyone's coming. They're looking for you, and you made it pretty easy once we found your trail. They're right behind me." Jay wrapped his arm protectively around her, drawing her closer to him. He kicked at the piles of snow, spreading them out. "Come on, let's start back. We'll head them off before they get here and start asking questions."

She allowed herself to be led, despite the increasing pain as she left the location of the body behind her.

It didn't want her to go.

They never did though.

She felt like she was suffering from some sort of withdrawal from the drugged haze of the echo she'd discovered, and the farther she walked, the stronger it gripped her.

But her thoughts, at least, started to clear again as the headache intensified, and as they did, she knew that Jay was right. The discomfort was nothing compared to what she would feel if she had to answer invasive questions from her friends about what she'd been doing, about what she had been searching for in the snow.

Claire was the first one to reach them, although Chelsea and Mike weren't far behind, meandering at their own slow and steady pace, hand in hand. Obviously not *everyone* had been worried about Violet's whereabouts.

"Oh good, you found her!" Claire exclaimed as she reached Violet and Jay, picking her way carefully through the path of footprints. "Where were you?" she asked Violet.

Violet was leaning her head against Jay's shoulder, trying in vain to block out the throbbing pangs of the echo as it called for her to return again. The vibrations, the impatient itching beneath her skin, continued to draw her back into the woods, and it was a struggle not to answer that call. She clung to Jay to resist it.

Jay kept moving, following the trail back toward the clearing from which they'd come. "She just went for a walk," he answered Claire, "and got turned around."

Claire wrinkled her nose as Jay brushed past her, half-carrying Violet now. "Why didn't you just follow your tracks?"

Violet heard Claire's question, and she vaguely caught the sound of Jay's voice thundering against the side of her head, but his actual words escaped her.

Cold sweat prickled against the top of her lip. The chills that seized her had nothing to do with the climate.

Shadows tugged at the periphery of her vision and then slowly squeezed tighter and tighter, until she was swimming in a vortex of darkness. She felt herself falling, and it seemed like forever before she finally stopped . . . landing in a heap against something solid . . . and warm. . . .

CHAPTER 29

WHEN VIOLET OPENED HER EYES, SHE WAS INSIDE the cabin. Four anxious faces were staring back at her.

And one mildly disinterested one.

Apparently, Violet's "mishap" had even enticed Megan from her bedroom.

"Look who's back," Chelsea said as she plopped herself onto the armrest of the threadbare couch Violet was lying on. Violet couldn't help noticing that Chelsea's voice had returned to its normal range—the Mike-free range—and was filled with concern.

"How are you feeling?" Jay asked next, kneeling down in front of her so they were eye to eye.

She felt better just seeing him there.

Violet ran her fingers tentatively over the back of her neck and then gingerly touched her fingertips to her temples. There was no pain. It was gone now. All of it.

All that remained was the lingering pull to go back into the woods.

"I'm okay," she insisted. And when he didn't look like he believed her, she added, "Really. I feel fine now."

"I'll get you some hot cocoa," Chelsea offered, and Violet realized that Chelsea must have been genuinely worried. She felt like she'd been seeing this side of Chelsea a lot lately.

Claire went with Chelsea to the kitchen, where they fumbled around trying to get the gas stove lit, until Megan, who had been hanging silently in the background, went in to help them. The younger girl moved expertly within the small space of the kitchen, lighting the burner and locating a pan for them, and, ultimately, Claire and Chelsea stepped aside. Megan seemed comfortable with that arrangement.

"What happened?" Violet asked Jay, when Mike went to join the girls in the kitchen, giving them a moment alone in front of the fire.

Jay shook his head, his expression dark. "You tell me. One minute you were leaning on me, and the next you passed out. It freaked the shit out of me."

"Claire actually screamed," Chelsea added, rejoining them. She sat down on a wooden chair across from Violet. "I can't believe you didn't hear her. I'm with Jay though—it was pretty scary. You're lucky he caught you before you hit the ground."

Violet cringed. She glanced up at Jay, humiliated. "You . . . *caught me*?"

He nodded, and she could tell from the look on his face that he was enjoying this part. A lot. "You're welcome," he said with a completely straight face.

She looked at him again and rolled her eyes, stubbornly refusing to thank him after he'd already so clearly patted himself on the back.

Megan came back in, carrying a mug of hot chocolate, and Claire trailed behind her.

"Be careful," Megan warned quietly, handing it to Violet. "It's kind of hot."

Their fingertips brushed as the mug exchanged hands. Violet locked eyes with the younger girl. "Thank you." She imparted as much meaning as she could in the two simple words and hoped that it was gesture enough, even if only for herself. She felt bad for the things she'd thought about Megan, for the hateful things she'd suspected her of doing.

Megan pulled her hand away and glanced down nervously. "You're welcome." Her voice was timid and hesitant.

"So she gives you hot chocolate and you thank her. I save your life and get nothing. That's messed up," Jay complained.

Violet smirked at him over the top of her hot cocoa. "Hers tastes better," she teased, blowing on the steaming liquid and then taking a sip. "Besides, I think you've already thanked yourself."

Claire interrupted the two of them, handing Violet a napkin. "So, seriously, Violet, what happened out there?"

Violet shook her head, trying to piece together those moments after Jay found her in the woods, after she'd discovered the location of the echo. She remembered the intense pain that she'd followed, the call of the body, and the mind-altering, drugged feeling once she'd located it. And then Jay dragging her away, and the pain coming back again, followed by her vision tunneling. And then . . .

"I just got dizzy, I guess," she finally answered, knowing it was a weak excuse. "I'm okay, though," she repeated, this time trying to sound more convincing.

Lame or not, no one asked any more questions; they seemed to accept her story.

Violet still felt distracted by the echo, despite the distance that now separated her from it. For now, though, all she could do was try to ignore it.

When they decided it was time to put dinner together, Mike and Jay went outside, to a small storage shed out back, to get more wood for the fire.

"Is your dad gonna be here for dinner?" Claire asked Megan, who was doing her best to remain inconspicuous in the open space of the cabin.

Megan simply shook her head in response, barely making eye contact as she answered.

Chelsea cast a questioning look in Violet's direction.

"Do you know where he is?" she pried, even though it was evident that the girl was uncomfortable.

Violet recognized Megan's discomfort. It seemed to radiate off of her. She didn't *want* to be noticed; she didn't *want* to be included. She hovered, wordlessly, soundlessly, on the periphery, existing in quiet solitude.

She's so sad, Violet thought. *Sad and lonely.* Violet wondered if she'd always been that way.

"He's in town. He'll probably be out late." Megan practically whispered the words.

"What does he do, hang out at a bar all night?" Claire attempted to joke.

Megan looked up at Claire, her face serious. "Sometimes," she responded.

Mike came in then, unwittingly shattering the strange hush that had fallen over the girls. Jay followed right behind; each of them had their arms piled high with logs. A wheelbarrow with more logs sat beside the back door, and Violet and Chelsea both jumped up to help them, stacking the wood neatly beside the hearth.

It was a convenient diversion from the awkwardness caused by Megan's starkly honest answer.

So what did that mean, exactly, about their father? That he was a drinker? An alcoholic? That the kids were frequently left on their own to fend for themselves?

It would explain Megan's ease in the kitchen and her isolating demeanor, wouldn't it? That she and Mike were used to taking care of themselves?

Violet's shame deepened.

Dinner was simple: grilled cheese sandwiches and potato chips. Of course, it was Megan who had to fire up the stovetop. And Megan, again, who managed to grill the sandwiches without burning them. Chelsea's attempt didn't end quite so expertly, and her sandwich was more charred than grilled. Violet's was even less admirable. Jay fared better, making something that was at least edible. But Megan proved to be something of a culinary whiz. Or at least a grilled-cheese-sandwich whiz.

So Jay helped Megan at the stove, and that was the only time Violet saw Megan going out of her way to interact with any one of them. She asked him quiet questions while they worked, and she smiled hesitantly when she responded to his playful banter.

It reminded Violet of why she'd suspected Megan of stalking her in the first place. Besides all her other suspicions, it was obvious that Megan had a little crush on Jay. Maybe more than a little one. And Violet felt immediately guilty for even entertaining the thought again.

She knew it hadn't been Megan.

Violet and Claire set the table while Jay and Megan made dinner. Mike and Chelsea "tended to the fire," which turned out to be equivalent to Violet and Jay "doing homework," so when they were called to get their plates, they were glassy-eyed and distracted.

After dinner, Mike and Chelsea were assigned to clean up the mess, which *actually* meant "cleaning up the mess," since they hadn't done anything to help with preparation. Everyone else went to sit in front of the fire.

Violet continued to feel pulled by whatever she'd discovered beneath the cover of the trees, buried under the frozen layers of ice and snow. She wondered briefly how she was going to resolve this predicament . . . it was an animal she couldn't get to, couldn't rebury. She still didn't understand why the draw to find some was so much stronger than others, why some creatures, like the deer by the roadside, could let her pass while others wanted so badly to be found that they continued to lure her, long after she should have left the radius of their reach.

She hoped beyond hope that the need to find this body would simply fade over time, releasing her eventually from its indefinable grip.

It was already past nine o'clock by the time they were finished cleaning up and were settling in for the night. Outside the snow had stopped falling, and even though the sky was dark, the ground shimmered eerily, capturing strands of light and reflecting them like tiny pieces of glass. It created a ghostly backdrop.

They had rearranged the furniture and spread their sleeping bags around the floor in front of the fireplace. There was one bedroom, which Violet presumed was where Megan would sleep, since that was where she'd been hiding earlier, and a small overhead loft, where she guessed Mike's dad stayed. When he was there.

But, even though she had a bedroom, Megan didn't

retreat again. She stayed with the group, lingering on the fringes, sitting without making a sound in a chair as far away as she could get from them and still be considered in the same room.

As often as she could, Violet tried to include Megan in their conversations. But Megan was reluctant, answering in as few words as possible and then falling silent again, stubbornly evading Violet's attempts to befriend her.

When it grew late, one by one they began finding their way into their sleeping bags. Violet crawled into hers, beside Jay, and eventually Megan went down the short hallway to her bedroom.

Conversation dwindled, and then disappeared into silence, until all that remained was the crackling of the fading fire.

CHAPTER 30

THE RAIN WOKE HER, BUT IT WAS THE DULL ache that kept Violet from falling back to sleep. It reached up through her neck, gripping the base of her skull with sinewy fingers.

And with it, something else caught her attention. A light that intruded on the night.

It saturated her eyelids, no matter how tightly she held them shut. But it wasn't the light itself that forced her into awareness. It was the pattern. The discontinuity of it.

It was flashing.

An icy chill swept over her as that realization dawned, and Violet struggled against the sudden urge to panic.

Hard as it was, she forced herself not to react. She lay there, unmoving, pretending *not* to be awake.

There is an explanation, she chanted inwardly, repeating the words over and over. There had to be a rational explanation.

Footsteps shuffled across the wooden floor, and Violet held her breath, listening to them, following them in her mind. She thought about waking Jay, but she was too afraid to breathe, let alone move.

And even though the pain in her head was less intense than before, she recognized it immediately. It was clear, unmistakable.

It was the echo from the woods. Or rather the imprint, coming from the person responsible for burying whatever Violet had found today. But that wasn't all. There was something other than the light and the pain that Violet couldn't quite pinpoint.

She heard the footsteps stop in the kitchen, and the jangling of keys as they clattered onto the countertop.

Violet slowly—*so, so slowly*—pried her eyelids apart, her pulse clamoring wildly as she tried to maintain the pretense that she was still asleep. Every movement she made felt obvious and overdone, and she was afraid that whoever was in there would notice her. Lying awake, trying to steal a glimpse.

The flashing continued, making it difficult to remain still, as her body physically reacted to each pulse of light. Her head pounded incessantly.

When her eyes finally opened, she saw a man. Or at least, she saw the back of him, tall and thick, still wearing a heavy red-and-black-checked wool jacket. He swayed slightly, even though he was standing in place, his hand resting on the edge of the counter. And from where she was lying, Violet could smell the thick scents of stale tobacco and beer that he carried on him.

He turned then, staggering over his own clunky boots, and Violet lowered her lashes, waiting for several breaths to be sure he hadn't spotted her there, and when she looked again, she saw a face she recognized instantly.

It was Mike's face.

Or what she imagined Mike might look like as a weathered, middle-aged man.

It was his father, Ed Russo.

And the light flickering from his skin was unnaturally intense, painfully brilliant. Still, it might have been bearable, had Violet not known the cause of it.

She remembered the night she'd first awakened to that flashing glow, and she wondered how a man—how *this man*—could be responsible for the death of the small cat she'd discovered at her house.

And why . . . ?

The questions both haunted and terrified her.

And now what? Now they were *here*, in this remote mountain cabin, *together*? How could this be a coincidence?

She didn't know what she should do now. She felt trapped by the circumstances—the weather, her location, her proximity to this *killer.* She didn't have any way to reach the outside world, not without going into town to call for help, and she didn't think it would be wise to go alone.

So what were her other options? To wake Jay? To tell the others that Mike's dad had killed a cat and left it in her yard for her to find?

How would she explain that? *Why* would he have done something like that in the first place? And why Violet? As far as she knew, this was the first time she was laying eyes on him.

And then there was the note. And the phone calls. Did she really think that this man, *Mike's father,* was responsible for those too?

Besides, he certainly didn't seem aware of her now, didn't seem to care that she was right there.

Her head was spinning—*reeling*—and the relentless ache was making it harder and harder for Violet to concentrate. She felt dizzy. But worse, there was something more now, something she could no longer ignore.

From the moment that she'd been awakened, the moment that this man had stepped into the room with her, Violet had been overwhelmed by the compelling urge to go back out into the woods.

Back to the echo.

Violet stayed still until long after silence descended over the cabin once more, long after Mike's father had gone up to the loft and she heard him settling in for the night.

And then she waited even longer, just to be certain, before she slowly, cautiously, eased herself up from her sleeping bag, trying not to disturb the others around her. She didn't want to wake Jay; she knew he would try to stop her. But she couldn't stay here.

Her entire body quivered with need as the pain in her head was completely overcome by the absolute, all-consuming drive to search out the echo again. Even the flashing that came in bursts from the loft above was simple to ignore in the face of her crushing desire to locate whatever was buried in the snow.

The fire was still burning, and Violet realized that someone, probably Mike or Jay, had added more wood to it during the night. Yet, despite the fire, Violet was freezing. And the idea of going out into the nearly arctic temperatures was unsettling, but not deterrent enough against the primitive craving that Violet could no longer deny.

She dressed quickly, layering herself in her heavy winter clothes, before grabbing a flashlight and moving soundlessly across the floor with her boots in her hand. She didn't breathe as she eased the back door open, careful to keep the latch from making a sound. She dropped her boots in the snow, and stepped into them as she closed the door softly behind her.

The bitter night air cut through her lungs with her first breath. Shock rolled through her body in a vicious spasm, and the warmth that she'd hoped to carry with her, bundled within her thick down coat, was leached out in one harsh gasp.

Even her bones felt icy and brittle.

She tugged the edges of her hat down as far as she could and wrapped her scarf around her face, breathing into it to create a temperate pocket.

She made her way toward the shed, not sure what she expected to find in there, but hoping there would be something, *anything*, to dig with that she could carry with her.

The decaying shed was dark, and the ancient wood smelled musty even in the cold. Violet turned on her flashlight so she could see inside. Firewood was stacked all the way from the dirt floor to the ceiling against one entire wall. Against the others, there were old boxes, piled one on top of another, tools of various kinds, many of which she didn't recognize: a snow shovel that she doubted would be useful, rusted cans of paint, an old broom, and a rickety wooden ladder. She'd wanted a real shovel, something with a pointed tip capable of penetrating the solid ground, but there was nothing like that.

She did, however, spot something that might prove just as useful. An ax leaned against the pile of wood, with a blade that, sharp or not, would at least break through the compacted ice to reach the dirt below.

Violet clutched the handle in her gloved hand before turning her flashlight out and leaving the shed behind her.

Violet walked, her boots crunching in the icy snow, for as far as she could in the glow that radiated from the windows of the cabin. She didn't want to turn on the flashlight until she had to. She didn't want to draw attention to herself, even though everyone inside was still asleep.

But there was no moon to illuminate her way, and it was dark beneath thick cloud cover. And eventually, when she was too far from the house, she had to use it anyway.

The beam cast a reflective gleam up from the ground like a fine, ethereal mist. At any other time Violet would have thought that it was wondrous and beautiful. Now, however, she was too caught up in her purpose to appreciate the wintry spectacle.

The ax grew heavy in her hand, and she hefted it up, leaning it against her shoulder to ease the burden of its weight.

There was only a moment of relief for Violet, after she was released from the pain of the imprint in the cabin she left behind—the one Mike's dad carried. She knew it was only temporary though, that it would reclaim her as she moved closer to the cover of trees, where the body lay hidden. Yet she was powerless to stop herself from moving toward it.

She didn't need to see her trail through the snow to find her way, the echo found her again easily, seeking her out. Calling to her.

Magical, Violet thought, *the desires of the dead*. And even as the pain reclaimed her, she was acutely aware that the nature of her ability was nothing less than miraculous.

In this moment, it was a thing of beauty.

Just like before, the pain peaked, and the narcotic sensations bled into her system, releasing imaginary toxins that made her light-headed with relief.

She had reached the hidden body.

She thought of the little cat in the box and wondered, for the first time, what was down below her, buried within the frozen ground she stood upon.

Mike had said that his father was a hunter, and Violet assumed that meant large game—elk or deer, rather than quail or rabbits.

Or small, harmless cats, Violet thought bitterly.

She let the haze reclaim her as she dropped to her knees.

PRIDE

MEGAN LISTENED IN THE DARK AS DOORS opened and then closed again. She had grown accustomed to being a sentinel of the night. Long-bred habits were hard to break.

She'd heard her father come in, and she knew from the sound of his unsteady movements around the cabin that he'd been drinking.

She stayed awake long after he'd gone to bed and his nighttime sounds had ceased.

And then there was something else. Another sound.

At first, Megan thought it was nothing. One of her brother's friends getting up to use the bathroom.

But it wasn't.

She listened. Hard.

It was barely noticeable, and if she hadn't gone to her window, she might have missed it altogether. Someone had left the cabin.

No, not someone. Violet.

It was strange seeing Violet walking away, dressed for the weather and disappearing into the uninviting night. Just days ago, Megan might have felt differently about what she was witnessing, about seeing someone who she'd despised fading into the freezing shadows.

But now . . . now she felt something she hadn't expected to feel. Curiosity.

And concern.

Violet had been kind to her when she'd deserved nothing but condemnation, even if Violet was unsure of the offenses that Megan had committed against her. Still, Violet had welcomed Megan into their group, forgiving whatever she had once suspected and trying to start anew.

Megan felt guilty for everything she'd done to Violet.

It was an odd mixture of emotions. Unfamiliar sensations crept over her in unwelcome waves.

Megan reached beneath her pillow and pulled out the tiny pink collar she'd hidden there. She fingered it—lovingly—stroking it slowly between her thumb and forefinger as she closed her eyes.

She missed her little cat, the stray she'd been secretly feeding, secretly loving. She missed the way it waited for her, counted on her, loved her in return.

It was the first time Megan had been needed. Really *needed.*

But her father had taken that from her too.

He wouldn't allow her to be loved.

He was too selfish to allow her anything good, so he'd taken care of the problem, not by arguing and demanding that she chase the cat away, but by simply leaving it in the trash for her to find.

Now all she had left was the collar she'd bought for her cat and a bitterness that refused to leave her alone.

Her father had never admitted to what he'd done, and Megan had never confronted him. But she'd known it was him.

She had been sickened when she'd discovered her little cat there, filled with rage. But her next step had been misdirected, she realized now. Misguided. It wasn't Violet's fault that Megan's life wasn't what she wanted it to be. It wasn't Violet she should loathe.

It was him. It was her father she hated.

Megan recognized the sound of his footsteps making their way back down the creaking staircase from the loft.

Her stomach clenched tightly as she launched herself beneath her covers, expertly feigning sleep as she had so many nights before.

But it wasn't her room he visited.

She listened while, not as silently as Violet, her father moved gracelessly through the cabin and out the back door.

She hurried to look through the frosted panes of her window as she watched him awkwardly making his way through the snow, a shotgun in his hand.

Following in Violet's footsteps.

CHAPTER 31

VIOLET CRINGED AS THE AX STRUCK THE FROZEN earth, sending a tingling sensation up her arms. The ax felt too heavy in her hands, the weight too solid for the task.

She'd positioned the flashlight in the snow so that it was shining over the spot where she was trying to dig.

She was having a hard time holding on to coherent thoughts. They were vaporous, drifting like opaque threads of smoke, only to vanish like shadows whenever she tried to grasp them. This particular echo had an indefinable intoxicating effect on her that seemed to suddenly intensify . . . its grip on her tightening, clutching her in its embrace.

But she was already here, answering its call; why would

it get stronger now? Unless . . .

His voice, deep and haggard, confirmed what she'd guessed—she was no longer alone.

She wasn't sure how he'd managed to sneak up on her—if it was the lack of clarity that plagued her brain or if it was the lingering pain filtering in around the edges. Or simply that she was too absorbed in trying to find her way below the surface of the icy ground to notice that something had changed in her surroundings.

That something was wrong. Terribly, terribly wrong.

"How did you know?" The man's words grated harshly through the night.

Violet's head cleared briefly as she jerked back from her task, fear temporarily jolting her from her stupor. She didn't need to ask who he was; when she saw him standing there, the broken bursts of light emanating from beneath the hood of his coat gave her that answer. She noticed it was raining again, that she could hear the same heavy drops that had awakened her.

No, she realized belatedly. *It isn't raining; it's too cold to rain.* It was only the sound she heard.

She glanced down at her gloved hands, at the ax she held there. She wasn't sure what to say. Terror blocked her throat, strangling her.

He spoke again, this time quieter, his voice ravaged by something that sounded like sorrow. Maybe even regret. "How did you find her?"

His questions didn't make any sense, and Violet struggled to pay attention.

Her? Violet tried to remember what she knew—which wasn't much—about hunting, about the laws that hunters were expected to abide by. Weren't they supposed to hunt only the males? Wasn't it illegal to kill the females?

She clenched her teeth, forcing herself *not* to succumb to the alluring pull of the echo, the venom that promised to deaden her senses.

He stumbled as he took another step toward her, and Violet could see his red-rimmed eyes behind the flickering light, and the dark circles beneath them. From this close, he looked so much older. And so very tired.

He stared back at her without seeing.

Violet remembered that he'd been out—presumably drinking—and she wondered if he felt half as blurry as she did.

She thought about moving away from it, from the echo beneath her feet, in an effort to gather her wits. But the prospect of facing that pain again, amplified by the presence of the man who carried the matching imprint, was unbearable. She preferred to remain drugged.

His voice, when he spoke again, was riddled with anguish. "I loved her. And a long, long time ago, she loved me too. I didn't want to do it."

Violet was losing the battle to understand what he was telling her. His words felt like nothing more than pieces of an unsolvable riddle to her addled mind.

She opened her mouth to ask him what he meant, but she couldn't seem to formulate the thoughts into words, and instead she sat there, gaping dully.

"She promised to love me forever. She made a vow. . . ." His voice became bitter, angry. Spittle gathered at the corners of his mouth, and Violet could tell that he was no longer talking to her. He gazed over her head, lost in his memories. "But she lied. And then she told me she didn't love me anymore. She said she . . ." His voice broke. ". . . she said she wanted *him*. He *ruined* my life." His jaw clenched.

Violet's eyes dropped down to his hand, which dangled limply at his side. She saw the shotgun he leaned against, clutched in his palm.

Her head started to clear as she shivered. Her blood felt electric within her veins and she was suddenly, *lucidly*, aware of her surroundings . . . and of the man standing before her. She was terrified by what she was witnessing, even though she still wasn't certain what it was that he was confessing. But she knew, deep down in her heart, that he was telling her something she probably didn't want to hear. That no one should ever have to hear.

Still, he didn't look at Violet. "But I loved her," he whispered, lost in his past. "How could she just leave like that? How could I just let her leave?"

Violet couldn't tear her eyes away from the weapon, and her heart pounded painfully, thrumming violently. Loudly.

"I didn't mean to hurt her," he admitted, his gaze finding Violet, trying to convince her, beseeching her to understand.

Violet's heart exploded within her chest, and she was shaking all over as she waited to see what he wanted from her. What he planned to do to her.

She nodded, telling him that she believed him.

"I couldn't let her take my children away from me. I couldn't let them start a new family with him." His eyes became fevered as he explained. "They love me, you know? And I tried to explain that to her, to tell her that she was wrong, that I *could* change. But she'd already decided. She said it was too late. She said I was never going to see them again." He paused, looking confused, asking Violet, *"Never see them again? How could she do that to me?"*

He frowned and shook his head, determination set in every hard line of his face. "I tried to talk to her, and when she wouldn't listen, I tried to stop her. I didn't mean to hurt her." He cried then, the sentence trailing off on a fractured sob. "And afterward I brought her here, so that she could be in the one place she'd always loved. Forever . . ."

He gripped the handle of the shotgun so tightly that his fingers turned white as he glanced up at Violet. "I'm really sorry that you found her," he explained sadly. "I didn't want anyone else to die."

CHAPTER 32

JAY ROLLED OVER IN HIS SLEEPING BAG AND stretched his arm out to Violet. When his hand swept over the cool surface of her pillow, he opened his eyes.

In the glow of the fading embers from the fireplace, he could see that she wasn't there, that she was no longer lying beside him. *She must have gone to the bathroom,* he thought lazily, as he shifted on the floor and waited for her to return.

He listened to the even sounds of sleep all around him. Mike's deep breathing bordered on snoring, and Jay thought about nudging him—maybe more of a punch in the arm—to get him to stop, but he decided he would rather be alone with Violet when she came back, and waking Mike would be counterproductive.

He wasn't sure how long he lay there, how much time had passed, but eventually he realized that it was too much, and he got up to see what was taking her so long.

When he looked down the hallway, to the open doorway of the darkened bathroom, his stomach sank.

Violet wasn't in there.

He hesitated briefly outside the closed bedroom door—Megan's room—thinking that maybe . . . *maybe* Violet had slipped in there to talk to Mike's little sister. *Why*, he didn't know. But he had to find out.

He tapped as softly as he could, trying not to wake the others. There was no answer.

He took a deep breath, steeling himself as he turned the knob to peer inside. The lamp beside the bed was on, and the bed was unmade but empty. Nobody was in the small, chilly bedroom.

Panic took hold. Something was wrong. *This was all wrong.*

He hurried back out to where his friends were asleep, and this time he grabbed Mike's arm, leaning down to wake him. "They're gone. Megan and Violet, they're not here," he whispered loudly.

Mike was groggy and slow to grasp what he'd said. "What—" He held his arm in front of his eyes, as if the diffused light from the lingering fire was too much for him. "What are you talking about?" he croaked.

"Jay, *where's* Violet?" Chelsea asked as she sat up, rubbing her face.

"I don't know," Jay answered, his voice getting louder.

"She wasn't here when I woke up, and I checked your sister's room," he said to Mike. "She's gone too."

Mike sat up now, grabbing his sweatshirt from the floor and tugging it over his head. "Is my dad here?"

But he was already going to the front of the cabin to see for himself. He came back and double-checked his sister's room before hurrying up the stairs to the loft above.

"Well, his truck's here, but he's not," Mike stated, fully alert now.

"Where do you think they are?" Claire asked, hugging her pillow to her chest.

Mike shook his head. "There's really nowhere to go out here." He looked to Jay for suggestions.

But Jay was already putting on his snow gear. He knew where Violet was; he should have known all night long that she'd try to go back out there after she'd discovered that echo . . . the pull was too strong for her to ignore.

"You and Claire stay here," Jay told Chelsea. "Put some wood on the fire, and if Megan and Violet come back, you guys just stay put. Mike and I will be back as soon as we can."

The confusion on Mike's face was evident, but he got dressed anyway, following Jay's lead.

When the two of them stepped out the back door, into the punishing cold of the night, there were three clear, and distinctly separate, sets of fresh footprints in the snow.

CHAPTER 33

"ARE YOU SAYING SHE DIDN'T LEAVE US?" IT WAS Megan's broken whisper that shattered the deadly calm hanging in the night air.

Violet wasn't sure whether to be relieved by the interruption, or whether she should scream at Megan to run.

Even in the eerie glow of the flashlight lying in the snow, Violet could see the tears streaming down Megan's face as the other girl struggled to understand what was happening. She stared at her father disbelievingly, revulsion and sorrow evident in her features. "Are you saying that she's . . ." She pointed to the ground, to where Violet had been digging. ". . . *here?"* The last word was empty, absent of any real sound, but Violet still heard her, and felt the girl's pain.

"Megan, *please* try to understand. She wanted to take you kids away from me. She wanted to separate us, but I couldn't let her do that. I couldn't let her take you . . . not with Roger. He was scum. He used to beat your mother, and I couldn't risk him hurting you too. I don't know why he had to come back and ruin everything. . . ." He took a step, closing the distance between them. He tried to reach out to her with his free hand, but she drew away, shrinking from his touch as if his hand were contaminated. "I love you. . . ."

Violet took the opportunity to get to her feet. She felt shaky, wobbly from the echo's drugging effect. For the moment, however, she was clear enough to think—fear keeping her thoughts somewhat in focus—but she wasn't sure how long that would last, how long the adrenaline could stave off the intruding sensations.

"You don't *love* us!" Megan screamed, finally finding her voice. "How could you *hurt* her? You're no better than him. You're worse! She was our mother!" Tears streamed down her cheeks. "She wouldn't have let him hurt us! How could you?" she howled. *"How could you?"*

"*I do! I do love you!* You're my princess. I couldn't live without you!" He tried again to touch her, his hand grazing her cheek.

Megan jerked, falling backward and landing in the snow at Violet's feet as she tried to get away from her own father. That was when he noticed Violet again, and his face twisted, contorting with hatred. *"This is your fault,"* he hissed. "This is all because of you! If you hadn't come, we would have been fine!"

Megan sobbed. "We weren't fine. We've never been fine. *You killed my mother!*"

Violet's eyes were wide, her heart thundering inside her chest. She wanted to explain that this was all a mistake, a misunderstanding—anything that might make him go away—but he was already lifting his shotgun to his shoulder, aiming it directly at her.

Violet shivered, from fear and from cold. She was frozen in place. The phantom rainstorm continued to pour as she wondered what *her* echo would be.

"*What the fuck?* What are you doing?" The distorted sound of Mike's voice rushed past her like a violent wind. She heard the thud of body colliding with body as Mike threw himself against his father, shoving him against the trunk of a nearby tree.

Megan got to her feet. "She didn't leave us. She didn't run away. He killed her," she sobbed, pointing at her father.

Mike glanced at Violet, confused. "Who?" And then he turned to Megan, taking in her state, and it was as if someone had flipped a switch. His confusion vanished.

"Is it true?" Mike moved his hand to his father's throat, pinning him to the large tree trunk. *"Is what she said true?"*

His father just closed his eyes, and even though he didn't deny the accusation, his answer was evident.

And then Violet felt Jay as he arrived only seconds behind Mike. He gathered her into his arms, reassuring himself that she was safe before pushing her behind him to shield her.

Mike tore the shotgun from his father's hands. The older man didn't even fight for it; he just let it go, as if he were giving up. As if he were already defeated.

Mike took a step back, releasing his grip on his father's neck with a rough jerk, and his dad's head cracked against the tree. The sound rattled around them.

"How could you hurt her? How could you do that to us?" But even while he spoke, Violet watched as Mike expertly released the handle of the shotgun, checking to see if there were shells inside.

From where she stood, Violet saw the same thing he did, and she knew that the gun was loaded.

She half-expected Megan to say something, to object to where this was going. The look on Mike's face as he squared off with the man who had just admitted to murdering his mother was chilling. The fact that he was armed was something shades darker than unspeakable.

But Megan just stood there, slipping silently into the backdrop, vanishing in plain sight. Even her eyes had gone blank.

Violet clung to Jay, afraid to even breathe.

Mike's father crumpled to the ground. He sobbed openly, bawling into the brisk air, his hot breath making puffs of steam as he begged his children: *"I'm so sorry. . . . Please . . . forgive me."* His words came out in wheezing jags. *"I don't deserve to live. Please just kill me. . . . I don't want to go to jail. . . ."* He buried his face in his hands.

As Mike pointed the gun at the top of his father's bowed head, his hands were visibly shaking.

"Mike," Violet heard Jay saying as he took a step forward. Violet wanted to stop him, but she was too late. "Don't do anything stupid," he begged his friend.

She wondered how Jay could sound so calm, so rational, when she doubted whether she could even speak at that moment. The nebulous feelings of the echo infringed on her again as she fought against them, fending them off.

Mike's glare shifted to Jay, his eyes glittering strangely, madly. For an instant, it was as though he'd forgotten that he wasn't alone . . . that it wasn't just him and his father. He frowned at Jay, baffled.

Jay put his hands up in front of him as he moved closer still.

In her head, Violet screamed at Jay to come back to her, to protect her, to stay away from the volatile situation.

"You don't want to do this, Mike. Trust me. He's already confessed, and he'll go to prison for what's done. Don't make things worse by hurting him."

Mike's answer was flat. "I wasn't planning to *hurt* him."

Jay took another step closer, understanding the meaning behind Mike's words. "I know. But think about your sister." Jay glanced over to where Megan stood quietly, silent tears slipping down her cheeks. "She needs you, Mike. If you *do anything* to your father, they'll take you away from her, and then who will she have?"

Something frantic flickered in Megan's eyes. Fear, perhaps. And need.

Mike looked too and saw her, *really* saw her standing there, broken. He hesitated, his shoulders falling slightly as the rage on his face splintered into something softer.

Megan didn't move, but her eyes never left his.

When Mike looked back at Jay, he nodded. "Take the girls back to the cabin and then go into town for help. I'll stay out here and wait for you."

"You won't do anything to him?" Jay asked, wanting some sort of assurance that Mike wouldn't shoot his father.

Mike stared back at Jay. Seriously and with resolve, he answered, "I promise."

Violet didn't mean to, but she once again found herself leaning against Jay as the torturous withdrawals from the echo hollowed out the inside of her skull.

What was surprising to Violet, however, was Megan's reaction. The younger girl refused to let go of Violet, clinging to her other hand while Jay kept them moving through the snow at a steady pace. Violet couldn't tell if the grip was meant to lend to—or to draw support from—her. All she knew was that Megan held on tight.

And after everything the girl had been through, Violet had no intention of letting go. Somewhere along the way, while the ache was almost too much to bear, Violet swore she heard Megan whispering something to her, something so quiet that only Violet was meant to hear it.

It sounded like: *"I'm sorry."*

But Violet was too weary to be certain.

As they moved away from the trees, cutting a path out into

the open, the pain began to wane, only slightly at first, and then with each step, Violet could feel relief blooming within her like a flower. She breathed deeply, relishing the release.

Up ahead of them, the night sky around the cabin was fractured by strange incandescent bursts. But these lights were different from the imprint that radiated from Megan's father's skin. These were the kind of lights that *everyone* could see. Red and blue flashing lights that illuminated the crystalline landscape with hues of indigo and crimson.

The police were already there. *But how?*

Behind them, the blast of the shotgun cracked sharply, deafeningly. Violet and Jay both startled, jerking reflexively as their feet stopped moving in the snow. On the other side of her, Violet felt nothing from Megan. Not even a flinch. She only stopped moving because they had.

And they knew, all three of them, that any beauty that snowy night had only been an icy illusion.

The cabin before them suddenly ruptured in a frenzy of activity. Where it had been quiet just moments before there was a sudden outpouring as people rushed toward them, erupting through the back door like an agitated swarm. Flashlights bounced along the ground, finding them where they stood, frozen in the night.

In the bustle, Violet recognized uniforms among the crowd. She saw her uncle and her parents, who were running through the snow to reach her.

And, somewhere, amid the moving and shifting faces that swallowed up the three of them—her and Jay and Megan—she saw Sara Priest.

CHAPTER 34

FOR VIOLET, THE REST OF THE NIGHT WAS DREAM-like and disjointed. So much had happened already, and she still had so many questions.

Her parents had explained to her about the phone calls they'd received from Sara Priest, who had given them the mistaken impression—just as she had when she'd met Violet—that she was with the FBI.

First, apparently, Sara had just left a message for Violet to call her, a message that they had relayed to the convenience store owners, since they couldn't reach Violet's cell phone. And, later, the more pressing phone call—the urgent, middle-of-the-night one—telling them Violet was in trouble, that she needed help. Sara had also suggested that they call Violet's uncle, and that the three of them meet her, along with the local authorities she would be contacting, up at the remote cabin.

They didn't know Sara, or what her relationship to Violet was, but in that moment, hearing that their daughter might be in danger, they hadn't stopped to question her. It was enough to know that Violet might need them.

They were relieved to find their daughter safe and alive. And horrified that Sara had been right, that Violet *had* been in jeopardy, and that someone else may have died there that night.

They held Violet so tightly that she felt like she might shatter. It had never been so good to see them.

Chelsea and Claire were beside themselves with relief, both of them crying when they realized that Violet, Megan, and Jay were unharmed.

None of them knew for certain what had happened to Mike. He was still out there.

But by the time the officers had gone in search of him, he was already emerging from the frozen woods.

Chaos ensued.

Violet strained to see him, to get a glimpse of him, as she listened to the commotion that his sudden appearance created. She heard voices shouting, demanding that he show his hands and that he keep them raised.

Mike obeyed listlessly, and Violet noted that his eyes were now as vacant as his sister's. His outstretched hands were empty.

She sensed nothing at all from him. No curious smells,

no abnormal colors or lights, no anomalous sounds.

No imprints at all.

Violet eased herself away from her parents and edged closer to where Mike was already being handcuffed. She wanted to get near him. She needed to know what had happened out there. She searched him, studying him. She scoured him to the depths of her ability and came back with nothing.

"What do you think?" she heard the familiar voice asking from beside her.

Violet shook her head, confused. "I don't think he did it." There was a pause, and then she glanced at Sara, remembering something that needed to be said. "There's a body out there, other than their dad's. I think Serena Russo has been buried there for a long time," Violet stated flatly, feeling hollow now too.

Sara blinked, and Violet could see the questions there, the ones that Violet knew she could answer now. When all this was over with, she would tell Sara everything. "Can you show me where?" Sara asked.

Violet led Sara back into the woods, back toward the echo that had drawn her in the first place.

They couldn't get close; the area was already being cordoned off, and despite her pull with law enforcement, even Sara was asked to stay back. It didn't matter though; they were close enough.

Mike's dad was there, in the same spot he'd been in when Jay had led Violet and Megan away. He still bore the imprints of the lives he'd taken before his death.

And Violet sensed the new imprint too, vibrant and fresh. Surrounding his lifeless body, covering him in ghostly clusters and hovering above him with vaporous, spectral wings, were butterflies. Hundreds and hundreds of beautiful, unearthly butterflies.

Violet's body hummed with each beat of their delicate, sheer wings.

The gun lay awkwardly beneath his arm.

Violet knew that Mike hadn't shot his father. She would have seen this imprint on him . . . and it hadn't been there. Instead, his father bore both the imprint *and* the echo of his own suicide.

Sara reached out to touch Violet's arm, misunderstanding the pained expression on Violet's face. "You don't have to look at him," she explained gently.

But Violet wasn't looking at him. It was the *other* echo that was causing her to shudder with ache.

"She's there." Violet pointed to the spot nearby. "He killed her and buried her there."

Sara nodded, and Violet realized that soon it would all be over. The pain, the discomfort, the unsettled feeling of a body craving peace.

Once Serena Russo was properly buried—at long last—Violet would be released.

"It was him, you know?" Sara explained as they turned to leave. "Ed Russo was responsible for killing Roger Hartman's dog."

Violet tried to respond, but already the pain was unbearable. Sara had no way of knowing.

"We finally reached Hartman, and he told us that Ed Russo had been harassing him ever since he moved back to the area, stopping by his work and his house, making threatening phone calls. Hartman let us listen to some of the messages." Sara didn't seem surprised when Violet reached for her, holding on to her arm for support, and Violet was in too much pain to worry about appearances. Sara continued, without missing a beat. "Drunken ramblings, mostly. But he accused Hartman of poisoning his wife's mind and destroying his family. In the last message, he brags about killing the dog. Pretty ugly stuff."

But Violet already knew. She had witnessed the echo—the ghostly rain—firsthand.

She frowned, still curious about one thing. "How did you know I needed help?" she questioned Sara. "What made you come all the way up here in the middle of the night?"

Sara glanced up then, but not at Violet.

She looked ahead of her, to where the trees became open field again. There was something strange in her eyes when she saw the person standing there, something Violet couldn't interpret. A secret of her own, perhaps.

Violet followed Sara's gaze and saw Rafe there, waiting for them in the snow with his hands stuffed deep into his pockets. It was the first time Violet had realized he was there. His serious blue eyes watched them cautiously, warily.

Even in the dead of night he looked mysteriously out of place.

When Sara answered Violet, her voice was hushed, her words cryptic and heavy with meaning. “Someone told me you were in danger.”

EPILOGUE

VIOLET STOOD ON THE OTHER SIDE OF THE GLASS and studied the men before her.

Again, they couldn't see her. And again, she was battered by several sensations at once. She stepped closer, until she could see her breath against the barrier that separated her from them, and she pressed her palms against the cool surface, closing her eyes. Concentrating.

There was only one sensation she was searching for in the midst of all the others.

She listened carefully, the sound of her own breathing steadying her as she disentangled one imprint from the rest.

Beautiful. Poignant. Melodic.

The evocative strings of the harp.

It was him, the man who had stolen the little boy from his family in Utah and left him to die inside the shipping crate on the waterfront. Violet would recognize him anywhere.

She opened her eyes. "There," she said, pointing to the man at the end of the row.

Sara nodded. "You're right. That's impressive, Violet."

Violet smiled. "So I passed?"

"I told you, it's not a test."

She took a step away from the glass, distancing herself even as the men were being led from the other room. "Yeah, but it kinda was."

Sara didn't answer. She didn't need to. Violet knew even if Sara refused to admit it.

Violet had expected to feel relief; she'd already known that unburdening herself, at least to Sara, would make her feel better. But what she hadn't counted on was that she would feel so . . . *alive.*

She tingled with a new sense of purpose. And even though she hadn't officially accepted Sara's invitation to join their group, Violet knew that, in a way, she already had.

She still didn't understand exactly what it was that Sara's team did, or how they operated, but after witnessing Sara in action that night at the cabin, Violet knew that Sara definitely had influence with the authorities. She'd witnessed Sara giving orders to the local sheriff's office and had watched her interacting with the FBI agents who had later arrived on the scene.

Even if she didn't actually work *for* the FBI, Sara Priest had proven that she was a force to be reckoned with.

And, more importantly, Violet knew she could count on Sara, could trust her. That was a lot for Violet.

As far as Mike and Megan, they were already gone. They'd moved to Oregon to live with an aunt who'd offered to take them in.

Megan had admitted to everything. She'd admitted that she'd hated Violet at first, that she was jealous, and had wanted to frighten her. She confessed to leaving her dead cat at Violet's house as a message. She confessed to the note and the phone calls as well.

Violet had reached out and forgiven Megan, knowing that the younger girl had already suffered enough, from years of living with an alcoholic father and then discovering that he'd murdered her mother.

Megan would need a lot of therapy to undo the damage her father had done, and Sara assured Violet that they would do everything they could to get her the help she needed.

Mike, on the other hand, admitted to nothing.

And although no one could dispute his story, that his father had wrestled the gun from his hands to take his own life, Violet suspected something else, something more disturbing. She couldn't help remembering the way Mike's father had begged Mike to end his life, to let him die, and she wondered if Mike hadn't just agreed, offering his father an alternative to prison.

And Violet wasn't sure she blamed him if he had. She

wasn't sure that his father didn't, in some way, deserve what he'd gotten, and that Mike and Megan didn't deserve the peace of knowing that they would never have to face their father again.

She honestly didn't know. . . .

As Violet gathered her things, Sara asked her to call later.

Violet nodded, for the first time agreeing, and she wondered again how she would fit into their group.

In the hallway, Rafe stood waiting for them. Waiting for Violet.

He held out his hand to her, and in it Violet saw the folded pink note that she'd given to Sara when she'd asked for her help. She looked at it curiously.

"Here." He spoke in the quiet voice she'd grown accustomed to. It seemed to suit his brooding nature. "I don't need this anymore."

Violet tentatively reached out her hand to take it from him, her mind speculating as to why he'd had it in the first place. She'd spent plenty of time wondering about his role in the group, so how did the note fit in?

Her fingertips brushed against his and, not for the first time, she felt that tremor of something pass through her, something electric.

He pulled his hand away quickly but glanced up at her, meeting her gaze.

Violet smiled at him unsurely. "Hey, I want to thank you. You know, for bringing help that night. I owe you one." She didn't say anything else, and she didn't wait for a response. But as she started to walk away, leaving him standing there in the hallway, out of the corner of her eye, she saw him smile knowingly.

Violet didn't need an explanation as to how he'd known she was in trouble, just as she didn't want to go around explaining to others what she could do.

It was enough to know that they were a part of something else now.

Together.

"That was fast," Jay said as Violet got into the car.

"I told you I wouldn't be long."

"Good, 'cause I think we're gonna be late," he answered, glancing at the clock on his dash.

Violet sighed. "Is this about the party?"

"I already told you: There is no party." And then he grinned at her. "Besides, if you don't act surprised, Chelsea's going to kill me."

"*Ugh!* I hate parties."

Jay reached over and slipped his hand around the back of Violet's neck, pulling her toward him. She could smell the mint he'd been chewing on as she leaned into him.

"Come on. None of them got to celebrate your birthday with you." He kissed her once, softly, sweetly, on her cheek. "Let them have their little party; it won't last long." He kissed her other cheek and then her chin, and Violet felt her resolve slipping.

"We'll be out of there in no time." His lips brushed her

forehead; his eyes smoldered as he gazed down at her. "And then afterward"—he found her lips, lightly teasing her—"we can have our own party."

Violet sighed in defeat, losing herself to his very persuasive argument.

"I think we're gonna be late," she whispered, surrendering at last.

ACKNOWLEDGMENTS

First, I have to thank my ever-patient agent, Laura Rennert, for always being in my corner, cheering me on every step of the way . . . thank you!

To my editors at HarperCollins, Farrin Jacobs and Kari Sutherland, thank you for your support, guidance, and unfailing good humor . . . you've made *Desires of the Dead* something we can all be proud of!

Thank you also to my fabulous marketing, publicity, and design team at HarperCollins, which includes my *super*-publicist Melissa Bruno—who works tirelessly to put my books in the hands of, well, pretty much everyone—and Sasha Illingworth—the incredibly talented designer who has created not one but two amazing covers for my books. I cannot thank you all enough!!!

To everyone at the Debs and the Tenners, for always having my back! To Jacqueline and Tamara, I couldn't have survived the launch of *The Body Finder* without the two of you! To Shelli Wells, for being as good a friend in real life as you are online. A special thanks to all *The Body Finder* Street Teamers who went out of their way to spread the word. And to Reggie, try to keep this one away from the bathtub!

I also want to thank my dad, Gerry, from whom I learned the gift of gab (among other things), an important trait for any writer . . . thank you. And my brother, Scot, who taught me that an annoying little brother can grow up to be a best friend.

And again, to my mom, Josh, Abby, Connor, and Amanda . . . because you're always there, loving me as much as I love you!

THE BODY FINDER

Kimberly Derting

A GIRL WITH A MORBID ABILITY

When a murder is committed it leaves a unique echo . . . on both the victim and the killer. Most people are unaware of these but Violet Ambrose has always been able to sense them.

A SERIAL KILLER ON THE LOOSE

Now that Violet's town is in the thralls of a serial killer the echoes of the local girls he has murdered are haunting her.

AND THE BOY WHO WOULD NEVER LET ANYTHING HAPPEN TO HER

The only shining light is Violet's best friend Jay. She's started falling for him and his fierce protectiveness gives her hope that he may feel the same . . .

With the police at a loss, can Violet use her ability to stop the killer or is she in danger of becoming his next victim?

978 0 7553 7895 1

headline